FUN LESSONS

LEANNE TREESE

Moxie Publishing

To my daughter, Katie. This novel's first reader and a sensitivity consultant for important topics in this book

CHAPTER 1

R*ebecca*
"Black sheep of the family. Nice to meet you." I thrust my hand toward Mark. Bangle bracelets, bright and colored, shake with the movement.

He waves in my direction. "Stop."

"Well, I feel like it." I grip my wine glass and glance at the suited, straight-faced lawyers gathered to celebrate Mom's swearing-in. She's now officially The Honorable Helene Chapman, newest judge in the Superior Court of New Jersey. Every person I see is in something dark and conservative. Not me. My dress is bright green and too tight. In fairness, the event was billed as a cocktail party, not a rush-here-from-the-office gathering. Suffice it to say, my dress choice does not feel as fun and festive as it did in the dressing room of TJ Maxx.

Mark, the nicer of my two older brothers, pulls at the lapel of his suit jacket. "Hey. You're the only interesting one in the family. The rest of us are pretty vanilla."

"What about Aunt Kimmy?" My father's sister is anything but vanilla.

"Immediate family," he corrects. "Come on, admit it. We're boring."

"Not boring. Successful."

Mark shrugs. "Depends on what you count as success."

He clinks his wineglass against mine and I smile. Mark always tries to build me up. And he isn't wrong. I *am* more colorful than my parents or siblings. The four of them are variations of one another, all with the same dark brown eyes and hair, the same lean build. The three men stand at 6'0", my mother at a respectable 5'8". They all work in esteemed professions—Mom and John in law, and Dad and Mark in medicine.

I'm a college dropout.

I can't help but think that Mom and Dad were feeling pretty good about their genes and parenting skills until I came along. Two for two, right? Then I came howling into the world, a colicky baby with wild red hair and big green eyes. I missed the tall gene. And the super slim gene. Also, the smart gene, the conservative gene, the golf gene, the "work a room" gene, and every other conceivable gene that would make me feel like I belonged in my homogeneously perfect family.

Mark leans toward me. "We should probably mingle," he whispers.

"Then I'll have to walk in these heels." I gesture to the two-inch black pumps I'd bought for cheap in hope they would make me look slimmer and taller. Instead, they hurt (read: kill and might forever scar) my feet.

Before Mark responds, Mom makes a beeline toward us, an older gentleman's arm linked in her own. "Mark, Rebecca, I'd like you to meet The Honorable Henry Tuffin. We'll be working in the civil division together." She unlinks her arm from Henry's; he shakes our hands.

"Looking forward to working with your mother," he says.

"She'll be a great asset to an already strong bench, I'm sure,"

Mark says just as woman with a name tag steps up and whispers in his ear.

He holds up a finger. "If you'll excuse me. I'm needed in the kitchen." He extends his hand to Henry. "Nice to meet you, Judge Tuffin."

Mark steps away. I pull at my dress, shift my feet, and half smile, the combination of which, I'm sure, makes me look even more uncomfortable than I feel.

"So, what is it that you do, Rebecca?" Judge Tuffin leans forward with interest. His eyes are kind.

I open my mouth to answer; Mom speaks instead. "Rebecca is taking a gap year from college." It's her favorite way around the fact that I dropped out. Over two years ago.

Judge Tuffin smiles. Wrinkles crease around his kind eyes. He looks a little like I'd imagine Santa might. "Smart woman. You only get so many chances at freedom in a lifetime." He nods toward me. "And what will you do with this gift of time, Ms. Chapman?"

I look at Mom, expecting her to answer for me again. She doesn't, and encouraged by Judge Tuffin's demeanor, I dive in. "I'm a musician. A singer, actually. I'm auditioning for a new reality show."

The judge nods; I continue. "It's called *Country Clash*. Bands are going to compete against each other for audience votes. On television."

"Sounds impressive."

I'm about to say more, how only ten percent of the people who sent in videos were extended an audition, but Mom interrupts. "Rebecca's also working as a—" she pauses. I can almost see her search her brain for what it is that I do.

"I'm a social media consultant," I supply.

"Yes," Mom says, seemingly relieved. "Rebecca puts little bits and bobs on Facebook and whatnot." She waves a hand dismissively.

Little bits and bobs? She couldn't have given a more conde-scending explanation of my job if she'd tried. But for Judge Tuffin and his still-kind eyes, I'd have called her out on it.

"What company do you work for?" the judge asks.

"Mrs. Fishes."

His face lights up. "Mrs. Fishes. I love that brand. When fish is the dish!" He says it in the singsong verse from the commer-cials. "Great line. Did you have a hand in it?"

I almost laugh. The tagline—always accompanied by scantily dressed women and shirtless men holding fish dishes—is prob-ably more famous than the company itself. "I can't say that I did," I acknowledge. "But it is catchy."

"Sure is." Judge Tuffin smiles.

John (older brother number two and considerably less nice) materializes, his hand extended. "Judge Tuffin." He nods at me, barely, then immediately launches into legal topics I know nothing about. We're joined by several more people, and soon the conversation is drowning in legalese. Case names. Legal terms. Precedents.

Boring.

Boring.

Boring.

I yawn without meaning to. It starts out small and ends up a yowler, the exaggerated kind with a noise, almost like I'm faking. After, it's dead silent. "Sorry." I wave a hand, then inex-plicably, yawn *again*.

Mom's eyes are daggers.

"Excuse me."

I slip out of the circle. Okay, slip is a misnomer. I hobble out of the circle, my cheap shoes digging hard into the backs of my heels. I take a few steps then look down to make sure I'm not bleeding. I'm not, but with the contorted movement, the V-neck of my dress slides open and my bra (black and lacy, thank you very much) pops out on the left side. My boobs are not the smallest, so the whole thing is a bit of show. I yank the material back in place, but I'm pretty sure the open-mouthed man at the bar saw. And the man next to him. Possibly the bartender.

My bra peeking out momentarily (or not momentarily) would not ordinarily bother me. In my own environment, I'm confident. Brash. The kind of woman that would proudly wear a form-fitting green dress to a party inhabited by serious lawyers in suits of black and gray. I'd make a joke out of the bra peek-a-boo—wardrobe malfunction anyone?—and the double yawn and Mom's absurd "bits and bobs" comment. None of these things would bother the real me.

Problem is, the real me disappears around my immediate family. I feel like the Wicked Witch of the West doused with water. I start out as a wholly intact person and end up a puddle. The funny, no holds-barred country music singer vanishes. She's replaced by the dyslexic kid who struggled in school, the one teachers inevitably asked—"You're not (insert superior brother's name here)'s sister, are you?" Once again, I become the teenager who failed her written driver's test, the one who wears blend-into-the-wall clothes, who scrapes by with mediocre grades.

So, whereas the real Rebecca would laugh at boobgate, home Rebecca is mortified. My face feels hot. I turn away from the bar and begin a gingerly walk toward the bathroom. My left heel starts to bleed for real.

Once inside the sanctity of the enormous room, I sit on a puffed cushion and press a wad of toilet paper to the afflicted spot. Lily, my high school best friend who, against all my advice, married my brother *John* last year, pushes out of a bathroom stall.

"Hey Bec." She stands by the sink and washes her hands super thoroughly. "What happened to you?" She shuts off the water and pulls a paper towel from the dispenser.

"I bought cheap heels and a peekaboo dress. Pretty sure I'm going to hide in here the rest of the night. Join me?"

"Absolutely." She fishes inside her purse, pulls out a Band-Aid, and throws it at me. "I'll get us cocktails."

Lily strides out and returns with two gigantic frozen daiquiris, the kind we used to drink without alcohol as little kids. Each is garnished with a tiny umbrella and a perfect swirl of whipped cream. She hands me one.

"You're an angel."

"So they say." She plops into a chair so fancy it has no business being anywhere near a bathroom. In fact, the entire powder room is a tribute to excess with plush carpet, thick-framed gold mirrors, and floral wallpaper that should look dated but looks regal instead.

I grip the drink with both hands. "My mom described my job as putting bits and bobs on Facebook."

Lily squints—her thinking face. "Bits and bobs. What does that even mean?"

"I don't know."

She leans back and crosses one leg over the other. "Did she tell people you were taking a gap year again?"

"Yup."

She rolls her eyes. Mom adores Lily (she's an environmental engineer and strangely devoted to my brother). Still, Lily knows how much my parents' lack of support for my music hurts.

"How's the audition practice going?"

"Pretty good."

"I can't wait for you to get on *Country Clash*." She holds her drink up.

I smack mine against it. "Me either."

I spend a good deal of my free time rehearsing or dreaming about the show. And, though I don't want to ruin my chances with bad karma, a decent amount of ha-ha-look-at-me-now thoughts creep into my psyche. It's probably unhealthy, but hey, the audition is just eight weeks away. I'll finally know if I can return home with my head held high. Or if I should get the first plane ticket out of here.

Lily and I sip our drinks in comfortable silence. A few women come in but, if any of them think it's strange we're drinking in the bathroom, they don't say.

Lily's phone pings. She pulls it from her purse. "Ugh. John. He wants to introduce me to someone." Her fingers fly over the keys before she tucks the phone back in her purse and pulls out foam flip-flops, the kind you get after getting a pedicure. She holds them out. "You should wear these once you leave."

"Okay." I take the flip-flops. "Why do you have these?"

"John picked me up at the salon and, I don't know, I thought they might be useful. You know how I am."

I nod. "Right. Borderline hoarder."

"I prefer the term environmentally conscious, but yes, I try to repurpose things."

"Thanks." I give her a quick hug and she powers out of the room with her empty daiquiri glass.

I sit alone a moment, then pull out my phone and send a text in the family chat: *Not feeling the best. Going to catch an earlier bus back home. Congrats Your Honor. XOXO R.*

I make my way to the bus stop in the foam flip flops, throw the cursed $9.99 heels in a bin on the way. Most of the time, I don't care that I don't have a driver's license. I bike, take Ubers, and walk. It's good exercise and I like to think I'm helping the environment. But, as I shuffle along in foam flip-flops not meant for walking, I admit the truth: having a license would be glorious.

I see the bus ahead and start to run as well as I can. The driver's face is illuminated by a streetlamp, his mouth twisted in a scowl. I hurry, nearly trip getting up the stairs. I scan the bus.

I'm about to sit next to the love of my life.

And I'm going to hate him.

CHAPTER 2

I *an*

    The bus driver pushes the lever; the door slides open with a loud squeak. I glance up from the photo of Audrey on my home screen. *Three* new passengers enter the already crammed and super-hot bus space. I internally groan. I hate crowded spaces. And people. And heat. People in hot crowded spaces? The worst.

A heavyset man with a big suitcase struggles down the aisle, maneuvering his stuffed black bag in a manner so painful I *almost* feel like I should try to help. Suitcase man is followed by a teenager with thick makeup. She's doused in what I can only guess is an entire bottle of floral perfume. The last passenger is a woman in a tight green dress. She's holding two pieces of foam in her hands. She scans the aisle, noticeable green eyes flicking from seat to seat to seat. I glance at my computer bag and duffel. I'd spread them across the seat next to me with the express purpose of keeping people out. She gestures to the items.

"Hey. Move your stuff." She gives the directive with authority.

I whip my head up and meet her eyes. They are *really* green. "Excuse me?"

"I said, move your stuff." She nods toward the back of the bus. "It's full in here, let's go."

She pushes at my computer bag. More out of surprise than chivalry, I move it and the duffel out of the way. The woman slides, collapses really, into the seat next to me. Her hair is a pretty shade of red. She's not wearing any shoes. I stare at the chipped blue polish on her bare feet. Are you even allowed to ride public transportation without shoes?

"Where are your shoes?" I blurt. She half turns her body and the V-neck of her dress gapes open to reveal her bra and a bit more of her cleavage than I think she'd intended. "Your dress." I point to the gap in material where black lace is clearly visible.

She rolls her eyes. "Lots of unasked-for observations about my appearance over there." She points to the top of my oxford shirt. "Well, here's one for you, Oxford. You don't have to button your shirt up to the tippy top."

"Buttoning your shirt to the top and not wearing shoes are two different things."

She shrugs. "Are they? Is there a law against being barefoot?"

I glance at her feet. "It's unsanitary."

"Says who?"

"Every person in civilized society."

She scans her eyes down my body. "You know, Oxford," she says finally, "it's been a long night." She pulls the material of her dress back across her chest. "I'm a little tired of uptight pricks like you. So if you don't mind, I'm going to listen to some music." She pulls wireless headphones out of her purse, plugs them in her ears, and leans back.

Uptight.

I bristle at her description. It was the exact word Audrey, my girlfriend, had used when she'd insisted we "take a break."

I pull up my most recent text message chain and scan

through. The last one, from me, posted one hour ago: *Hey, Aud. Almost to the consultant job. Miss you.*

No answer.

To that or my three preceding texts.

We *had* agreed not to speak for the two weeks I'd be at the consultant job. But I'd figured texts were okay. It's not *really* contact. Right?

I conjure an image of Audrey. Long, strawberry-blond hair, freckled nose, slight build. A receptionist at a doctor's office who'd suddenly and inexplicably changed. She went from a woman who loved nights in and her two cats to one who wanted to "see the world" and "live a little." I wasn't ready for the change.

I figure it will be fine. By the time I get back, Audrey and I can have a rational conversation and figure things out. As a gesture of good faith, I'd left her my car; hers is unreliable. Which, of course, is why I'm on the bus smushed next to a stranger.

Country music pings from the woman's headphones, loud enough that I hear Rex Armstrong, one of my favorite singers. Not that I'd tell her that. I sit back, listen to the lyrics, close my eyes. The rhythm of the bus jostles my body. I forget I'm on the bus, lulled into a half-sleep where Audrey is very much present and no longer angry with me.

"Last stop!"

My eyes fly open. I half expect to see Audrey. I see *her* instead. The shoeless woman. She's sitting across from me now, the foam pieces haphazardly placed on the seat beside her. She must have moved while I was sleeping.

I look to the front of the bus. The driver stands, his hand gripped tight around the lever to the now open door. The woman and I are the only people on the bus besides the driver, and the bus itself is parked in a row with dozens of others. The realization comes to me with a start. This is not a bus *stop*. This is a bus *depot*.

"Wait," I call out. "Why are you at a depot?"

The driver shrugs. "Done for the night."

Oh.

OH.

I'd assumed the bus would run all night. I feel ridiculous but take solace at the fact that the woman looks even more startled than I do, eyes comically wide.

She leans across the aisle. "Do you know where we are?"

"Your guess is as good as mine."

She looks to the driver. He pushes at the lever of the already open door, a big hint to, well, get off the goddammed bus. "You're in Moosham, New Jersey," he volunteers. "It's on the schedule."

The schedule. Right. Something people riding a bus should check more carefully. It probably gives important information like when the bus stops running for the night.

I gather my things and step off. The woman, still barefoot and holding the foam pieces, does the same. The parking lot is all gravel. She hobbles a few steps, then sets the foam pieces on the ground. She puts her feet on them and tries to walk. It's clear they're broken.

I forge ahead but feel like a jerk. It's a long way across the parking lot to the sidewalk and main building. I take a few steps, turn around. "Are you okay?"

Her face shoots up. She looks at me with a scowl. "Yes. Why?"

"Your shoes are broken." I pause. "I mean, *are* those your shoes?"

She shakes her head. "You've got quite the obsession with footwear, Oxford."

"Sorry."

She swipes the foam pieces off the ground, takes a step forward, and winces. That has to hurt. Plus, there might be glass bits and who knows what else. Very unsanitary, for real.

I eye the sidewalk, still a good distance ahead. "Do you need help?"

"And how would you help me? What, are you going to carry me to the sidewalk?"

"I would."

She narrows her eyes, puts her hand on her hip. "Why?"

"Because this whole scenario with your feet on the dirt and the pebbles and everything is giving me the willies."

A smile tugs at the corners of her mouth. "The willies? First, did you actually use that phrase? And second, it's just a little dirt."

I make a sour face without meaning to; she stares at me. "You really have a delicate constitution there, don't you, Oxford?"

I hold up my hands. "Just trying to help."

"Well, aren't you gallant? Trying to save a damsel in distress from the horror of walking barefoot *on the earth*. Thank you, but I'm good." She hop-steps toward the sidewalk.

Fine. I'm from Nebraska. In The Cornhusker State, you're *supposed* to help out fellow citizens. Not in good old New Jersey, I guess.

I pull out my phone and summon an Uber from the app. I stride to the sidewalk, stand under the streetlamp twenty feet from the woman. She taps at her phone.

I stare at her profile. She seems to notice my gaze. I look away.

This woman. She's gotten under my skin.

My phone buzzes; Audrey's picture flashes on the screen. I try to answer, too fast, and practically drop the phone. "Audrey. Hi."

"Ian. You have to stop texting me." She's irritated.

"I thought you would want to know I arrived."

"We're on a break."

"I know." I put my free hand over my ear and turn my back to the woman. I lower my voice. "I just thought, you know. It's not like we don't care about each other."

She sighs. I imagine her twisting a lock of hair around her finger, a nervous habit I'd always found endearing.

"Ian, please," she says, her tone more pleading than angry now. "Give me the space I need."

She clicks off. I stare at my phone like Audrey's somehow inside it.

"Ouch."

The woman's voice interrupts my thoughts. I look at her.

"Just saying," she continues, "that sounded harsh."

"How could you even—" I start, then wave at her like a dismissal. Minutes pass. We don't speak despite our being in the same situation, neither of us having realized the bus route stopped at midnight.

A white Honda CRV pulls up. A wiry man with a Phillies baseball hat jumps out and clicks open the trunk. "Hey. I'm Carl."

"Hey, Carl." I hurl my suitcase into the trunk and slip in the passenger seat. The woman is still leaning against the streetlamp, headphones now plugged in her ears. It's dark. She's alone. Does she even have a ride coming?

I turn toward Carl. "Can you hang on a minute?"

"Sure thing, man."

I pop out of the car. "Do you have a ride?" I yell across the parking lot.

She lifts an eyebrow. "Are you offering?"

I don't know where she's going. I don't know *her*, actually, and I stall my words. Am I offering to give her a ride? I don't even know. But I can't leave her stranded at a bus depot in the middle of the night.

She nods toward a car pulling into the lot. "Don't sweat it, Oxford. My ride's here." The second car pulls in behind Carl.

"Thanks for the almost offer." She winks in my direction before disappearing inside the vehicle.

CHAPTER 3

R*ebecca*
    The day after Mom's swearing-in, I think I see
GUY FROM THE BUS. Twice. Once perusing
vegetables at Shoprite and the second coming out of a coffee
shop.

Of course, the guy isn't him. He's just on my mind because I
ended up with a gash on my foot from the dash across the
parking lot. The gash reminds me of him, which I think says all
I need to about the impression he made on me.

It's now Monday morning and I've been summoned by Aunt
Kimmy. Aunt Kimmy, my father's sister, is my *favorite*. Blond,
brash, and unapologetic, she's everything my family isn't. She
received ownership of Mrs. Fishes (originally CM Fish Co.) as
part of her divorce settlement. Her ex-husband, I'm pretty sure,
thought he'd unloaded a dud. Kimmy proved him wrong. In the
span of five years, she transformed the company from a fledg-
ling local business to a nationally recognized brand, mainly due
to marketing campaigns centered on sex. Kimmy hired all
women to work in corporate; men worked the docks. She hired

me as a social media consultant two years ago, when I dropped out of school.

I carry two tall lattes into her office. She looks up from an ornate gold desk. "Hey Bec. Just in time."

I set the coffees on her desk.

"Do you mind getting the door?"

"Sure." I push the door shut and move to sit in a comically fluffy chair in front of her desk. The chair, like everything else in the office, screams stereotypical femininity. It's a pink space with hues of gold, fresh flowers always on the desk. Floral prints adorn the walls. Pink fish swim in a giant corner tank. If you didn't know Kimmy, the space might seem absurd for a company CEO. But it's very on brand. Kimmy's the poster child for "anything boys can do girls can do better," a mantra made all the more powerful by the fact that she looks, acts, and decorates "like a girl."

She grips the latte and leans forward. "I'll get right to it. You know Mrs. Fishes has a parent company, right?"

"Right." I *definitely* know this. The acquisition of Mrs. Fishes by megacompany LCR had been huge news.

"LCR," Kimmy continues, "has received some complaints about the culture here."

"What? Why?"

She angles her head toward the gold-plated mirror next to her desk, fingers a lock of hair. "Apparently, it's too feminine. Men don't feel included." She pulls an emery board from her desk, rubs it on the edge of a manicured nail.

"Like a good old girls club?"

"Exactly." She sets the board down. "Like the fish industry hasn't catered to men for years." She rolls her eyes. "Anyway, to address the problem, LCR has sent a sensitivity trainer from some consulting company to give us tips."

My eyes bug out.

"I know. It's two weeks. We'll hear what he has to say and

then he'll be gone." She leans back in her chair. "Can you be a doll and be the point person while he's here? I don't want to deal with him more than I have to."

"Sure," I say automatically. There's almost nothing I won't do for Aunt Kimmy.

"Don't feel like you have to go crazy or anything. Maybe take him to dinner tonight as a welcome?" She pulls open her desk drawer, retrieves a credit card, and holds it out.

"Sure." I take the card from her outstretched hand.

Kimmy stands and smooths out the wrinkles in her fitted suit skirt. "All right then, I'll introduce you."

I follow Kimmy out of her office. She glides down the hall in three-inch turquoise heels like they're sneakers. I follow in my denim skirt, bright yellow shirt, and faux blue glasses. A small scarf, patterned with tropical fish, is tied around my neck.

Kimmy stops in the doorway of an office. I peer around her and spy a man at a desk pushed against the far wall. His back is to me, but I can tell he's tall. He's got good hair, thick and brown. I stare at it a moment. Really good hair. The kind you'd want to run your hands through.

"Mr. Ledger," Kimmy calls, "I'd like you to meet one of my associates, Rebecca Chapman. Rebecca, this is Ian Ledger."

I step in front of Kimmy and shoot my hand out just as the man turns around.

The smile leaves my face as soon as I see him.

Ian is Oxford. GUY FROM THE BUS.

"Nice to meet you, Rebecca." No recognition crosses his features as he grips my now dormant hand.

"Sure."

"Rebecca will be your point person for the next two weeks," Kimmy continues.

"Great," Ian says. He releases my hand. Still no inkling of recognition.

"Well, I'll leave you two to it," Kimmy says. She slips out of the office.

As soon as she's gone, Ian gives a dismissive nod in my direction. "I'll look for you if I need something." He swivels back toward his computer.

My feet root to the floor. It's insulting, his apparent lack of recall. We sat next to each other for at least an hour. We were stranded at a bus depot. He offered to *carry* me. Honestly. Am I that unmemorable?

"Don't you remember me?" I blurt.

He swivels back and meets my eyes. "Yes. I do."

The directness of his response takes me by surprise. "And?"

He looks at my feet. "I see you've rectified your footwear issue." He nods to my shoes. Clogs with flowers. "Sort of."

"I never had a footwear issue," I retort. "And what's wrong with these shoes?" I gesture toward them.

He shrugs. "Nothing. If you want footgear that's completely useless in case of an unforeseen emergency."

"What emergency?"

"I don't know. That's why it's unforeseen."

I say nothing, flustered. He's besting me.

"They're loud too," he continues. "I heard you coming well before you got to my office. Clop. Clop. Clop. Clop." He bangs his hands on his desk in rhythm with his words.

"I—" I stamp my foot. CLOP. The sound *is* loud and I lose my train of thought.

Ian smirks. "Anyway, I recall seeing you. If that's your question." He turns and continues typing.

Seriously? I turn on my heel and make my way out of the office. The clog clopping sound, which never bothered me before, seems obnoxious. I collapse into the chair in front of my desk, which of course, is right outside Ian's door. I toss my bag on the floor and stare at the sticky note affixed to my computer, September 8 in my messy scrawl.

Otherwise known as the day of my *Country Clash* audition.

Otherwise, otherwise known as the day I start living my dream.

Or the day that it ends.

CHAPTER 4

I*an*

I walk out of my temporary office, sensitivity quizzes
in hand. As always, I'll hand the questionnaires out
personally and introduce myself. I hate doing it—meeting new
people is not my forte—but I find people are more honest if
they've spoken to the person who made the questionnaire.

The first person I see is Rebecca. She's staring at her
computer, sheets of auburn hair around her face. It's straighter
today, not curled like it was on the bus. She pushes glasses with
electric blue frames up the bridge of her nose.

I can't believe she works here.

She's crept into my thoughts more than once since the bus
ride. And not in a good way. It's how she made me feel. Like I
was tense and uptight. The *exact* qualities Audrey wants me to
change.

I move to her desk. She looks up and her eyes are such an
intense shade of green that I momentarily forget to speak.

She stares at me a moment. "Did you need something,
Oxford?"

"It's Ian."

"Sure, E."

"*Ian*." I hold out a quiz. "It's a sensitivity questionnaire."

She pulls the quiz from my hand, scans it, then reads the first question. "True or false. It's okay to tell jokes in the workplace." She sets the questionnaire down and whips her head up. "How is that a question?"

"What do you mean?"

"I mean, some jokes have to be okay to tell, right?"

I lean forward and tap the blank spaces under the question. "That's why there's room to elaborate. The questions are designed to make people think."

"So, it's less of a questionnaire than a springboard for discussion?" She scans the paper then looks at me again. "Okay. How's this? Knock, knock."

I roll my eyes.

She rolls hers back at me. "I'm trying to participate in *your* survey, E." She pauses. "Let's try again. Knock, knock."

Fine. "Who's there?"

"Centipede."

"Centipede who?"

"Centipede in my stocking."

I scrunch up my face. I get the punchline just as she says it.

She leans forward. "Get it? *Santa* peed in my stocking. Could be insulting. Or no?" She tips her head like she's thinking hard. "I think it would be a good one for discussion. Right? I mean, by the look on your face, you seem highly offended."

"Just get the questionnaire in by the end of the day."

"Aye, aye, captain." She gives me a salute.

I move to step away, catching sight of her computer screen as I do so. I stop. On the screen are two bright yellow cartoonish fish facing each other. One has eyes fringed with dark lashes, red and puckered lips, and a fuchsia boa. The other is wearing a cowboy hat and a red bandana. Their lips almost touch. Over the two of them, in bright orange bubble letters, is a tagline: Get Fresh with Mrs. Fishes.

She glances at me. "Yes?"

"Is that a new logo?" I nod toward her computer screen.

"It's an idea for a social media campaign."

"Why are you gendering the fish?"

She twists around in her chair and meets my eyes. "Fish have genders."

"But these are stereotypical genders."

She shakes her head. "They look cute. And the graphic goes with our tagline." She turns back and hits a few buttons to give the female fish a lipstick to carry. After, she turns back, looks at me, and lifts an eyebrow. "Better?"

I know I should leave it. This image and tagline will never get approved by LCR. But I somehow can't help myself. "Why does Mrs. Fishes need a social media campaign centered on outdated sexual stereotypes?"

She widens her eyes in a way clearly meant to be sarcastic. "Oh my gosh, you're right." She taps vigorously on the computer keys. A football appears under the fin of the male fish. She angles the screen in the direction I'm standing.

"Do what you want. It's not very twenty-first century."

She shifts her feet in the absurd flower clogs. "I'll bear that in mind. By the way"—she points to her neck—"I thought we talked about the buttons on the bus. No need to go all the way to the top."

Instinctively, I touch the top of my button-down. "I'm good."

"Maybe a funky color then? Instead of beige? You'd look good in lavender." She bumps the woman at the next desk who, honestly, I hadn't even noticed until this exact moment. I've been too engaged with Rebecca.

"What do you think, Jeanine?" she asks.

Jeanine, an older woman with stiff gray hair and a thick shirt embroidered with daisies, looks mortified. "Sure. But honestly, you look fine in beige."

"Thank you." I hand Jeanine a questionnaire, introduce myself, and move on. Ignoring Rebecca as much as possible seems the best course of action.

I pass out my questionnaires. I eat lunch with Kimberly in her office and feel like I'm inside an explosion of pink, gold, and fluff. She's wearing a form-fitting suit jacket with a lacy camisole, and every time she leans forward (which seems to be a lot), I get an ample view of her cleavage. I try not to look. But it keeps happening, and it becomes more awkward to avert my eyes. I don't want to seem like I find the cleavage offensive, but I don't want to look like a pervert either. So, I hurry through lunch and rattle off a fake meeting to leave early.

I walk back to my office, shut the door, and collapse into my chair. Sometimes, like right now, I really dislike my job. Too much thinking about what could be insulting or offensive makes me crazy. And uptight, apparently. On the other hand, *not* thinking about it, not trying to understand the experience of others in a thoughtful way, can lead to discrimination. It's my mission to minimize that.

I bury myself in a PowerPoint presentation I'll give later in the week. I forget about the time until Rebecca bursts in. She waves a credit card. "Winner, winner, chicken dinner."

I look up. She smiles.

"Kimmy wants me to take you to dinner."

I check my watch. Five on the nose. I normally work until at least six.

"She made us reservations at The Lobster House."

I love seafood. I do not want to have dinner with Rebecca. She's under my skin enough as it is. I wave my hand. "Thanks, but I'll get takeout."

"Nope. No can do."

She taps the credit card on the edge of the doorframe, leans against it after. Bare legs are visible from the tops of her clogs to the end of her pretty short denim skirt. I can't figure out if she looks cute or sexy. Or neither. She's an enigma.

"I'm under strict instructions to take you out," she says.

"Really. I'm good."

She nods at my desk. I follow her gaze to the oversized framed picture of Audrey I'd placed there. One of her outside at the park, freckles spread across the bridge of her nose, wind blowing at her hair. It's my favorite but it's too big for the space, the frame way too ornate for an office. Embarrassingly, it looks kind of like the start of a shrine.

"That the girl you were talking to at the train station?"

I bristle, recall my scolding conversation with Audrey. There's no way Rebecca could have heard that. Right? I angle the photo away from her view. "It's not your concern."

She shrugs. "She's cute. Nice skin. Looks like it would burn. Does it burn?"

"It does—" Ridiculously, I start to answer the question.

"Come on," Rebecca says, waving a hand forward. "I'll bet *she's* having dinner out."

She nods toward Audrey's picture with her chin, and as much as I hate to admit it, she's probably right. Audrey most likely is eating out. Or doing something else spontaneous. One thing she's surely not doing: eating takeout alone.

Okay. Eating dinner with a coworker—even if it is Rebecca —is exactly what I'm supposed to be doing during "the break." When the break is over, I'll be able to entertain Audrey with details of the people I met, the places I went, and the things that I did. If nothing else, Rebecca is an entertaining caricature. I can't imagine an evening with her would be boring.

I stand. "Fine. You lead the way."

CHAPTER 5

R*ebecca*

The server seats Ian and me at a circular table on the deck of the sailboat of The Lobster House, Cape May's most iconic seafood restaurant, conveniently within walking distance from Mrs. Fishes. A bright sun sits in the center of the sky, its rays dotting the surface of the surrounding ocean water. A warm breeze pushes at gentle ocean swells, rhythmically rocking the boat. Soft classical music plays from speakers; the scent of cooked seafood infuses the air. The energy of the restaurant is relaxed, one of sundrenched people on a summer getaway. The atmosphere is so ideal, I wish I were on a date. But, of course, this would require me to have a real, flesh and blood boyfriend, which I don't. So, it's dinner with Ian. Better than dinner alone.

Maybe?

His head is buried in the menu. In fairness, there are *a lot* of choices. He flips from page to page of the book-like, laminated menu. His hair falls in front of his eyes. I note it has a bit of a wave, something I hadn't observed before. The top button of his oxford is undone, and his sleeves are folded and pushed to his mid-arm. The casual vibe suits him. He looks, for the first time since I met him, like his muscles aren't tensed.

A perky college-aged server materializes in front of our table, pen and pad in hand. She has lavender highlights in her hair, a tiny nose ring, and turquoise earrings so long they pull at her lobes. "I'm Carly. Ready to order?"

I glance at Ian, still flipping through the menu. I'm about to ask for more time when he shoots his head up. "I'm good."

I order crabcakes, Ian a seafood platter; we both order wine. Carly writes the information on a pad and walks back toward the kitchen.

I look at Ian. "How'd you get through the menu so fast?"

"I didn't." He shakes his head. "But I used to work in a restaurant. A night like tonight is big for tips. I can't be taking too much of her time." He shrugs. "I figure I'll get a bit of everything with a seafood platter. You can have some. It seemed pretty big."

"Thanks." I digest his intent to help Carly. The small act of compassion fleshes him out, makes him seem like more than uptight GUY FROM THE BUS. I soften a little.

Carly returns with our wine and a huge basket of fresh, warm rolls and sets both on the table. I grab a roll, break it in half, and direct my attention back to Ian. "Were you a waiter at the restaurant?"

"Sure was. Six years at Mr. Steak in Carlisle, Nebraska."

"Wait." I hold up a hand. "Are you from *Nebraska*?"

"Born and bred."

He says the words with a purposeful midwestern lilt. It's funny; it surprises me. I didn't expect him to have a sense of humor.

"Nebraska," I repeat.

"It's not Mars."

"And you still live there?"

"I do."

I pop a piece of roll in my mouth, chew, and swallow. "Sorry. Had to unpack that for a moment."

"Haven't met any Cornhuskers, huh?"

"No." I huff out the word.

"Almost two million people live there, you know."

His mouth curls into a half smile and I wonder if he's teasing me. Do two million people actually live in Nebraska? I have no idea. I change the subject. "Tell me about Mr. Steak."

"It's the nicest restaurant in Carlisle. You can't go by the name. Everything in that area starts with Mr.—Mr. Steak, Mr. Donut, Mr. Bike, Mr. Pizza." He pauses. "Mr. Taxes."

"Mr. Taxes?"

"Yup. Owned by a woman, ironically."

"Why wouldn't she just name it Ms. Taxes or Mrs. Taxes?" I pause. "Miss Taxes?"

He shrugs. "Not sure. I think one business was successful using it, so it caught on. Or maybe people are just unoriginal. I don't know." He picks up his wine from the table. "Oh. There's Mr. Pet too. Forgot about that one."

"No Mrs. or Ms.?"

He twists his glass by the stem. "Not a one."

I lean forward. "Hmm. A little sexist, don't you think? Is that what got you started in your sensitivity training? Trying to right the ship with Carlisle's Mr.-Mrs. thing?"

Ian's expression turns serious; he straightens. I get the distinct impression I insulted him. I wave the half roll, still in my hand. "Sorry. I didn't mean to offend you."

"It's fine."

I leave it. Ian probably didn't get the joke. Maybe he doesn't have a sense of humor after all.

It's silent for a beat, then another. I'm grateful when Carly materializes, expertly balancing a tray crammed with food dishes. All ours. "Plates are hot." She places one after the other on the table. "Anything else?"

Ian looks up. "Not for me, Carly. Thank you."

"Me either."

Ian grabs a plate of scallops and scrapes a bunch on his plate. He takes salad next, then coleslaw, then crab legs. "So how about you?" he asks finally. "I worked at Mr. Steak. What was your first job?"

"Babysitting." I say automatically. "I was *the* neighborhood babysitter growing up."

"Really?"

"You're surprised."

He stabs a scallop. "You seem like the kind of girl who would have better things to do on a Friday or Saturday night."

My face reddens. I assume it's a compliment, the fact Ian thinks I'd have had better things to do in high school than babysit. Truth is, I didn't. The confident, brash side of me—the one Ian knows—is recent.

I finish my wine, and as if she were waiting in the wings, Carly materializes with another open bottle. "More?"

I hold up my glass. Ian does the same. It's probably not a good idea. I have a very low tolerance for alcohol. But the atmosphere pulls at my resistance, and I take a sip from my newly full glass.

"What's your best babysitting story?"

"Hmmm." I pop a scallop in my mouth and think. "I know," I say, setting my fork on my plate. "The Newhouses. They had four boys and always had me babysit during events at their house. They never wanted 'the children' underfoot." I make quotation marks with my fingers.

"Of course not."

"This one time, Mrs. Newhouse was having a fancy coffee for some charity group. The boys had all sorts of reptiles that Mrs. Newhouse let them get in lieu of a dog." I roll my eyes. "Like that's the same thing. One of the kids actually named his snake Fido."

Ian smiles. "Cool name."

"It was. Anyway, during the coffee, all the reptiles got out."

He lifts an eyebrow.

I shoot my hand out. "I know what you're thinking, but they unlocked their cages *before* I got there. I had nothing to do with the escape."

"So, what happened?"

"I made the boys look for them."

"They listened to you?"

"Yeah, they listened to me. I ran a pretty tight ship, but I was fun. If they behaved, we always did cool stuff." I pause, thinking back. I'd always liked babysitting. There was a creative component to it, thinking of fun and different things to do. Obstacle courses, dinosaur digs, making solution for giant bubbles out of dishwasher soap and glycerin. I was good at that job, one of the only things I have talent for besides music. And my parents were proud of my babysitting prowess until their friends' children aged out of needing sitters.

"Anyway," I continue, "they found them all but Fido."

"The snake?"

"Yup. That snake was over two feet long so I couldn't figure it out. I mean, we looked everywhere. I finally made an excuse to go into the room where the coffee was and I see it, wrapped around a plant, right by some lady's head."

"No," Ian hisses. "What did you do?"

I lean forward, enthralled with the storytelling. "I told the kids we'd make homemade ice cream if they put on an impromptu talent show in the yard. Most of the guests were moms. If little kids want to have a talent show, you've got to watch, right? So, the ladies go out to see the show and I get Fido. End of story."

Ian nods appreciatively. "All right. I'm impressed. Better than any story I've got from Mr. Steak."

We continue to eat, spooning from every plate on the table

like we're accustomed to eating together. We finish the second glasses of wine and order dessert—chocolate cake for me, carrot cake for Ian. The vibe is casual, fun even. I don't know what it is. The atmosphere. The food. The fact that Ian is—maybe—not as big a douche as I thought.

"What do you do in your free time, Ian Ledger?" I ask, then put my hand up. "Wait. Wait. Let me guess." I rub my chin like I'm thinking. "Puzzles," I shout.

"Nope."

"Sudoku."

"Never."

"Model trains."

"No."

I lean back and rap my fingers on the table. "Stamp collecting?"

He laughs. "No and please stop. I cook. I'm a big runner. I love astronomy."

Carly returns and sets down two massive pieces of cake. Without thinking, I slice each in half, try both. If Ian finds it objectionable that I'm eating *his* carrot cake, he doesn't say.

Ian stabs a piece of carrot cake with his fork. "Oh. And I like most music."

"Really? I'm a professional musician." I say this like I get paid to perform. Which I don't. Unless you count a few free drinks at local bars.

He draws his head back, seemingly surprised. "Wow. Genre?"

"Country."

"I love country."

This, of course, opens a whole new thread of conversation. I babble about my favorite musicians and songs and the concerts I've been to. Posters I had on my wall as a kid. "I'm trying out for *Country Clash*," I say, and feeling some weird need to prove it, I pull up the invitation on my phone and slide it over to Ian. He inspects the screen.

"Really cool, Rebecca," he says, still looking at the phone.

I bask in the compliment.

"What instrument do you play?"

"I don't." I slice a piece of the chocolate cake with my fork.

He tips his head, a quizzical look on his features. "Don't you have to?" He looks at my phone and back up at me.

A shot of adrenaline shoots through me. Ian hands the phone back, a tiny part of the invitation now enlarged on the screen. I read it to myself: "To audition, every candidate is required to be proficient in a minimum of one musical instrument." There's an explanation as to the meaning of proficient but I don't read it. I can't read it, actually. The letters are dyslexic jumble, and the font is tiny.

I press my hand on my forehead and stare at the jumble of letters on my phone. My stomach clenches. My heart tingles. My mind whirs with alarm. The fun atmosphere fades away and all I can think is: *I have to learn to play an instrument in eight weeks.*

"Are you all right?"

I glance up. Ian's looking at me, his face etched with concern.

Suddenly, irrationally, I'm angry with him. Viscerally angry. Like *he* missed the requirement. The reasonable part of my brain, buried deep under the panicked part, knows this makes no sense. It's a classic "kill the messenger" response. But my shocked and frenzied mind—the one internally screaming *NOOOOOO*—can't access rationality.

"Rebecca?"

"We should go." I stand and wave at Carly with wild arms. "Check, please."

CHAPTER 6

I*an*

Rebecca signs the check with a single swipe of the pen. She puffs out a series of breaths like she can't catch her own. Her face is flushed.

The sudden change in her demeanor is disconcerting. "Are you all right?" I ask again.

"Fine." She drops the thick, puffy folder with the bill on the table, the rim of the credit card peeking out the top. "Let's go." She pushes back her chair.

"Hey." I nod toward the table. "Don't forget the card."

She pulls it from the folder and grips it in her hand. Without a word, she strides forward, weaving between tables toward the door. Her steps are as fast as they can be with the clogs, which is not all that fast. They clomp, loudly, on the restaurant floor. Given our prior conversation about the clogs, the scenario seems like it might be funny. It's something I'd tease her about except the glimmer of joviality we'd shared is clearly over. I can't help but think I said or did something wrong.

She spills out on to the sidewalk, still flushed and breathless, and stands in front of the boat. It's dark now, her face bright in the moonlight. I stand in front of her, mouth open like a stuffed fish. Finally, I ask, "Are you mad at me?"

She rolls her eyes. "What are you, a teenage girl?"

"Why a teenage girl? Why that stereotype?" As soon as the words leave my mouth, I wish I could stuff them back in.

She throws her head back like she's laughing but she's not. "You're too much, you know that, Oxford?" She takes a breath. "Oh, and by using the term 'oxford'"—she makes quotation marks with her fingers—"I definitely intend to stereotype you as an uptight prick."

She turns and pushes past families waiting outside The Lobster House. She heads in the only direction you can go, down the asphalt path which leads to the main road. No way am I following. I'd overtake her—she's slow on the clogs—and I'm pretty sure that wouldn't go over well.

I move to a bench and stare at the bay, streaks of moonlight on the surface of the rippled water. There's a fishy, salty aroma which should be unpleasant but somehow makes the atmosphere feel more authentic. Seagulls swoop and dip; their distinctive calls fill the air.

I pull out my phone and google *Country Clash*. I scan information about the competition. Successful audition candidates are paired together by judges to form bands which will compete on live television for audience votes. The winning band gets a record contract and a million dollars.

Whoa.

I re-read the information, make sure I saw it right. Yup. A record contract AND a million dollars. No wonder Rebecca's a little off-balance about her audition. I've pieced together that she missed the instrument requirement, and though I have no reason to care, I feel bad.

I can play guitar, but she probably wouldn't want my help. I'm only here for two weeks anyway.

Leave it, Ian.

The directive is clear in my mind.

I stand, shove my phone in my pocket, and walk in the general direction of the town. Kimberly—or Kimmy, I guess—booked a bed-and-breakfast for me. "A staple of the Cape May experience," she'd said. The chosen B&B, Shelly's by the Sea, is a massive Victorian home three blocks from the beach. The architecture, like most of the homes in Cape May, is ornate: a gingerbread house with green siding, swirly pink trim, and a wraparound porch with rockers and ferns. It's the kind of house Audrey would love, and I've already taken at least a dozen pictures to show her after "the break." I take photos of more homes as I walk, all majestic in the moonlight.

Shelly's comes into view. A talkative husband and wife who I met briefly yesterday sit in rockers on the porch. Both grip thick glass tumblers. I tromp up the stairs and head straight to the door, careful not to make eye contact. I'm supposed to work on being friendly; I just can't do it tonight.

I pull open the door and feel like I dodged a bullet. I spy the staircase which leads to my room and literally salivate at the thought of being alone. No awkward conversations or dead silences. No trying to be "on" when I desperately want to be "off." No dinners with strangers who may or may not hate me.

A voice calls out.

"Ian!"

It's Lou, one of the proud owners of Shelly's.

"How was your night?" asks Sue, Lou's wife, the other proud owner.

I turn around. Lou and Sue are behind the reception desk with matching white hairstyles and Shelly's polos, a huge pink shell on the left pocket. Both look unabashedly thrilled.

"Good," I say.

"Night cap?" Sue asks.

I wave at her. "Nah."

"You could join the card group," Lou suggests, nodding toward a table in the foyer where a group of guests are mid-game around a circular table.

"Some guests are going on a haunted tour of Cape May, if that's more to your liking." Sue smiles broadly.

It's clear Sue and Lou want me to choose *something*, that they can't, as B&B owners, fathom I'd rather sit alone than socialize. In fairness, people who typically stay in bed-and-breakfasts, and certainly those that own them, are probably joiners. The kind of people who make lifelong friends with strangers or enjoy spontaneous social activities. People who, after a long day, would be energized by cocktails or haunted tours or card games.

I am not that person.

"I'm good," I say.

"Breakfast starts at seven," Sue sings out. "We'll pair you with someone. Don't worry." She smiles, wide, and I make a note to have breakfast somewhere else.

I wave but don't turn around, hurry up the stairs, and find my room. I unlock the door (with an actual key!) and step inside. Like the house, the room is Victorian themed. There's a large mahogany poster bed, floral wallpaper, and a gas fireplace on one wall. All flat surfaces are covered with lace doilies. It's small but cozy with the only real downside being the size of the bathroom. I can only guess people of the Victorian era were very, very short.

I dress in boxers, brush my teeth, and collapse on the bed. For the first time since "the break," I don't automatically think of Audrey. Instead, I conjure an image of Rebecca in those ridiculous clogs, glasses with electric blue frames on her face.

My phone rings. I grab it from the nightstand in a fluid movement, thinking it's Audrey. She's come to her senses. She misses me. The break is over.

I answer the phone without looking. "Hello."

"Ian."

Not Audrey. My sister, Brenda. Not bad. She's at the top of my admittedly short list of people I'd like to get a call from.

"Hey, Brenda. What's up?"

"Just checking on you. How's the new job?"

Pots and pans clank in the background. Brenda and her fiancé, Julian, are caterers. They're always cooking something. Visiting them is a vacation for the senses, with all the food looking, smelling, and tasting so good it makes me wish I'd gone into a culinary profession.

I grip the phone to my ear. "It's fine. Two weeks."

"And the break?"

"Still on."

She lets out a breath. Brenda never thought Audrey was right for me, but to her credit, she'd only ever said it once. One and done so I'd know her opinion. Since then, she tries to be supportive, but we're close enough that I know the meaning of that exhalation.

"So are you being *friendly*?" The way she asks the question is mocking.

"Well," I say, shifting the pillow beneath my head, "I turned down an offer for nightcaps, a card game, and a haunted tour. How's that?"

"Sounds par for the course."

"I did go out to dinner with a work colleague."

"Ooooh. Progress. Do tell."

"Eh. Fine. I had a ton of great seafood."

I don't share details about Rebecca; my feelings about her are too mixed. Do I like her? Hate her? I somehow don't know. Fortunately, Brenda doesn't ask for details, instead fixated on my meal, the word "seafood" having set off a litany of questions on preparation and taste.

"Sounds like just the kind of food Julian and I want to offer for our frozen food meal service," Brenda says. "Job's still open if you want it."

I smile. "No thanks." Brenda brings up me working on a frozen food line every time we talk. I don't think she's serious. I don't know the first thing about frozen food.

"How's the hotel?"

"Not a hotel. A bed-and-breakfast." I describe the house, the gingerbread details, the giant wraparound porch, and my tiny bathroom. "Oh, and there's a disturbing stain on the ceiling," I add, staring at it. "I think it's water."

"And do you think it's going to leak in the night? Get you wet?" There's a trace of amusement in her voice.

I smile. Brenda is the *only* person who can make light of my worrywart nature without it seeming like an insult. "I don't know," I say with a mock concerned tone. "It's an old house. Plaster could rain down on me in my sleep. You should be concerned."

"I am concerned. I hope you survive the night." Pots and pans clank loudly. "Got to go. My soufflés are burning."

Brenda hangs up. I switch off the light and quickly fall asleep. Sometime later, I dream someone is knocking on the door. It's loud. And it keeps going. Louder. I open my eyes, and well, shit! Someone's in my room. Someone is IN MY ROOM. I bolt up, panicked, then make out the faces.

It's Sue and Lou.

Lou's wearing a headband with a miner's lamp in the center. The light from it shines in my face; I put up a hand to shield my eyes. It's surreal. I feel like I'm about to be kidnapped in a bizarre "bring this man out of his shell" social plot.

I glance at the clock. One friggin' a.m. "What are you doing in here?"

"Sorry, Mr. Ledger," Sue sings out.

"Leak in the ceiling," Lou adds. He looks up and his miner's light illuminates big drops of water, and a little plaster, dripping from the ceiling stain.

I knew it.

I can't wait to tell Brenda.

"We have another room all set up for you," Sue says. "Don't you worry."

Like another room is what I'm worried about right now.

Lou looks around. "We'll bring your belongings to the new room in the morning."

"All we need right now is you," Sue adds.

Now wide awake, I follow them down the hall and a windy staircase. Lou, still in the lighted miner's hat, swings open the door to a room. I step inside. It's huge. And kind of lived in.

"Make yourself at home!" Sue swings out her arms like being uprooted in the middle of the night and rehomed in what appears to be someone else's room is a big treat.

"Is someone in here already?"

"Nope. Just you," Lou says.

It's not until the morning, when I see framed pictures of Lou and Sue and various children on every conceivable surface, that I realize I'm in *their* room. Dentures on the sink, a bra discarded on the floor—they clearly left in a hurry. Standing in their lived-in, unprepared room—and having slept in their bed—feels almost worse than it would have to stay in the one with the leak. Not to mention, where did they sleep? It's all a little disturbing.

Kimmy calls at eight.

"IAN."

She's says my name like that, like it's in all caps.

"I'm so sorry," she continues. "I heard what happened."

"It's all right," I manage.

"Shelly's is full," she continues, "but don't worry. I have the perfect place for you to stay."

She goes on to describe a company-owned duplex in town. It

sounds perfect—read: isolated—and I readily agree to move over there for the duration of my stay.

"Oh, and you already know the person next door," she says.

I can't imagine that's right. I hardly know anyone here except—I think the name as soon as she says it.

"It's Rebecca."

CHAPTER 7

R*ebecca*

I swear I hear Ian outside. But it can't be him. It's 10:00 a.m. on a workday, the morning after our dinner at The Lobster House, and I've called out sick. Not a lie. I have been sick to my stomach since last night's revelation. Printouts for potential music instructors are strewn across my unmade bed, most of them too expensive or too far away.

"Looks good," the man with Ian's voice says.

"So sorry about the B&B," another voice says, and I sit up. It's Kimmy. I'd recognize her voice anywhere.

I move to the window, peek from behind the bedroom curtain. Yup. They're there. Kimmy, perky in a tight tan suit and floral stilettos, and Ian, disheveled with mussed hair and a T-shirt that pulls across a broad chest. He's got on gray sweatpants. If I didn't know better, I'd think this was the tail end of a booty call.

Kimmy moves to the porch; Ian follows. She pushes open the door to the other half of the duplex. Both sides of the house are completely furnished and owned by Mrs. Fishes. I live on one side; the other has been vacant for as long as I've been here.

The walls are thin, and I can hear Ian and Kimmy's movements on my side.

Feet pound up the stairs. Then down. They're talking; I can't make out the words. What are they doing here?

There's a rap at my door and I freeze. I'm supposed to be sick. And, while I feel sick, I don't have any of the trademark signs: runny nose, pale skin, cough.

A second knock. "You in there, Rebecca?" Kimmy yells.

I swing open the door and Kimmy steps inside, Ian behind her. She inspects my face. "You look awful."

"You really do," Ian affirms.

Well thanks *for that.* Maybe I do look sick. Hours of panic-stricken crying will do that to a girl.

"Ian had the worst night," Kimmy says. She places a manicured hand on his shoulder.

"Not the worst night," Ian protests.

Kimmy waves him off. "A piece of the ceiling at Shelly's by the Sea fell on his bed last night. He ended up sleeping in the owners' room."

"Wow," I say, looking at Ian, because I've met Lou and Sue. Not the kind of people I'd think he would bunk up with, the little I know about him.

Ian's face turns red. "I didn't know it was their room. They said it was a spare."

"Anyway," Kimmy continues, "Ian is going to stay next door for the remainder of his time here. Not sure why I didn't think of that before." She smiles brightly. "Plus, I have news on that front." She holds up a finger. "Spoke to corporate this morning. They're extending Ian's time. He'll be here eight weeks now, not two."

I digest the information, thinking that it's not that bad, that it's two months, when I look over at Ian. His mouth is agape, his eyes wide with shock. He looks like Kimmy just told him he'd have to live inside a portal to hell for the next fifty-six days.

Really?

I cross my arms.

Cape May is a seaside town. People pay money to vacation here. Homes sell for millions of dollars. But apparently, Ian Ledger would rather be in Nebraska. Living next to me for eight weeks is *that bad*. A landlocked state full of corn trumps being my neighbor.

"I'll have someone bring your things over," Kimmy says in Ian's direction. "And don't feel like you have to come in today if you're not up for it." She turns to me. "You should get some rest. You really do look awful."

She strides out on the stilettos, leaving Ian and me alone. I say nothing. He says nothing. It's incredibly awkward. Of course, there are a ton of things I could ask—like what is Lou and Sue's room like for starters—but I don't. I won't bail him out. He's *that* dismayed at the prospect of living next to me for a few weeks? Let him twist in the wind.

He stands still a few beats then inclines his head to our shared wall. "I guess I should get back."

"I guess you should."

He takes a step, stops, opens his mouth, and shuts it. The sequence is so stiff that it's painful to watch. He finally gives a lackluster wave and walks out.

* * *

By Saturday, I'm used to Ian being there, or rather, I'm used to ignoring him. The task has been made easier by the learn-to-play-an-instrument-in-eight-weeks dilemma, a predicament which has engulfed most of my waking hours for the past few days.

Now, I'm en route to a lesson with Margaret Caddell, the only instructor with affordable guitar lessons within walking distance.

I walk past giant Victorian houses in the early morning sun and recall the description of her company—Music All Around. The entity holds classes for preschoolers up to adults and, also, private music lessons in guitar, piano, tambourine, banjo, and harp.

I reach the studio. It's in a strip mall on the edge of town, sandwiched between a pizza shop and a fishing supply store. It's a bit far from my usual walking routes and I hadn't seen it before. But it looks clean with a blocky sign and music notes with faces painted all over the door. I approach and hear kids' voices—an early Saturday morning class, I guess.

I pull open the door. It's chaos.

A girl, probably my age, with a messy bun and a long flowing skirt, stands in the center of a couple of children seated on a colorful mat. Other children, more than half the class I'd estimate, run around the outside of the circle.

The girl locks eyes with me. "Are you Liz?"

I shake my head. "I'm not Liz."

Her face falls. I spy her nametag: Olivia.

"You're not the intern from Stockton?" She looks at me with such a hopeful expression, I actually *want* to be the intern from Stockton. "No. I'm Rebecca Chapman. I'm here for a guitar lesson with Margaret."

"Oh." Olivia scrunches her face up. "Did you book online?" A boy races by, a pair of drumsticks in his outstretched hands. "Hey, Scottie," Olivia yells, "please put those down." The command sounds more like a suggestion, and Scottie runs faster, drumsticks extended like skinny wooden horns.

Olivia claps, barely. "Hey. Settle down," she says with no authority whatsoever. Three kids sprint by her. One pigtailed girl hides behind me in what I can guess is an attempt not to be tagged.

Scottie rounds the corner, picking up speed. He's following another kid, also holding drumsticks. They're both running fast,

Scottie closing the gap between him and the other boy. It's bad. One of them is going to get impaled.

I look to Olivia. Her mouth is agape, her eyes following the boys. She looks like she might cry.

Okay.

Didn't want to do this, but I'm not going to stand here and let a kid be maimed. I put my index fingers in my mouth and let out a loud whistle. *Everyone*, including Olivia, stops to look at me. I feel a twinge of pride. I've still got it.

"Hey. On the mat. Now." I point. "Miss Olivia has a surprise, but she can't tell you about it until everyone is seated." The kids scramble because, as every former babysitter knows, kids love surprises. Doesn't matter if they're lame. I once rewarded kids with rocks.

I glance at Olivia. She's looking at me like I'm Batman.

I shrug, then whisper, "Where's Margaret? I don't want to be late."

Olivia shakes her head. "You won't be. Can you"—she looks around—"wait? I can explain after class."

"All right." The words come out slowly. I'm digesting the "explain" part. What is there to explain? I have a music lesson at ten with Margaret. Seems simple.

I move a dozen tiny character-laden shoes, most with light-up soles, to create a space against the wall. I sit and observe the class, which within moments of Olivia taking over, is again in shambles. She's the worst, at least at this. Her voice is too soft, her demeanor uncommanding. And she appears to have no rhythm, musical knowledge, or experience with kids. It's bad. Like witnessing a train wreck in person.

Scottie gets up; Olivia gives me a pleading look.

Whatever.

I may as well make myself useful.

I stand and grab a bucket full of triangles. "Line up," I command. The kids stop what they're doing. Tip two for dealing with little kids: they usually stop what they are doing if you tell them to line up. "Line up" usually means something good—recess, a game, or, in this case, getting a super old metal triangle.

I hand each kid a triangle and a striker. When they're all seated, I teach them to play "Jingle Bells." Doesn't matter that it's not Christmastime. It's an easy piece that every kid recognizes. They love it.

"How did you do that?" Olivia whispers. Her voice holds such reverence, I feel like I did something way more important than teach a bunch of preschoolers to play the easiest song in the world on the simplest instrument ever created. Still. Not gonna lie. It feels good.

Parents start to roll in while the kids are playing the song. It's clear what they think: *Junior is a prodigy! Sign up for music lessons! Carnegie Hall, here we come!*

It's kind of funny, but touching too, and I wonder briefly if my parents ever looked like that when it came to me. Given their reaction to my decisions in recent years, the idea that they were once proud of me—that they thought I had potential for *something*—seems far-fetched. Maybe they always knew I'd underachieve, that I was the "let's make the best of it with this one" child.

Children leave with their parents one by one, tiny hands encased in safe, large ones. One pigtailed girl with round glasses gives me a hug. Her arms barely make it around my waist. She smells like strawberries.

"Come on, Charity," a woman, presumably her mother, urges, pulling at the girl. She looks at me. "Sorry," she says sheepishly.

"No problem." I give Charity a small embrace.

"See you next week," she sings and skips out of the room. She's the last child to leave, and once she's through the door, I turn to Olivia. "So, what's the deal with Margaret?"

"Umm." Olivia adjusts her bun; the effort makes it look even messier. "Margaret's my Gram Gram," she volunteers.

I nod, not sure how I'm expected to react to this information or the fact that Olivia refers to her grandmother as "Gram Gram." I wait for her to elaborate. She doesn't. "Where is she?" I ask finally.

"Gram Gram's ninety-three." Olivia shakes her head. "She doesn't give lessons anymore."

I rub the back of my neck and digest this. Margaret does not give music lessons.

Margaret does not give music lessons.

Reality sets in. Margaret, the only person giving music lessons I could afford within walking distance, *does not give music lessons.*

"Why can you book lessons with her on the website?" I demand.

Olivia swoops forward and picks up a stray triangle. "No one ever books the private lessons. People just know, you know." She shrugs.

"Can she make an exception? I'm in a bit of a bind. It would only be for eight weeks. Seven even."

Olivia scrunches up her nose.

"Six?"

"Gram Gram's old, you know."

She doesn't elaborate, but I get the gist. Gram Gram is not going to be able to help me.

"Anyone else? Guitar lessons?"

Her eyes light up. "Guitar? I play guitar." She taps her chest. "I mean, it's been a few years, but I'll teach you what I know."

No.

After observing Olivia's utter lack of musical or other talent for the past hour, there's no way. No way.

"There's no one else?" I blurt.

She tosses another triangle toward the bucket. It misses.

"Nope. It's just me and sometimes a girl named Flo."

I survey her. Maybe she's a guitar genius hidden inside an inept person. A surprise nesting doll of talent. "How long did you play?"

"Couple months. I remember all the chords though." She sings a song about the chords. Off-key.

Oh my God.

"I'll think about it. Thanks." I move toward the door.

"Rebecca," Olivia sings out, and for a moment, I think she's going to advocate for herself. My mind whirs with excuses other than "you're bad" when she asks, "Would you want to teach a class here?"

CHAPTER 8

I *an*
Through the razor-thin walls that separate my shared duplex with Rebecca, I hear her playing the guitar. I'm in the family room, reclined on a semi-comfortable couch, an open thriller on my chest. I assume Rebecca is in the same place, on her side of the wall. The sound is loud. It's not music. It's plucking. She's been at it for hours.

I shouldn't care. I don't care. Except that I played guitar in a band with my high school buddies for years. I know what the instrument can and should sound like, even for beginners, and it's nothing remotely like the sound coming through the wall. Again, I'd offer to help except Rebecca appears to detest me. Whatever glimpse of normalcy, friendship, whatever it was we'd had during our Lobster House dinner has vanished and we're back to the dynamic from the bus. I'm the uptight asshole. She's the kind of girl who gives the middle finger to societal norms.

There's a horrid sound, which I assume is meant to be a C4. Rebecca curses. There's a loud bang on her side of the wall.

My phone rings. I sit up, swipe it off the side table, and spy the caller. Audrey. My heart leaps. I press my ear to the phone.

"Ian." Her voice is tight.

"Did you get my message?"

"Messages, you mean?" I can practically see her eyebrow lifted, hip jutted against her kitchen wall.

"It's eight weeks now. Not two. I thought you'd want to know."

"Of course, I'd want to know. One message was enough."

"The break is much longer," I say, stating the obvious.

"Yes."

The word is caustic; irritation slides down my gut. The break is *four times* longer. That should mean something. Right?

"Sorry," Audrey says. The word is like a salve on a wound.

"I think," I start, encouraged.

"We should continue the break for the eight weeks," Audrey commands, and pop, the hopeful bubble in my chest bursts. "It's going to work, or it isn't," she continues. "The more time we have to figure things out, the better."

I don't comment. It's not me who needs to figure things out.

"I'll still go to Brenda's wedding," she says. The offer comes off as charitable.

"That's big of you," I retort.

"Ian."

"Doesn't it bother you? Not seeing each other for eight weeks? Not even talking?" She doesn't respond and my emotions start to pick up speed, a tumbleweed of confusion and hurt. "I miss you, Audrey. I see little dogs or those fat pastries you like or these big, beautiful homes in crazy colors. I want to share it with you. I want you to visit. I don't think I can wait eight weeks."

The silence that follows stretches out. I pull the phone away from my ear and check it to make sure it hadn't disconnected.

"I went on a date, Ian."

The statement feels like a punch in the gut. "It's been a week."

"It was just one date. I don't know if it will go anywhere."

My mind teems with questions—who, when, why?

"You should date too."

What? This conversation is so far astray from what I thought it was going to be that I can barely think. I seriously thought Audrey would come here to visit, that the prospect of being apart for eight weeks would be too much. Instead, she's suggesting I date.

"I don't want to date anyone else."

"Come on, Ian. Don't make this harder. I need to be sure we are as meant to be as you seem to think we are. I can't do that if we're still exclusive."

I shut my eyes.

"Ian?"

I know what I say in the next moment means something. Railing and protesting and acting all jealous (and I am very, very jealous) will only drive her away. I take a deep breath. "Okay."

"Okay?"

"I mean, not okay, but I'll try to understand, all right? If this break is important to you, if seeing other people is important to you—" I pause, not ready to say the rest of it. I plunge forward anyway. "Then okay. I'll still see you at the wedding?"

"With bells on."

She clicks off. I put my phone face down on the coffee table. My heart feels shattered, shards of emotional glass course through my body. I try to force away images of Audrey on dates, but a parade of them crosses my mind anyway. The calm I'd cultivated during those final moments of the call morph into the beginnings of anger.

I am mad at the break. At the change in Audrey that precipitated it. I'm mad at this assignment. I'm mad at the extension. I'm even mad at Rebecca, plucking at strings.

Pluck. Pluck. Pluck.

The sounds are so discordant, they couldn't possibly qualify as music. The noise grates on my emotionally charged brain.

Pluck. Pluck. Horrible chord. Pluck.

Honestly. Does she not realize people—mainly me—have to listen to this crap?

Suppressed anger overflows and my sympathetic nervous system, the one that has no sense, takes over. I stand, grab my sneaker, and hurl it across the room at the wall. THUD. It hits, the impact more, louder, than I'd intended. There's a scuff mark on the wall where it hit. Its existence, the ugly black mark on the pristine white wall, feels like a last straw, a red flag in front of a bull. I pick up the other sneaker and throw it just as hard. Two marks now. I stare at them, breathless.

It's silent. No plucks. No chords. Then: "Screw you, Ian."

"Get good," I yell at the wall.

No response. I pace, waiting for Rebecca to yell back, every part of my reptilian brain wanting the conflict to continue. My fists are balled. I'm sweating. My nostrils flare.

Nothing.

I pace the length of the room, catch a glimpse of myself in the foyer mirror. My face is red, my hair askew in a way that's disconcerting. I look like a madman.

I sit. Take a deep breath. Another. Slowly, my emotions start to calm. I'm still confused and angry, but not at Rebecca. Embarrassment courses through me. I'd thrown my shoes against the wall. I'd told her to "get good." Musicians don't say things like that to each other. Putting yourself out there is hard enough.

The silence stretches on. I perch on the edge of the couch, head in my hands.

Pluck.

She's started again.

Pluck.

It's still bad but I listen more carefully, incline my head toward the wall. A bit of a melody emerges, and I smile despite everything.

CHAPTER 9

R*ebecca*

      I push open the door to the porch to wait for my Uber in red rubber boots adorned with ladybugs, denim shorts, and a navy tee. I spy Ian in the rocker. He's got a bottle of red wine in his hand.

"Rebecca."

"Ian." I move to the railing, my back to him.

"Nice night."

"Sure is."

"Might get cool later."

"Might." I don't turn around.

Though he'd apologized, I've been like this since the "get good" comment. I'm knowingly (and unfairly) blaming my musical dilemma on Ian because, if I don't, I'll have to take responsibility for it myself and I can't do that right now. So, like the proverbial terrible pet owner that kicks his dog after a bad day at work, I give Ian the cold shoulder.

I do wonder where he's going. He's typically casual outside of work but tonight he's dressed up in crisp khakis and a polo shirt that looks freshly ironed. It crosses my mind that maybe he and I are going to the same place, Aunt Kimmy's freedom party (thrown annually on the day her divorce was finalized). But no. The event is for good friends and family only. Kimmy barely knows Ian.

I glance at him, hand gripped tightly around the neck of the wine bottle. Curiosity gets the better of me. "So. Where are you off to? A social for the local debate team? A button tradeshow?" I point to his polo, buttoned to the tippy top. Again.

He fingers the top button, pulls at it until it comes loose. "I'm going to a party."

"Crashing, I assume? Good outfit choice. Very nondescript."

He opens his mouth. He's got the expression of someone who wants to say something pithy but, for the life of him, can't think of anything. There's a beat of silence. Two. He says nothing.

I feel bad. Like I just yelled at a puppy.

A car slows down and stops. I pull out my phone to see if it's the make and model of my Uber, but before I can confirm, Ian stands, hops down the stairs, and pulls open the door. His ride, I guess.

"Have a nice night," I call.

"Thanks."

He slips inside the car; it drives away. I move to the rocking chair. With the distraction of Ian removed, I'm forced to think about tonight's dilemma. I need money for music lessons. Real ones. There's no way I'm asking Olivia, and teaching myself has been a disaster. I'd ask Kimmy for a loan, but she's already given me a job and a free place to stay. My pride won't let me ask for more.

It has to be my parents. They'll be there tonight. The event is always over the top with an overflowing buffet and an open bar with top-of-the-line liquor. It's a tribute to how outstanding the food and drinks are that my parents overlook the "theme" aspect of the event. Last year's motif was "Cape May Cowboys."

This year it's a foam party; I don't know what that entails. The invitation said to wear clothes that could get wet.

My ride pulls up, and minutes later, the driver drops me off a block from Kimmy's. She lives in a five-bedroom house on the end of Beach Avenue. Aside from every state-of-the-art feature a person could imagine (including a coffee bar she activates from her phone), the home features panoramic views of the Atlantic Ocean. And there's an actual yard with grass, a luxury at the Jersey shore.

I walk toward the house, rehearsing ideas for my loan mantra:

I know you don't approve of this idea but—

I'll pay you back just as soon as—

If you could just hear me out—

Ugh. I'm so in my head about the upcoming conversation that I'm practically at the house before I comprehend how crazy it is.

Every inch of the normally grassy backyard is covered white foam, four feet deep, buttressed by a moon bounce with six multicolored slides. There's a woman behind a face-painting station and a man snaking through the crowd, fashioning balloons into animals.

Most guests are still on the enormous, two-tiered deck, save a handful of children and one couple slathering each other in foam, both of whom have faces painted with tiger stripes.

I scan the deck and see my parents standing at a wrought iron table. I'm not ready to see them yet. More accurately, I'm not ready to ask them for the money. I need to be fortified first.

I push into the house in search of strong alcohol. I ram into a broad chest and look up. Shit.

"Hey Rebecca."

I nod. "Ian."

He smiles like a Cheshire cat. "Just refreshing your mom's wine." He tips his head toward the wineglass in his hand.

I throw him a quizzical look.

"Kimmy introduced us." He pushes past me to the deck. He maneuvers through the crowd of flip-flopped, T-shirted party guests to my parents' table and sets the wine before Mom. He fits with them, actually, all three in clothing more dressy than a foam party warrants, all with the same stiff posture, the unspoken sentiment—"can you believe how undignified this is?" —on their lips.

I order a Long Island Iced Tea from a bartender who looks like he stepped out of an ad for cologne or underwear or a motorcycle or something. Long hair. Intense blue eyes. Broad shoulders. He's got a name tag. Tristan. Typical Kimmy to hire a drop-dead gorgeous bartender. The catering staff is likely equally hot.

Tristan hands me a thick tumbler and smiles as if the small act has actually made his day. "Enjoy."

"Thanks." I sip the drink—perfect—and move to edge of the room. I peek out the window. Ian is standing with my parents, all of them engaged in conversation. Ian's speaking, more animated than I've ever seen him, not that we've spoken much. My parents looked captivated and my dad, not known for his sense of humor, actually guffaws.

What the hell?

I take a long sip of the drink, push open the door, and move toward the group.

"Darling," Dad greets when I join the trio. "Ian was just telling us about the pumpkin slingshot event in his hometown." He shakes his head and gives Ian the Richard Chapman shoulder pat of approval. "Crazy."

I suck down the rest of my drink.

"How are *you*?" Mom asks. There's an emphasis on the you which makes the question feel condescending.

"I'm good." I pause. Now's as good a time as any. At least, if Ian's here, he can attest to how badly I need the lessons. "Actually—" I start.

I'm interrupted by a man dressed as a clown, complete with the red nose and floppy shoes. "Balloon animal?" He points to a plethora of balloons sticking out from a polka-dotted pocket.

Mom smiles. "Sure. Why not?"

I glance at her, surprised. Sad as it sounds, saying yes to a balloon animal is one of Mom's more spontaneous acts. She's usually too serious for such frivolity, and the shift in mood makes me hopeful that maybe, just maybe, she and Dad will be receptive to my request.

The clown pulls out a fistful of colorful balloons and fashions a pink one into a dog. He hands it to Mom. She nods appreciatively. High praise.

"Can you make a frog?" Ian asks.

In the surprise of Mom engaging with the clown, I'd forgotten Ian was here. Does he seriously want *a frog?*

"Can't do a frog," the clown answers. "I can do dogs, swords, and flowers."

"I can show you a frog," Ian offers.

What?

The clown shrugs, then hands him the balloons and pump. Ian blows up a few green and yellow ones and starts to twist. It's weird. A secret talent, I guess. I'd never have pinned Ian as a balloon animal guy.

"Rebecca."

I twist my head back to Mom.

"I was asking if you got the email I forwarded from Elenore."

Elenore. One of Mom's friends who just so happens to be a college consultant. Elenore never fails to have information about some college program which would be "perfect for me." I did see the email. I deleted it.

"Actually, I wanted to ask you something," I say. "I need to borrow money."

Dad blows out a breath.

"For music lessons," I add. "Guitar lessons. I need them for the audition."

Neither speak. I hear Ian's low voice—he and the clown are geeking out over animal balloon design.

"It's just—" I start, about to launch into my error, explain why I'm so in need of lessons at the last minute.

"Rebecca," Dad says, his voice kind but firm, "we're glad to give you money, but it has to go toward college. We're not financing a venture with wildly uncertain returns."

"It's just eight weeks until the audition. I could pay you back."

The look of pity on Dad's face makes me feel two feet tall.

"Honey," he says, "it's time to get serious. You've spent two years on this pipe dream."

Pipe dream.

I know that's what it is.

But it's my pipe dream.

CHAPTER 10

an

I A half hour after Rebecca disappears, my capacity for human interaction is saturated. I've set a clear goal for the evening: stay a minimum of two hours or meet five new people, whichever comes first. I haven't achieved either, but I won't be able to forge ahead socially if I don't catch a break.

I grab a beer, slip past the growing group of "people in foam," and head toward the beach. It's a quieter spot than the one near Shelly's by the Sea, far from the beachfront hotels and main town. I plop in front of sand dunes, my body in the soft earth. I twist around and look at Kimmy's house, make sure the spot isn't visible from the yard. I don't want to be rude and, according to Audrey, leaving a party in the middle for some desperately needed alone time is impolite and "lame."

I'm working on it.

I twist off the beer cap, tuck it in my pocket, and take a sip. The sky, clear and black, is dotted with stars. I scan for constellations and planets. Stargazing relaxes me. Something about the vast space, the fact that there are entire other worlds beyond our own. These same stars were in the sky thousands of years ago and, presumably, will be for thousands to come. I've got a small telescope at home which helps me see more. Still, I can make out the main constellations with my naked eye—Big and Small Bear, Orion. These same stars will be visible in Nebraska in a few hours. Will Audrey be under them? On a date?

I shake the thought from my mind and shut my eyes. I inhale the scent of the sea and listen to the sound of the waves crashing on the shore.

"No longer saving the world one balloon animal at a time?"

My eyes fly open. Rebecca's standing before me, the absurd ladybug boots half-covered in sand. I'm surprised she's talking to me, given how little she's interacted with me these past few days.

I shrug. "I'm taking a break."

"But there are *so* many animals to make."

"True. But I've got to sharpen the saw, you know. Don't want to get animal balloon art burnout."

"Animal balloon art burnout is the worst."

I smile; she smiles back, her features illuminated by the moon. She looks pretty, probably because she's not scowling at me. "Care to sit?" I pat the sand next to me. I half expect her to flip me the bird, but instead, she plops down. I'd caught bits and pieces of the conversation with her parents. Rough. I could tell it had been hard for her to ask them for the money. Worse was the fact that they'd said no. What had they called her music? A pipe dream. Right. No wonder she's out here on the beach with me.

I reach in my pocket and pull out the wad of balloons that Stan—the balloon guy—had given me. I hold them up. "Want one?"

"A balloon animal? I thought you were taking a break?"

"I'll make an exception for you, just this once."

She lifts an eyebrow. "How gallant."

"What do you want?"

"What can you make?"

"Anything."

She tilts her head. "Seriously?"

"Okay, anything within reason."

She gazes at the ocean a moment. "How 'bout a seahorse?"

"Easy." I pull a yellow balloon from the handful and blow into the end until it's full, but not too full. I tie it closed and start twisting. I haven't actually made a seahorse before—it's not the first animal that comes to mind in Nebraska—but I've done enough of these that I can figure it out.

Rebecca digs her fingertips into the fine sand, pulls out a half seashell and inspects it. "So where'd you learn to make balloon animals? Mr. Balloon?"

I laugh at her reference to our conversation at The Lobster House. "My mother," I say, "is a party planner. Kids' parties, weddings, showers." I hold up the half-twisted balloon. "My sister and I both learned to do this. Family trade, you know."

She stares at me a beat. "Your mother is a *party planner*. How does that compute?"

I smile, pleased that, in the little time we've known each other, she's picked up that forced social events and I don't mix.

Yet.

"Brenda, my sister, got all the social genes. She loved Mom's events, schmoozing the guests and all. It was easier for me to be in the background, twisting latex into creatures." I do a final few twists and hand her the seahorse.

She takes it from my extended hand. "Impressive."

"Thanks."

We sit in silence. Crashing waves and party music fill the space around us. "About the other night," I start.

She waves the seahorse at me. "No good conversation ever started with 'about the other night.' Forget it."

I shake my head. "I shouldn't have said that. I'm sorry."

She shrugs. "It's okay. I suck. I know. That's the problem."

"You're not that bad," I insist.

She rolls her eyes. "I am and you know it."

"You're holding the chords too hard," I volunteer. "And you need to tune your guitar. I can guess you're not holding it right either."

She angles her head and squints her eyes. "Ian?"

"I've played the guitar since I was twelve. I was part of a band."

"A band?" She arches an eyebrow. I can practically see the wheels turning with all the sarcastic remarks she's holding back.

"Yes. A band. In high school. We called ourselves Replacement Parts." I shrug and give the explanation before she asks. "One of the guys' dad owned a company that specialized in rebuilding old autos. We practiced in his garage." My mind flashes back to the garage a moment, the smell of automotive oil, old parts strewn about the floor, hanging from the rafters. We'd spent hours in that garage, composing, playing, talking. "I can teach you."

"Really?" She leans forward.

"Yes. Please let me teach you. I need to improve the sound on my side of the wall."

She pushes at my shoulder. "Jerk."

I shrug.

She looks up a moment. "I don't have much money. How much would you charge?"

I shake my head. "I'm not charging you, Rebecca."

She shifts. "What's in it for you then?"

I lean back, my hands outstretched behind me. It hadn't occurred to me that Rebecca would want this to be a quid pro quo, that she wouldn't just take the lessons. I like that though; I'd be the same way. I close my eyes and think about things Rebecca could help me with. The answer is almost immediate.

"I do have something you could help me with but"—I point at her—"no laughing."

Her face twists into a smirk. A laugh bursts out, and I can't help it, the sound makes me smile. I slap the sand. "I haven't even told you yet."

"I know. I know," she says, composing herself. "I'm just getting it out now. In case it's funny."

I point at her. "Don't make me retract my offer."

She waves. "I won't. I won't. Sorry. Go on."

"My girlfriend and I are on a break."

"Girlfriend." She inhales a breath. "Girlfriend. The one in the picture on your desk?"

"Yes. Audrey. The break was her idea. She thinks I'm a little," I pause, "stodgy. Like an old man in a twenty-eight-year-old body."

A smile inches across her face.

"Hey," I say.

"Sorry." She composes her features.

"Anyway," I continue, "my sister is getting married in eight weeks and Audrey's coming to the wedding. I'd like to show her a different side of me. One that's, well—" I search for the right word.

"Fun," Rebecca supplies.

"Yes, fun. And you seem, well, fun."

"I seem fun?"

"Yeah. The crazy clothes, the electric blue glasses. You seem like the kind of person that would head up a cha-cha line or go cliff diving."

She doesn't say anything.

"I mean those things as a compliment."

"I know. Thanks." She picks up a pile of sand, lets it slide through her fingers. "So," she says slowly, "you would give me guitar lessons in exchange for"—she's quiet a moment—"fun lessons?"

I sit up straighter and nod. "Yes. That's it. Guitar lessons for fun lessons."

She smiles, head nodding. "Guitar lessons for fun lessons." She's quiet a moment, almost like she's weighing the deal. She stretches her hand in my direction. "I like it. You're on."

I shake her hand. "Great. When do we start?"

She extricates her hand from mine, stands, and brushes sand from her clothes. "We're going to start right now."

CHAPTER 11

R *ebecca*
   "Now?"
   "Now."
Ian stands. We walk toward Kimmy's. Music pulses; the sound of shrieking laughter cuts through the still night. The balloon seahorse swings in my hand.

I'm cautiously optimistic that Ian can teach me guitar. He doesn't seem like the type of guy who would say he could play the guitar if he couldn't *play* the guitar. He's too serious for that. The idea that my issue might be solved—for free—bolsters my mood. Plus, the fun lessons. I love that idea. In eight weeks' time, Ian's going to fun the heck back into his old girlfriend's life. I'll make sure of it.

We near Kimmy's property and stop at the edge. New foam jets out from machines on the roof, landing on the grass in a soft haze of white that looks like snow. Dozens of brightly colored plastic balls bob on the surface. People race through the existing foam, more are in line for the slides. Everyone is soaked. It's chaos.

I angle my head toward Ian. "How do you feel about foam?"

He shoves his hands in his pockets. "I have not yet formed a strong opinion on foam. You?"

"Love it." I nod toward the screaming mass of people.

Ian stiffens.

"We're definitely going in the foam, Ian. It's *fun*."

He gives me a sheepish grin. "Why do I get the feeling I'm going to regret this deal?"

I point the seahorse at him. "You are *not* going to regret this deal. By the time I'm done with you, you'll be so fun, Audrey won't recognize you." I glance at the mass of inebriated people in the foam. "Tell you what," I say, "we'll get drinks first."

We grab drinks from Tristan—another Long Island Iced Tea for me, a craft beer for Ian. I put desserts for both of us from the newly replenished buffet on a thick paper plate. We sit at the same wrought iron table my parents had been at earlier. They're nowhere in sight. I assume they went home. I note that neither of them thought to tell me, even by text. Nice.

"So, what's the problem with this?" I nod to the four feet of foam and screaming people on the lawn.

"What do you mean?"

"I mean, what's the hesitation? Do you not want to get your clothes wet? Is it the crowd?"

He takes a bite of a cookie and swallows. "I don't mind getting wet. I'm not a fan of crowds but I can deal." He pauses. "The hesitation is—" He stops. "Promise you won't make fun of me?"

I bug my eyes out. "Honestly. Have I been that bad?" I lean forward. "I won't make fun of you" I hold up two fingers. "Scout's honor."

"You know the symbol is three fingers, right?"

"Fine." I add a finger. "Scout's honor."

He sips his beer, looks at the foam pit, then back at me. "Okay. So, I brave the crowd and get all wet. I'm in the pit. What happens then? Do I just start throwing foam at random strangers? Do I make myself a foam beard and just hope someone will comment?" He grabs another cookie from the plate. "I can get in the mix. I don't know what I'm supposed to do once I get there."

I slice off a piece of chocolate cake with my fork and think about his question. What would I do? Get in the foam. Get wet. Then what? The idea of hurling handfuls of foam at strangers suddenly seems ludicrous. As does starting a game of tag. Or making a foam hairstyle.

"You can't think about it," I say decisively. "You have to let the situation unfold naturally. If you think too much about it, you'll freeze up."

"If I think about it at all, I'll freeze up."

"Fun Ian won't. Lean into it."

He holds up his beer. "Thanks for the specifics."

"You'll see." I drain my drink and stand. "Come on. Let's go."

He follows me down the deck stairs. We stand on the few inches of grass not covered by foam and look at the commotion. I open my mouth to suggest he take off his nice polo (most of the men are shirtless), but before any words come out, Ian sprints toward the mayhem, arms in the air like he's on a roller coaster. He runs until he's in the center. He grabs a handful of foam, swipes it over his head, and molds it into a shark fin.

Unexpected.

And pretty fun.

I laugh, trudge in, and stand next to him, his polo and khakis covered in strips of white. "Nice. Like the spontaneity there."

"Trying not to think about it." He swipes a colored ball from the foam and throws it at me.

"Hey," I say, catching it.

He throws another, starts running, then stops and throws a third one. It hits me squarely on the chest. I grab it and chase after him. A girl joins me, then her companion. In a matter of seconds, the pit is a mass of ball-throwing, mostly inebriated adults. There aren't any rules until a man yells "dodge ball" and the chaotic group miraculously morphs into a circle.

"Guys in the center," I shout, and as if guided by some foam-party deity, all the men and a few teenage boys congregate inside a tight circle of women. Balls fly at a rapid speed. I spy Ian and hurl a green ball in his direction. He dodges. I try again and fail. Two, three balls fly at him. Miss, miss, miss. He's impressively good at dodge ball.

I stop and watch him a moment. He's smiling. And laughing. It's a good look on him, a mighty improvement over his normal colorless expression.

A girl hits his back with a yellow ball. He gives her a high five, sloshes out of the circle, and stands next to me. "How am I doing?" he asks, breathless. He's drenched, his khaki shorts and polo cling to his skin.

"Good. *Very* fun." I pause. "Are *you* having fun?"

He smiles in my direction. His smile's a bit lopsided. Endearingly lopsided, actually. And he's got a dimple, something I've never noticed. Probably because he's never smiled in my presence quite like this.

"I am having fun," he confirms.

A woman races by me to catch a ball and I step back. "Should we try the slides?" I nod toward the inflatable mass.

That smile again. "Absolutely."

Ian runs through the foam toward the slide. I follow. We scramble up the inflatable stairs to the top of four separate slides.

"Race ya!" I say and push off with my arms. I slide down, fast because I'm soaking wet. I let out a whoop.

"Hey!" I hear Ian's voice behind me. He slides into the foam a moment after me. "Rematch."

He scrambles to the stairs. I race after him. We repeat the sequence until we're both breathless and sweaty despite being wet.

"Good workout," I pant.

"Yeah." He breathes hard. "Take a break?"

We trudge out of the foam. I pluck two plush terry towels from a bin. "Very nice effort," I say.

"Thank you."

"I'd almost think you were already fun."

He shakes his head. "That was a stretch. Trust me."

I spy two free Adirondack chairs by Kimmy's stone firepit. I nod toward them. "Sit there?"

Ian nods. He grabs long sticks and marshmallows from what appears to be a s'more station and hands me a set.

I put the oversized marshmallow on the end and hold it gingerly above the flames. Ian does the same. After a moment, I bump my marshmallow against his. "Thank you for saving me from having to ask one of my brothers for money for music lessons," I say quietly. "*That* would have been humiliating."

He twists his stick over the fire. "Not the musical types?"

"Nope. We got two lawyers and two doctors in the family." I pull back my stick and take off the marshmallow. "Oh. And me." I roll my eyes. "My parents are so proud."

"They ought to be." Ian puts a chocolate bar and two graham crackers on the arm of my chair. "Music is hard. It's extremely math-based you know."

I snort.

"I'm serious. Music and math are both pattern-based. But with music, there's that undefinable emotional component that's almost impossible to get right. It isn't frivolous. It's friggin' hard."

I wipe the sticky marshmallow residue from my hands on the towel, Ian's words in my head. *It isn't frivolous. It's friggin' hard.* No one has ever validated music like that for me. It always seemed silly and easy, not like medicine or law.

"Thanks," I say.

"You're welcome."

We eat our s'mores in silence but it's not awkward. It's comfortable. And I'm tired. Running through foam, dealing with my parents, and consuming too much food and alcohol will do that to a girl. It's all caught up to me. I shut my eyes.

When I come to, the crowd has thinned, and my head is leaning on Ian's shoulder. I jolt up. "Sorry, I—" I start.

"It's all right," he says. "You seemed tired."

"I was tired," I confirm. I refuse to weird out over falling asleep on Ian.

"Not everyone is a master of foam," he adds.

I sit up. "So you're a master of foam now?"

"I'm not the one who fell asleep after an easy foam workout."

I laugh. Ian's funny. And he is fun. I don't know what his girlfriend is talking about.

"Should I call us an Uber?" he asks.

"Definitely."

We share the Uber home, and after, stand on the porch in front of our respective doors. It feels like the end of a date. If it were the end of a date, I'd kiss Ian right now. But it isn't and it's Ian, a man I detested just twenty-four hours ago. I push any thoughts of kissing from my mind.

He smiles, big enough that the dimple is visible. "See you tomorrow?"

"See you tomorrow."

CHAPTER 12

*I*an I approach Music All Around at 11:00 Saturday morning. Rebecca teaches a kids' class there. A new weekend job, she'd said.

I stand outside the front door along with a mass of parents. Most peek through the storefront window on tiptoes, necks craned. Over their heads, I spy Rebecca. She's got on a T-shirt with the words "Music All Around" on the front. Her hair is bunched up in a swingy ponytail, stray curls wisp around her face. She's singing "The Hokey Pokey" in a bold alto. At the "put your whole self in" part, she jumps into the center of the circle and wiggles. The kids do the same to a chorus of giggles.

Okay.

It's cute.

And impressive.

She opens the door after the song and parents filter in. She talks to them easily simultaneously ruffling kids' hair or accepting hugs from arms so tiny they only fit halfway around her waist. I'm by the door, mute. I feel—and probably look— totally awkward. Doesn't matter that I'm here to help Rebecca.

Or that, less than twelve hours ago, we were side-by-side, waist deep in a pit of foam. I have a natural proclivity toward discomfort. It's who I am.

Rebecca gives a high five to the last kid to leave, a towheaded little boy, and looks to me. A moment passes. She crosses her arms. "Cat got your tongue? Or are you bowled over with how incredible I look in my new 'Music All Around' tee?" She spreads her arms out wide then nods toward a box overflowing with shirts in the corner. "Take one if you're that jealous about it."

I laugh.

She swipes a tee out of the box and throws it in my direction. "Put it on. You look like you're dressed for a debate again."

I look down at my beige shorts and navy polo.

"I do not."

"Do." She moves forward, grabs the shirt from the floor, and pushes it into my chest. "This shirt is way more fun than the one you've got on. Consider this your second fun lesson."

I shake my head.

"Let's go."

"Fine." I pull off my polo and replace it with the T-shirt. I look down. The shirt features a dozen personified music notes. "What's with the notes?"

She rolls her eyes. "They're marching, Ian. Duh."

"Yours is plain." I nod toward her shirt, "Music All Around" in block letters across the front.

She smirks. "Yours is more fun. I'm already fun. You said so yourself."

"Oh. So, you don't need to wear fun shirts?"

"Exactly." She nods toward two guitars propped up against the wall.

I look down at the shirt again, at the procession of music notes with faces. It's ridiculous.

"Should we do this?" she asks.

"I'm ready if you are."

We sit in the only two adult-size chairs in the room, gray folding numbers near a wall with a mural of the same happy music notes displayed across my chest. Rebecca picks up one of the guitars then looks at me. "Wait. Play something."

"Me?" I put my hand on my chest.

"Yes, you. The only other person in the room. I want to see what my instructor can do."

I hug the guitar toward my body, adjust the strap. "I haven't played in a few years," I say preemptively.

She lays her guitar on her lap and crosses her arms. "All the more reason you should play something. Get the kinks out."

I close my eyes, run through all the songs I used to be able to play without thinking. After a moment, I start Willie Nelson's "On the Road Again." Muscle memory works its magic, and my fingers fly over the strings. I'm standing back in that automotive garage, the memory so vivid that I can practically smell the spilled gasoline, taste the stale popcorn we'd always thought was a cool treat. I sing out of habit, immersed in my own world.

I finish and I open my eyes.

Rebecca is staring at me.

I feel intensely self-conscious. She maintains her gaze. I go pink. Was I even in tune? I thought I was, but it has been a few years. Doubts flood my mind. I was probably awful. She's probably regretting the whole deal.

"You're good," she says finally.

I exhale. "Thanks."

"Really good," she repeats. "Why didn't you tell me?"

I swing my head toward her. "I did."

"You said you could play," Rebecca says, eyes still assessing me, "not that you could *play*. And I didn't know you could sing."

I shrug. "I did backup vocals."

"Backup." She scoffs. "Who was your lead? Keith Urban?"

I smile. Somehow, getting praise from Rebecca feels like a big deal. "Trust me then?"

She nods. "I trust you."

We go over open strings, basic chords, riffs, and scales. She's a quick learner; she knows music. As she practices the basics, I rack my brain for easy songs to start with. I teach her some of the chords for "Country Roads" by John Denver. She finishes one set and looks up. "Well?"

"Good." I nod.

"Really."

"Really. But"—I put my hand over hers—"you should stop."

She looks up, her face a scowl. "What? Why?"

"You'll get callouses on your fingers. Trust me." I move my hand from hers. "We should get tape for next time."

She stands and sets her guitar against the wall. "Next time being later today. I only have eight weeks, you know."

"All right." I stand. "Let's get tape then." I swipe my polo off the floor.

Rebecca shakes her head. "Nope. Got to wear the music note shirt. It's part of the lesson, remember?"

I stare at her a moment, the navy polo dormant in my hand. "Are you going to make me do ridiculous things and call them fun lessons for the next eight weeks?"

"Yup."

"Good thing I don't know anyone in Cape May."

"Yet," she says and pushes open the door.

We walk to Della's 5 and 10, a store with just about everything, in the center of the Washington Mall in Cape May. We get the tape for her fingers. After, she points to a white counter in the back with red twisty stools in front of it. A giant sign featuring menu items takes up half the back wall. There's a glass covered cake stand with a pyramid of freshly baked cookies in front of the cash register. "Lunch is on me," Rebecca announces.

I avert my eyes from the exhaustive menu and look at her. "Why?"

"For helping me."

"You're helping me too, remember?" I point to the shirt.

She waves in my direction. "Helping you is more fun. I get to make you do stupid shit."

"Can't argue with that."

We order burgers, fries, and shakes that come with stripy straws and big dollops of whipped cream. The server has on a white 1950s soda jerk cap. It's like we've gone back in time, and at any moment, an Elvis Presley song is going to blare out of the very authentic-looking jukebox against the wall.

"You should sing an Elvis song for the audition," I blurt with sudden inspiration. "It would be different. And you could make it country. Your voice is perfect for it."

She sucks in some of her milkshake, lips puckered around the top of the straw.

I shake my head. "Sorry. Not sure where that came from. I'm sure you have something planned."

She releases the straw, red lipstick left in the aftermath. "I have a few ideas. Nothing concrete. What are you thinking?"

"'Jailhouse Rock,' 'Love Me Tender.' You could do just about any of his songs. It's the country spin that would matter."

"I'll consider that." She lifts her milkshake glass. "Thank you, Ian Ledger."

I pick up my glass and clink it against hers. "You are very welcome."

After lunch, we walk the Cape May promenade, an asphalt path between the ocean and the town. The beach is already packed with families. Colorful umbrellas, sand toys, rafts, and beach chairs dot the sand. Sunlight reflects off ocean swells. I've stayed away from the beach during the day since I got here, thinking I wouldn't like the crowds or the heat. Typical lame Ian stuff. Now the atmosphere seems fun.

Ha.

I catch the thought.

FUN. I guess this whole fun lessons endeavor is working already.

Rebecca grabs my hand and pulls me into an arcade. "Three games of Skee-Ball."

I say nothing.

She inspects my face. "Ian Ledger, if you don't know what Skee-Ball is, I'm calling this off."

I stop in front of a PAC-MAN machine and look at her. "I know what Skee-Ball is."

"Cool. Let's bet on it."

"Bet on it?"

"Yes." She puts her hand on her hip. "It's not like I'm a professional Skee-Ball player or something."

"That's not a thing, but fine. What's the bet?"

"That."

She points to a flyer on the wall. The picture on it depicts a massive claw machine. The claws—the ones that normally drop so the participant can try to grasp a toy—have a full-grown man inside of them. He's got on a helmet and is suspended at least six feet over a sea of stuffed animals. There's one coming to the promenade next week.

I stare at the picture. It actually looks a little fun. I smile. There's that word again. FUN.

"Who goes in the machine?" I ask. "Winner or loser."

Rebecca puts a five-dollar bill into a change machine. "I want you to go in, so loser."

"Hey."

She shrugs and holds out a handful of coins. "Prove me wrong then, Cornhusker."

We play three games of Skee-Ball. Rebecca wins. Easily.

"I think you are a professional Skee-Ball player," I say after.

"Of course, I am." She takes a picture of the flyer on the wall, flips around the phone, and wiggles it. "Okay. Next week, when they bring the human claw here, you're going in."

I groan because I think she likes the thought that I don't *want* to go in the machine, but truthfully, I'm pumped. Being a participant in a human claw machine is nothing I would ordinarily do, but somehow, the activity being under the auspices of the fun lessons makes it easier for me to put myself out there. I have to do it, right? It's *a lesson.* And I'll make sure Rebecca gets some pictures so can I show Audrey. I'm conjuring what Audrey's reaction might be when Rebecca pulls at my hand.

"Next," she says and pulls us out of the arcade onto the promenade. We head toward a woman holding a giant tray outside a store called The Fudge Kitchen.

"Sample?" The woman holds up the tray. It's scattered with tiny fudge pieces on toothpicks.

"Yes." Rebecca plucks one off. "Can you believe my friend has never had fudge? He's from *Nebraska.*"

Fudge woman widens her eyes. "You've never had fudge?"

"Never," I lie because, frankly, lying seems more fun in this situation.

"Do they not make fudge in Nebraska?"

Her tone is pitying, and I shake my head. "Nope. Hard to get all the ingredients out there." *Where most food ingredients are grown...*

"Have the rest of the samples," Fudge woman volunteers, and before I can protest, or say I'll buy some, Rebecca swipes a bunch off the tray into her hand. "Get the rest, Ian."

I grab the remaining fudge pieces. "Thanks."

"Of course," Fudge woman says. "Enjoy."

"Thanks a million," Rebecca adds. She strides down the promenade and pops one in her mouth.

I catch up. "You know I've had fudge before, right?"

"I figured but who knows? Plus, free fudge." She winks.

"You are too much."

"So I've been told."

We walk on the promenade, and when the pavement ends, we turn and start back. It's comfortable. Typically, with someone new, I feel a need to say *something*. My mind races through topics, coming up blank. Most of the time, I make an inane comment about the weather. I don't feel a need to chatter about nothing around Rebecca. The silence feels okay.

When we get closer to Music All Around, Rebecca shoots me a look. "Practice again?"

"Sure."

We get inside. I pull the tape from the bag and hold it up. "Want me to show you how to tape up your fingers?"

"Yeah. That would be great."

She sits on the gray adult-size chair in the back. I kneel in front of the chair and pull her hand toward mine. Her fingers are slender, her nails plain. I take her index finger and start taping the ball of it, then wrap the tape a few times. I take her second finger and look up.

Her face is flushed, the stray bits of escaped hair from her ponytail frame her face. She looks at me with those green eyes and I feel—something. Attraction, tenderness. I can't put my finger on it.

"Let's go, Ledger," she says. "It'll be night before you're done."

Her words snap me out of my feelings. Right. It's Rebecca. The woman who barely tolerates me.

She practices for another hour, and after, we walk home together. It's the best day I've had since I got here.

CHAPTER 13

R*ebecca*

I press my cell against my ear and start talking as soon as Lily picks up. "What do you think? Cardboard boat race or Renaissance Faire?"

"What are you even talking about?"

"For Ian. The next fun lesson." Duh. That's my tone.

"Right." She seems to orient herself to the conversation. "Didn't you just make him do that claw thing?"

"Yeah. Last week."

I look at the duck Squishmallow, now named Mally, on my bed. Ian retrieved it from the machine, making a silly and unexpected show of moving his hands like claws. He'd given it to me after. A "thank you" for the lesson, he'd said.

"Do the Renaissance Faire," Lily says decisively.

I avert my eyes from Mally. "Why the Faire?"

"You said he was hot. Don't you want to see him dressed up in doublets and breeches and all that?"

"I never said he was hot," I protest, but the truth is, I do think he's handsome. I didn't before. He's grown on me. The dimple when he smiles, the cowlick he tries, and fails, to tame. He's got nice eyes. I hadn't noticed any of these things on the bus or his first few days in the office.

"Whatever," Lily continues. "He could joust. You guys could drink mead and eat those giant drumstick things. He could sing in a show or something."

I recall Ian singing "On the Road Again" at Music All Around. His deep baritone, textured singing voice. I'd be up for hearing that again.

"Okay. I like it," I say after a moment. "Can you give us a ride?"

It's silent and I know she's shaking her head on the other side of the phone. Unlike my family members, Lily has no tolerance for the fact I haven't tried to get my license again since high school. Once every few months, she texts a snapshot of the DMV with the caption "it's time." Almost always, I think about trying, then I remember standing at the kiosk at the DMV in front of the written test, the letters jumbling on the screen. Whichever brother took me would be in the waiting area and I could always see him in my peripheral vision. My nerves intensified, guessing started. I'd fail. After the mandatory six-week waiting period, I'd sign up for the test again, then the whole sequence of events would repeat itself. Humiliating.

"Don't tell me Ian doesn't have a license either," Lily says finally.

"No. His car's in Nebraska." I pause. "I guess we could get an Uber."

"No." Lily's answer is immediate. She hates Ubers. "I'll take you."

"Yes, Lil. It'll be fun. You can even plan the lesson."

"Can I make you both wear costumes?"

I pause. I should have known Lily would go there. She's a Halloween enthusiast, to say the least. She knows the best places to buy costumes at discounts year-round. Anything she picks will be insane. But maybe that's a good thing? Fun, right? "Sure."

"Deal."

* * *

ON THE MORNING of the Faire, I step out of the bathroom in my costume.

Lily claps her hands. "Oooooh. Perfect."

I shake my head. I'm not so sure. The dress is maroon and ankle length with a full skirt, fitted black bodice, and a French cut neckline. The sleeves are long and flowy. A gold headdress sticks up from the top of my head like a shield.

Lily steps forward and pulls my hair, which is down and in tendrils at her insistence, so most of it is in the front. "You look gorgeous."

"I look ridiculous."

"Nope. Gorgeous." She adjusts another tendril. "Now let's go get your peasant boy."

We step onto the porch and knock on Ian's door. He pulls it open, already dressed in his costume: white shirt with billowy sleeves, black pants, tall boots. He's got suede vambraces on his wrists and a fat leather belt.

My face flushes for no reason. It's just Ian. He's got the cute cowlick and the dimple but he's still *Ian*. No reason to get all flustered over the fact he looks kind of good—very good?—in his costume.

His eyes scan the length of me. "Wow. You look great."

I feel my face. Pinker. I know it.

"You both look amazing," Lily volunteers. "Get together. I want a picture."

Ian slings his arm around my shoulders and pulls me to him. I'm not sure I've been this close to Ian before, except maybe in the foam. He smells woodsy. A new cologne? Or maybe he just smells like that, and I'd never noticed. Kind of like the dimples and the cowlick.

"Smile," Lily says. She holds up her phone and clicks a shot.

She tips the screen toward us after, and I view the image. It's a good picture of me, a rarity. Ian looks good too. Really good.

"You look hot, E," I say, an effort to break my internal tension. If I say the words out loud, maybe the fact of them will seem less powerful.

"Thank you, m'lady," Ian says without missing a beat and I laugh.

Lily drives us the half hour to the Faire. The conversation is easy, mainly because Lily can't ask enough questions about Nebraska. Ian answers them all in his polite Ian way: "Yes, there are a lot of corn fields." "Yes, it's very flat." "Yes, the people are more friendly." He shares that the official Nebraska tourism slogan is: "Honestly, it's not for everyone," and Lily and I burst out laughing.

"It's not," Ian says, a smile on his face. "It's really not."

When we get there, Ian opens the passenger-side car door and peeks his head in. "May I assist you out of the vehicle, m'lady?"

I give him my hand and he helps me out. After, he links his arm in mine and we walk toward the entrance, Lily behind us with an unfolded map.

Being with Ian like this feels...nice? I don't know. It's different with both of us in costume, like maybe, in another time and place, we might have liked each other, even dated. We'd have at least made out.

"What's up first, Lily?" I ask.

She checks her watch. "Ian has a jousting lesson in fifteen minutes."

"A jousting lesson," Ian says, a bit of surprise in his voice. "Like on a horse with that spear thing?"

"The *lance?*" I correct.

He smiles. "Yes. The *lance.*"

Lily shrugs. "I don't know what the class entails, but it was almost full when I signed you up last night."

We get tickets at the entrance and step inside what feels like another world. Tudor-style buildings line asphalt paths dotted with giant buckets of flowers. There's a faux castle, a maypole, and at least a dozen food vendors. On a small stage, a group of musicians play folk music and a group of costumed Faire goers —perhaps having had too much mead—dance enthusiastically in front. A man recites poetry in a knight costume; a woman sits in front of an easel sketching a caricature.

"This way," Lily says. She extends her hand toward a colorful sign that says "Jousting Lessons" with a hand-drawn arrow under the words.

We follow the direction of the arrow into a tent filled with a dozen kids, mostly boys, ranging in age from around eight to twelve. A pile of foam pool noodles, decorative tape, cardboard pieces, and markers sit in giant bins in one corner. In the center, there are three narrow planks elevated a few inches off the ground with concrete blocks. A man dressed similarly to Ian stands near the front with what can best be described as a scroll.

I guess Ian is in this class. With these little kids? I glance at Lily, but before I can ask, the man with the scroll claps his hands. "Knights in training, may I have your attention."

The kids settle down. Ian takes a big step back. I think he is realizing the same thing I am—*this* is his class.

"Knights in training," the man repeats, and I force myself not to give my signature two-finger whistle.

He grabs a long instrument from a nearby table—one I'm proud to identify as a crumhorn—and blows into it. *This* settles everyone down and I make a mental note: get a crumhorn for Music All Around.

"Good day," the man says, and the kids parrot it back. "I am Sir Gerald. Ye lads and lasses are here to learn the art of jousting, yes?"

There's mild affirmation before the man starts taking attendance from the scroll, using the words "Sir" or "Lady" before each name.

Ian turns to Lily. "I'm not really signed up for this, right?"

"Yes, you are."

"There's no age limit on fun, Ian," I deadpan.

He leans on one boot. "The other day, you said today's lesson was feeling comfortable in costume."

I wave a hand. "There are multiple aims to each lesson. We only have a few weeks, you know."

"Right." He rolls his eyes, but in a way which makes me feel like he's amused more than annoyed.

Over the next half hour, Lily and I stand with proud moms and dads while Ian and the other jousting participants make lances out of foam pool noodles and decorative tape. They draw made-up family crests on cardboard shields with thick magic markers. Ian winds tape around his lance, alternating between red and white. He draws a rudimentary crest with a beer, a moon, a spatula, and a guitar.

"Pair up for jousting," Gerald yells.

The kids immediately pair up. Ian stands alone.

Gerald moves next to him. He grabs Ian's hand and holds it up. "We need a jousting partner for Sir Ian," he shouts.

Ian shakes his head. "I'm good. I'll watch."

"Nope. Nope," Gerald says as if Ian is just another ten-year-old instead of a man nearing thirty. "Jousting is the fun part. Can't miss it." He cups his hands around his mouth and yells, "Looking for a partner for SIR IAN. Sirs and Madams can go twice. Don't be shy."

No one moves but all eyes are focused on Ian, standing with a dormant lance in his hand.

"It's really okay," Ian insists.

"No. No," Gerald says. "I'll find you someone." He cups his hands around his mouth. "Sirs and Madams. Your attention."

Ian looks mortified. His face is pink, and I swear, he's slouching to look shorter.

"Sirs and Madams," Gerald repeats, his voice louder and more stern. "We need—"

I raise my hand. "I'll do it."

Gerald twists in my direction. "You, m'lady? *You* will take on Sir Ian?"

He looks incredulous. It irritates me. "Yes. Me."

"As you wish." He bends down, picks up a foam-noodle lance and a shield, and holds them in my direction.

I grab the items and move next to Ian. We're standing tall above a mass of children, in line behind one of the beams.

"You don't have to do this," Ian says.

I knock his foam noodle with mine. "You're not afraid to joust me, are you?"

"No. I just don't want you to feel dumb."

I do a mock lunge with the noodle. "Why would I feel dumb? Do *you* feel dumb?"

"Jousting in a class with little children? Of course not."

We move up in line. Ian makes a show of touching his toes.

"Good idea." I touch my toes. Ian does arm circles. I do a half twist. We one-up with stretches, high knees, and other completely unnecessary warm-up activities. We mock serious-ness the entire time. Some of the kids follow suit.

"Sir Ian and his partner," Gerald yells.

I step to the beam, a narrow plank on two concrete blocks about four inches off the ground. I recover my composure.

"Ready," Gerald yells, hands apart, "Joust!"

Ian and I move toward each other. I'm faster than him, and when I get close enough, I whip the noodle toward his groin area. He looks down in surprise. I knew he would. Men are *so* protective of their jewels. While he's distracted, I push him off the plank.

"M'lady is the winner," Gerald announces.

I jump off the beam and Gerald holds my hand up to a smattering of applause.

"Go again?" Ian asks.

We get in line to joust again. The second bout is more competitive, each of us wildly swinging noodles, blocking with shields, and moving back and forth on the narrow plank. Ian advances toward me, his bright yellow pool noodle raised over his head, the makeshift shield in front of his face. He looks so serious, like he might *be* in a joust for real, that I start to laugh.

He stops. "What?"

"You." I point at him with my noodle. "You're all like 'I have to win this joust.'"

He smiles. "And you're not?"

"Nope. I'll prove it." I move to look like I'm about to jump off.

Ian shakes his head. "Not falling for that, Lady Rebecca. You're going to pretend to jump off and then push me."

"Aren't you paranoid?"

"Am I? That's not what you are going to do?"

"It is," I admit.

"Come on guys. Enough." Lily strides over and pushes me off. "Let's go."

With her consent, we abandon the remainder of Lily's "lesson plan" and just enjoy the Faire for the rest of the afternoon. We ride the Sea Dragon Swing, a giant boat with seats that swings riders high into the air on either side. Ian competes in an axe throw, which they must do a lot in Nebraska because he wins both Lily and me plastic goblets. We race through a maze of hay, and after, try our hand at archery. We watch a show involving trained rats.

The stores and merchandise are endless. *Everything* seems like a good purchase. The stripy handblown glasses which go with nothing I own, the floral headband I may not ever wear.

Even a little stone troll calls to me. Lily buys a feathered hat and a set of perfumed oils; Ian gets himself a flute.

"Don't tell me you play the flute." I say.

"I don't. But it would be cool to learn, right?"

"It would."

"We should eat," Lily announces, adjusting her hat.

We enter the nearest pub and sit at a pocked, round table in the corner of a dark space made to look like a tavern for knights. Shields and weapons adorn stone walls; giant chandeliers hang from a dark-beamed ceiling. There's a bar across one side, a smattering of high-top tables in front of it.

All three of us order giant turkey legs (when in Rome) that come with green salads and alarming portions of coleslaw. We order mead served in overflowing pewter mugs. Lily holds hers up.

"To fun lessons."

"To fun lessons," Ian and I echo. We smash our mugs together hard enough that mead sloshes on the table.

"Was it too bad," Lily asks, "dressing up and jousting with a bunch of little kids?"

Ian sets his mug down. "Nah. I've had a great day. Axe throwing, the maze, that somewhat disturbing rat show—" He shrugs. "Today was *fun*. And I like the peasant costume."

"Well, you're pulling it off in a *major* way," Lily says.

Ian laughs, and though I didn't state the sentiment, my face goes red because I was thinking the same thing.

"I never would have thought to do any of this." He shakes his head. "I might have refused if it wasn't part of a lesson." He throws a rueful smile. "Thank you, ladies. Seriously." He holds up his mug.

We bang our mugs together again and dive into the meal. Conversation is lively, mostly about the day's happenings, and it's nice to see Ian so relaxed. It's almost like he pulled down a protective layer, giving Lily and me a glimpse into the person behind the hard outer shell. A person willing to sit on the floor and decorate a cardboard shield with a bunch of ten-year-olds. Someone who wants to try out the flute and has no issue walking around all day in knee-high boots and a peasant shirt saying things like "m'lady."

It's not until we get dessert—chocolate covered bacon slices, don't judge—that it dawns on me. I haven't thought about the audition all day. The tryout usually consumes my thoughts, worry sneaking in during moments of quiet, invading my inner peace in a way that feels insidious. Up until today, just now, the inevitable results of the audition have loomed huge in my mind.

Scenario one: I get cast on the show. My life is perfect, my family is proud of me, and I drive off into the sunset in some car I don't even know how to operate.

OR.

Scenario two: I don't get cast. I'm a failure, the family joke, destined to create gender-specific fish for seafood campaigns for the rest of my life.

I have a glimpse of how silly my attitude is, this all-or-nothing, black-and-white view of the audition results. I'm not ready to give up the viewpoint, not yet, but there's a tiny glimmer of realization in this moment. I'm not on the show. And I'm still having fun.

CHAPTER 14

I *an* head to the bar for another round of mead. Rebecca and Lily are giggling at the table. It's an infectious sound, and I smile even though I'm probably the subject of whatever they're laughing about. Doesn't matter. Their teasing feels like friendship, each of us now with a loosely defined role. Rebecca's the free spirit. Lily's the activist. I'm the uptight one but, instead of derision, my nervous idiosyncrasies are a source of gentle humor. It's the same vibe I get from Brenda, which I think is the reason today made me so happy.

The barista, in a classic barmaid costume, tight-fitting bodice and all, moves in front of me. "Good day, sir. What's your pleasure?"

"I'll take three meads, thanks."

"Aye." She nods and pulls pewter mugs from the thick iron rungs above the bar. She fills them with gold liquid and sets them on the bar.

"Once a woman, always a woman."

I pivot toward what sounds like an aggressive remark. The source seems to be a burly man standing with two others, the three of them crowded around two people. One of them is dressed as a fairy; the other has on a costume strikingly like my own.

"Leave him alone," the fairy says.

"HIM?" The man looks toward his companions as though he just heard the most preposterous thing in his life. "That's no him, am I right?"

His cronies don't affirm, exactly, but none of them tell the man to back off either.

"If you're born a woman, you're a woman," the man continues. "I mean, look at this. SHE'S trying to grow facial hair." He points at the man's face with the neck of his beer bottle. "This country, man, it's going to shit."

The veins in my head pulse. I should walk away. Men like this guy don't want to understand. It's not like a lecture from me will cause some great awakening. It would probably make things worse.

"I don't want my taxes going to this transition shit," the man says now, louder. "Right? I mean, *we're* paying for this. We the taxpayers." He looks around the bar, seemingly for agreement from what appear to be increasingly uncomfortable patrons.

My fists ball, and though I presume no one is taking the guy seriously, I can't stay quiet. "Tax dollars don't go for transition surgery," I say. "Most health insurances don't cover it either. Actually," I continue, unable to help myself, "most people transitioning save for years to get the surgery they need to feel the comfort in their bodies that you and I take for granted."

The man slowly turns in my direction. His face is red, his eyes black and beady. A potbelly protrudes over his jeans. I couldn't have imagined a better caricature of a bully had I sat down and designed one.

"Is that right?" he says and moves close enough that I can smell the liquor on his breath. He squints in my direction. "Are you one of them?"

"One of who?"

"One of them goddammed freaks."

Freaks.

Memories of that word—"freak"—shatter to the surface. I'm straddled between present and past. Without thinking, without even knowing I'm doing it, my still-balled fist connects, hard, with the man's jaw.

He stumbles back, knocking over a stool. Patrons behind him yell, and the man hurtles toward me, holding his face in one hand, the beer bottle in the other.

"Freak," the man says again. He lifts the beer bottle, brandishes it over his head like a weapon.

A crowd forms. I'm vaguely aware of Rebecca urging me to stand down. The barista is screaming.

"Frank," one of the man's friend's yells. He pushes past the crowd toward him.

Frank swings the bottle down in my direction. I dodge. The bottle slams on the bar and shatters. Shards of glass shoot into the surrounding area. People dodge like they're bullets, upturning stools, pushing into each other in their wake. Spilled beer forms a puddle on the bar. Frank lunges toward me; a man grabs his arms.

A hand on my elbow. Lily. "Come on Ian," she whispers. "Let's go."

I take a step back, then another. People fill in the empty space where I'd been. Frank struggles in the clutches of two men, nonsensical rants and obscenities spewing from the twist of his mouth. Lily leads me to the door; Rebecca's outside with our things.

"You don't want to be here if the police show up," Lily whispers.

"Why?"

She pulls me outside and starts walking. Rebecca follows.

"That guy may have escalated things," she says, "but you were the initial aggressor. You could get in trouble."

Oh.

I hadn't thought of that.

I hadn't thought of anything. I'd acted on instinct.

We snake back through the Faire toward the parking lot, our pace fast but not so fast as to draw attention. My heart beats hard, my body tense.

We reach the car and tumble inside. Lily starts the engine and peels out of the parking lot in a way that makes me feel like we're in a getaway car. If I wasn't so mad, the whole thing might seem funny. Who would have bet on me taking out a guy like Frank?

Rebecca whips her head around, peers at me from the front seat. "Are you all right?"

"My fist hurts. Otherwise, yeah, I'm fine."

"Good."

It's silent. I lean back in the seat, exercise the fingers of my hurt hand.

"What happened?" Rebecca asks.

"Guy was an asshole. I lost my temper."

"You decked him, Ian," she says. "I mean, you really decked him."

"Yeah."

I'd assumed Lily and Rebecca heard the man's comments, the ones which precipitated the punch. But maybe they hadn't. Maybe it seemed like their awkward, uptight friend hauled off and punched a man for no reason.

I open my mouth to explain, shut it. I don't feel like explaining why I did what I did. The social aspects of the day, fun as they were, already had me drained. The fight, my anger over the man and what I know is a pervasive attitude in our society, depleted whatever energy I had left.

An explanation—if they even want one—will have to wait.

CHAPTER 15

R*ebecca*

The morning after "the punch," Ian sits on the porch rocker in a T-shirt and sweat shorts. He's clutching a cloth-covered bag over his knuckles. Unfolded newspaper pieces litter the floor below him.

"You should have seen the other guy," I say, nodding at his injury.

He shakes his head; the corners of his mouth twitch upward.

I sit in the other rocking chair, my hands gripped around a steaming mug of coffee. "Why'd you hit him?"

I've wanted to ask the question since last night.

He shrugs. "He looked at me funny."

I tip my head.

Ian sets the cloth bag of ice on the plastic table next to his chair. "The guy was mouthing off to a gentleman transitioning."

Transitioning. I know the word. I can't place it.

"The guy was transgender," Ian supplies. "Transitioning from a woman to a man. He was being a jerk to the guy."

"Oh."

My response is inadequate; I'm still digesting. Ian's

passionate about equality. I know that. It's his *job*. But punching a guy? It just doesn't seem like something he'd do. At least from what I know of him. "Was it really bad?" I ask.

"I thought so." He sits forward, leans his elbows on his knees. "It probably seems extreme. Me punching the guy."

"A little," I say honestly.

He looks away from me, toward the sidewalk. A woman walks by with two boxy-headed Labradors. A yellow bird lands on the rail.

"My sister, Brenda," Ian says, shifting his gaze back to me, "grew up as Brendan."

Understanding cascades through me. Oh. This small snippet of information explains a lot.

"She transitioned the year after she graduated high school," he says.

"Was it hard?"

"For her, yeah."

"And for you?"

"For me? Yes. It was hard."

He pinches the bridge of his nose and hangs his head. However the transition happened, it's heavy for him. I don't know that I'm the person he wants to talk to about this and I don't push. We stare at the road, at the cars passing and the pedestrians walking and the stray bird that flies by.

Ian lifts his head. "I was a total douche about it," he says finally. "I'd just turned sixteen and I thought the whole thing was weird. I was ashamed. And mad. So friggin' mad." He shakes his head. "I remember the feeling like it was yesterday. I could barely look at her. All I could think is why? Why are you doing this?" He pauses. "And my parents, they were great, supportive and all that, and I kept thinking, am I the only one? Am I the only one who wants Brendan back? Crazy thing, the one person I would have wanted to talk to it about was my brother. And it felt like he was gone."

I sip my coffee. "I think a lot of sixteen-year-olds would be like that."

I'm not sure how I would have reacted if one of my brothers transitioned when I was in high school. Or now even.

Ian leans back in the rocker. "I know. But I stood idle while others gave her a hard time. A group of kids we both knew stopped in front of our house. Brenda was out front raking leaves. They got out of their car and taunted her, got right in her face, called her a freak. Over and over."

I put my hand over his. "Ian, I'm sorry."

He withdraws his hand, looks down and shakes his head. "I was there. In the garage. I saw it. I said nothing. I did nothing. I just—" He pauses. "I just let it happen." He looks up at me. "I don't know what I would have done if they'd hit her, Rebecca. I don't think anything. I think I would have stayed in the garage and let it happen."

"You don't know that."

"I do. That's the problem." He pauses. "So last night, when that guy called that gentleman a freak—"

I hold up a hand. "You don't have to explain."

"It's why I do what I do, you know. The job." He swings his head toward the sidewalk and blows out a breath. "Sorry. That was a lot."

"I'm glad you told me." I glance at Ian, his expression fixed on the sidewalk. "Do you and Brenda have a good relationship now?"

He looks at me. "We do. After months of me being a total ass, even moving out for a few weeks, she called me out on it. I said every hateful, emotional thing I could think of, no holds barred. I told her I missed Brendan. That I hated Brenda. I told her I was embarrassed, that she looked weird, that I'd never, ever, ever accept her as a woman."

"What did she say?"

"Nothing. I was shaking and crying. She sat on the bed next

to me and hugged me to her. And it was like some level of understanding uncorked inside of me. Brenda, Brendan. It didn't matter. She still loved chocolate milkshakes, hiking, dogs, and good puns. She loved to cook, loved stupid board games that no one else wanted to play. We still shared all the same family memories we'd had when she was Brendan. We were siblings. Gender shouldn't matter. I wasn't going to let it matter."

"Did you tell her that?"

He shakes his head. "I didn't have to. She knew." He pauses, a small smile on his lips. "We went to get ice cream."

"After the fight?"

"Yup. Huge sundaes with hot fudge and whipped cream." He leans back. "I've done everything I can to be a good brother since then."

"Ian," I say, unable to formulate exactly what I'm thinking. I'm ashamed, actually, that I'd judged him so quickly when we'd met. "I'm so impressed."

"Impressed that I was an asshole?"

"Impressed with everything you've done since. I mean, you care. Not just about Brenda, but about transgender people and what they go through." I shift forward, extend my hand, and put it on his knee. "You should be proud."

He meets my gaze a long moment before responding. "Thanks, Rebecca."

"You're welcome."

I retract my hand; Ian stands. "Should I make us breakfast? Omelets?"

"An omelet sounds perfect."

I follow Ian into his kitchen, identical to mine but in the reverse and *way* neater. His kitchen towels are folded nicely; there are no dishes in the sink, not even ones soaking, the kind I count as "done."

I sit at the kitchen table. There's a picture of Ian and Audrey in a silver frame on the edge by the wall. Both of Ian's arms are looped around her in a giant bear hug. She's cute, really cute, with dimples that match his. Their kids would be *adorable*. I'm looking for a flaw, any flaw, when Ian speaks.

"Fifth anniversary." He nods toward the picture.

I avert my eyes, embarrassed to have been caught staring. "Cool."

Ian pulls out a carton of eggs, olive oil, salt, and potato chips.

I eye the chips. "You're not putting potato chips in the omelets, are you?

He pulls a gigantic cast-iron skillet from a cupboard. "I am and don't judge." He grabs a bowl. "Brenda and her fiancé have a catering company. They taught me this recipe, and believe me, if I do it right, you'll never go back."

"I'll never go back to having potato-chip-free omelets after today?" I lean back in my chair. "I find that hard to believe but okay."

"I'm serious," he says, holding up an egg. "Your culinary world is about to change forever."

He cracks the egg on the side of the bowl, casts the shells into the sink. He repeats this six times then pours in a good amount of chips. He moves to sit across from me. "We have to wait five minutes for the chips to absorb the eggs."

I tap on the table. "I feel like you're making this up. Like all you had in the house were eggs and potato chips, so you decided to pretend it's an omelet recipe."

"I would do that, but not today." He holds up a hand. "This is a real recipe, I swear."

"All right," I say with a headshake, "but I may have to verify this with Brenda."

"You got it." He swipes his phone from the counter and punches at it. "FaceTiming her."

I wave my hands at him. "Don't really; I'm just kidding."

"Too late." He holds the phone, and a moment later, a

woman with short dark hair, an angular face, and striking blue eyes fills the screen. She looks sleepy. Did Ian just wake her up?

"Ian. To what do I owe the pleasure of this early morning call?"

He smiles. "Sorry. I'm here with my friend, Rebecca." He moves the phone; I wave at the screen. "Can you please tell her potato chip omelets are a thing?"

He moves the phone so I can see Brenda. I hate that my first instinct is to see if I can tell she was once a male. I wipe the thought away, ashamed, but with a bloom of understanding. If I, a person who prides myself on acceptance, had that initial reaction, how hard must it be for Brenda to navigate a world of less tolerant people?

"Potato chip omelets," Brenda says, "are glorious. Make sure Ian serves it to you with a nice dollop of salsa."

"I don't have salsa," Ian calls, not turning the phone.

Brenda inches her face forward; it takes up the entire screen. "He's a barbarian," she says in a quiet voice. "So, so sorry for him, but the omelet is good without the salsa too. Make sure he uses medium heat." She pulls the phone back and yells, "Medium heat, E," at the screen.

He turns the phone back. "Got it. Thanks."

"And have you thought about my proposal? Help Julian and me get a frozen meal service started?"

Ian moves to the table, picks up the phone, and looks at the screen. "I'm not doing that. I live in Nebraska, remember?"

"You don't have to live there."

He shakes his head. "Bye sis." He clicks off the conversation.

I stare at the phone, then at him, amazed. "Do you always do that?"

"Do what?"

"Call your sister early in the morning, ask a bunch of stupid questions, and hang up?"

He moves to the stove, drips olive oil in the pan. "More or less. Why? You wouldn't call your brothers like that?"

"My brothers?" I scoff. "The esteemed John Chapman, *Esquire* and *Dr.* Mark Chapman?" I shake my head. "No. I wouldn't call them to ask them if potato chip omelets are real."

He puts the eggs in the skillet, turns the heat to medium. "Do you call them at all?"

I don't have to think about it. I know the answer. No. I don't call my brothers. I call my parents once a week, Sundays, out of obligation. "I'm not really like the rest of my family." I stand, grab two plates, and set them by the stove. "You've met my parents. They're all into careers and education and all that. It's how they define success."

"Really?" He flips over an omelet. "Have they ever seen you with little kids? Like at Music All Around? Not that many people could command a classroom the way you can and still have the kids adore you." He steps back from the stove. "It's pretty amazing."

Amazing. Not a way I've been described, possibly ever, and I feel warm from the compliment. "Being good with kids is not being a success," I protest.

"I disagree. Most people suck with kids. I know I do." He points at me with his spatula. "You should invite your family to the showcase."

I let out a laugh. The "showcase" is a little musical demonstration we're having for the parents at the start of class Saturday. I can't imagine my parents or brothers wanting to attend. I can't even visualize them there.

Ian flips the omelets onto plates and gets us glasses of orange juice. "Seriously, Rebecca. You are an outstanding musician and an exceptional teacher. Your family should know that."

"Outstanding and exceptional." I wave a napkin in front of my face and speak in my best southern belle imitation. "Why Ian Ledger, you are making me blush."

He is making me blush, for real; I hope the comment is a good cover.

"Sorry for that, my lady, but it's true." He sets the omelet and juice before me. "Ta da." He stares at me intensely.

I pick up a fork. "Are you going to stare at me while I eat this?"

"Yes. I want to see the moment you decide never to eat potato-chip-free omelets again."

I shovel a bite into my mouth. Salty, not too much. Oh. Good. It's good. "Mmm," I say, nodding, then swallow. "Really good."

"Right?"

"Yes. Excellent."

He smiles.

I shovel in another bite, then a third, and swallow. "Really good."

He sits across from me. "Not going back, are you?"

"Not on your life." I hold up my orange juice glass. "To potato chip omelets."

"To potato chip omelets," he echoes.

We clink our glasses and drink. "And to families with all their complications," I add.

"Here's to that."

We clink again, finish the omelets, and make plans for the day. We have lunch, play Skee-Ball, and spend more time at the beach than I have in weeks. I attempt to teach Ian to body surf. He is the worst body surfer on the planet; I do not hesitate to tell him this. After the beach, we shower and meet back at Ian's for Chinese takeout. We start the documentary *Tiger King* after. It's strangely fascinating. One episode slips into another until it's a full-out binge. Which, of course, means ice cream. I scoop out big chunks into giant cereal bowls, and we sit, side by side on the couch, mesmerized.

It's a date without the awkwardness, and it's not until later that I realize that Ian and I spent the whole day together with no ulterior plan.

No fun lesson.

No music lesson.

Just us.

CHAPTER 16

Ian

"I did it."

I look toward the door. Rebecca's leaning against the doorframe of my office in a dress covered with yellow and orange fish. Today's glasses, faux I now know, are fuchsia.

"I thought about what you said," she continues, "and I invited my parents and brothers to the showcase Saturday."

I inch my chair forward. "Really? Are they coming?"

"My parents are. And John. Mark is on call at the hospital." She rolls her eyes. "You know, him being a *doctor* and all."

"That's awesome."

She smiles. "You're still going to accompany us on the guitar, right?"

"Hmm." I lean back in the chair and swivel. "Well, Saturday's showcase is the *only* thing I've got going on for the whole weekend. So"—I spring forward—"yes, I'll do it."

She laughs.

"Not that you couldn't. You can play enough chords now, you know."

This is true. Rebecca's a quick study, and she practices endlessly, a fact I know from our shared wall.

She shakes her head. "No way."

"You underestimate yourself."

"Nope. Nope. Nope. Not happening."

I want to say more. About how she's a natural musician. How I conjure her singing voice, deep and textured, when she's not around. How great she is with the kids. How happy I am when I see her, which, from a major introvert, is about as big a compliment as you can get. I hardly ever like seeing anyone. She's so blinded by her family's professions, by the words doctor and lawyer, that she doesn't realize how talented she is in her own right.

I want to tell her, but it feels like it's too much. We've only known each other a few weeks, and while I'm pretty sure I'm no longer in the despised prick category, I'm not sure how far I am out of it. Tolerable prick, maybe?

I keep my mouth shut.

* * *

WE WALK TOGETHER to the showcase on Saturday. Rebecca's in clothes I've never seen her wear—a navy golf shirt and tan Bermuda shorts. Her hair, usually in a swingy ponytail for class, is pulled into a bun so severe it pulls at the skin on her face. She's wearing such a stoic expression, if I didn't know better, I'd think she was going to a funeral. I half expect her to break into a dirge.

I rap my hand on her shoulder. "It'll be great."

"Yeah."

When we near Music All Around, her parents are already out front in what can best be described as cruise clothes. Her mother's short-sleeved blue sweater has a giant white anchor on the front; her father's in pastel madras shorts and a pink polo.

Lily and John are behind them. They wave at us. Rebecca lifts her hand. Barely.

Her parents nod and there's a general greeting—that fake "hi, how are you" kind of thing introverts dread—before we assemble inside. The chairs Rebecca and I had set up for the parents last night are in two neat rows in the back of the room. We'd gone to the beach after the set up. It was an exceptional night for stars with constellations clearly visible. Rebecca had been kind enough to let me blabber on about them for what I realize in retrospect was *way* too long.

As soon as they get inside, both her parents look around the space, heads swiveling back and forth. The scrutiny is palpable, and for a moment, I don't see the bright space that's normally infused with energy and music and laughter. Instead, all that's evident are the worn rugs, the cubbies with chipped paint, the baskets of musical instruments which have seen better days.

"Awesome space," Lily says.

Mrs. Chapman rubs her bare arms. "Nice, honey." The bare-bones compliment comes out stiff. Even I can tell she doesn't mean it.

Rebecca tucks a stray piece of hair behind her ear. "Right." She straightens the already straight chairs in a flurry of movement. After, she stares at the floor. God. She's nervous. I didn't expect her to be so nervous.

She straightens more chairs. Ones which, ironically, she'd made crooked with her prior effort. She wipes non-existent dust off one with her bare hand.

"You're in for a treat," I volunteer, "Rebecca is a supremely talented musician. And she's amazing with the kids."

Her dad rolls back on his heels. "Rebecca's always had a little talent for that."

I look at him. *Little*. Why little? Why not just talent?

Rebecca wipes her hands on her shorts. She bites a nail.

We stand in absolute, you-could-hear-a-pin-drop silence. I

shouldn't have suggested this. I did not know enough about the dynamic with her family.

Finally and thankfully, the door bursts open and a freckle-faced girl charges in, her parents laden with camera equipment behind her. Their infusion into the space breaks whatever dark spell Rebecca is under and she gives her first real smile of the morning. The atmosphere immediately lightens.

"This is all Charity could talk about all week," the mom gushes. "We're really looking forward to it."

"The kids are fabulous." Rebecca ruffles Charity's hair. "Please, take a seat." She gestures to the back of the room.

More children and parents filter in. I'm pretty sure Rebecca is hugged more times in the span of five minutes than I have been over the past year.

I steal glances at her family. John is buried in his phone. Her mom's head pivots around the room; it's hard to tell what she's thinking. Her dad is smiling. At least it looks like he is.

Once the room is full, Rebecca does her signature whistle. The kids, all between three and five, scramble into rows on the carpet. I grab my guitar and take my place in a chair at the front of the room. Rebecca stands before the kids, a finger in the air. "One, two, three," she whispers

The children sing "The Wheels on the Bus" and "The Itsy Bitsy Spider," all of them mimicking Rebecca's hand motions. I keep my eyes on her parents. Definitely smiling. I exhale a breath of relief on her behalf. Mine too. This was my idea.

After the two songs, Rebecca stops and explains the importance of music for kids this age. How clapping and instrument playing help develop fine and gross motor control, how singing fosters a sense of creativity and community, and how there's a correlation between musical education and excellence in math. She's slaying this.

After the speech, she passes out shakers and the kids sing

"Five Little Monkeys," tapping the shakers on the rug in time with the music.

The remainder of the class is parent observation. Rebecca sits on the floor with the kids, all of them singing and playing the instruments from the worn baskets. She runs a tight ship, but it's evident how much she loves the kids. They love her too. It's obvious.

When the class is over, parents profusely thank her; there's no shortage of kid hugs. Charity hands her a drawing of big and little stick figures on a rug. The larger one has green eyes and a ponytail, clearly Rebecca. The little one is Charity. Rebecca hugs it to her chest. "Thank you. I love it."

Once everyone leaves, she turns toward her family, Charity's drawing dormant in her hand.

"Way to go, Bec," Lily says. "That was awesome."

"Wonderful job, dear." Her mother smiles.

Rebecca turns toward her mom. "You think so?" She bites her lip, the need for reassurance so painfully obvious that I wonder again where the Rebecca I know is. How does a woman who just expertly commanded a class of toddlers, who educated parents on the importance of music, turn into a puddle of insecurity so quickly?

"Yes," her mother says, "very nice."

It's a compliment but it's dismissive, almost as bad as the term "little talent." These people. God. I want to shake them.

"Shall we go to lunch?" Her dad pulls out a money clip from the madras shorts.

Rebecca gives him a long look, almost like she's waiting for him to say something about the lesson. He doesn't.

"Lunch is great for us." John slings his arm around Lily.

Rebecca nods in a rapid movement I've never seen her make. "Sure. Sure." She looks around like she needs to clean up or do something, but she doesn't. She trained the kids to clean up after themselves.

We go to The Mad Batter, a restaurant on the first floor of one of the giant Victorian houses nearby. The hostess seats us at a table in the back, next to a window with panes of stained glass. Rebecca's dad orders a bottle of white wine and two orders of calamari for the table. He doesn't ask anyone if they want either of those things. Maybe it's something their family always gets?

The calamari arrives, along with the wine, and her dad pours glasses for everyone. I wait for the expected toast. Nothing.

I hold up my glass. "To Rebecca and a successful showcase."

"To Rebecca," everyone says. And that's it. No compliments. No questions. No accolades. I can't believe it. They have no idea how hard it was for Rebecca to invite them.

"How awesome was that class?" I say randomly.

Rebecca throws me a look of death.

"Nice job, honey," her dad says.

The remark is condescending, the kind of thing you say to a toddler, and I feel like a jerk for setting Rebecca up like this. I vow to be silent.

The server drops off the ordered-for-us calamari and we eat in an awkward half silence, bland conversation peppered between bites. It's brutal.

"So, Rebecca," her mother says, "I have some exciting news."

She picks her head up. "Yeah?"

"Yes. I've been able to secure you a place in the one-year paralegal studies program at Bella University." Her mother smiles wide.

Rebecca says nothing, a fork and knife frozen in each of her hands.

"It's very hard to get into," her mother continues. "All graduates are practically guaranteed a job." She leans forward and lowers her voice. "And your brother's firm will hire you." She nods toward John.

John swallows. "Real estate," he says without explanation.

Rebecca's head pivots from one family member to the next.

None of them look remotely abashed. Only Lily has the decency to look embarrassed.

"And when is this golden opportunity supposed to start?" Rebecca asks.

"Two weeks." Her mother leans forward, toward Rebecca, "someone dropped out."

Rebecca pushes her chair back. "Well, great. Glad I can fill that spot and train for a job we all know I'd be a disaster at. The dyslexia is real, you know. Not to mention I'd hate that job. And I have my audition coming up."

"You can still audition," her father says. "You'll just have something to fall back on. You know. In case." He shrugs.

"In case what?" Rebecca demands.

"In case you don't make it, sis," John says. "Aren't there, like, a gazillion people trying out?" He pops a calamari in his mouth.

"In fact, no." Rebecca stands. "There aren't that many people because I already passed through the first step. Something you would know if you showed any interest in my music at all." She stands and throws her napkin on the table. "Thanks for coming to the showcase. I have to go."

CHAPTER 17

R*ebecca*

Ian's footsteps are behind me. I keep walking, head down, my heart thumping with angry beats.

I can't believe them.

A paralegal? At John's firm? I couldn't have conjured a worse career fit had I tried. And the attitude about the audition. Like an audition for a show that's going to be on national television with a million-dollar prize is akin to a high school play or community theatre production.

"Rebecca, wait." Ian moves beside me, his breath heavy. Neither of us say anything for a few beats. "Sorry. That totally sucked."

I glance at him, shrug. "My parents are like that. Careers are everything to them. At least the ones they deem worthy are."

We snake through the streets, neither of us talking. When we reach the porch of the duplex, Ian grabs my hand and looks at me. "You've got to get on that show, Rebecca."

His expression is intense. "Ian Ledger," I say with the hint of a smile, "are you being a cutthroat?"

"You bet I am. We should double up on the lessons."

"You're the boss," I say, glad he suggested it. I'd wanted more lessons; it hadn't felt right to ask. "And I have to figure out what to wear."

"For the audition."

"Yeah. I have to have a look, you know. I can't show up in something like this." She waves her hand down her body, gestures to the very un-Rebecca-like outfit worn for the benefit of her family.

"Would you want Brenda to help you? She's great at this kind of thing."

"Sure." I shrug like I don't care, but I'm touched that he wants to help. At the same time, it's a bit sobering that Ian, a man I met just a few weeks ago and intensely disliked at first, cares more about my dream than my own family.

He strides up the porch steps and pulls out his key. "She'll love it. I'll call her later."

"Great." I move to my door. "By the way." I unlock my door and push it open with my hip. "Your next fun lesson is tomorrow."

"Tomorrow?" He bugs his eyes out. "What are we doing?"

I lift an eyebrow. "I don't know."

"How do you not know?"

"I don't know exactly," I say, my tone purposely cryptic, "because we're taking a mystery bus tour."

* * *

THE NEXT MORNING, I rummage through my things to find the items the tour suggested we bring: sunscreen, change of clothes, sunglasses, towels, umbrella.

Some mystery.

It's pretty obvious we're going to the beach, which is silly because we *live* at the beach. I assume most of the tour-goers do, too, because the tour takes off from Wildwood. Whatever. At least a beach day will get my mind off yesterday's debacle.

I throw a bathing suit in a knapsack.

When we load onto the bus an hour later, Ian and I end up sitting in the identical seats we had a few weeks back, the night I had no shoes. He'd been an uptight prick in my mind back then; he's layered now. It's like they're two different people: Oxford Ian from the bus and this new one. Still uptight, but funny and kind and a little more handsome than I gave him credit for on night one.

He pulls the knapsack off my lap and looks inside. "Hmm. Do you think we're going skiing?"

A round-faced woman pokes her head over the seat. She looks older, in her sixties maybe, and has bits of pink highlights in gray hair. "It's too hot for skiing," she volunteers.

"Oh," Ian says. "Maybe snowboarding then."

She points at him with a blue fingernail. "Funny. I'm Shirl."

"Hey Shirl. I'm Ian. This is Rebecca."

I twist around in my seat. "Hey."

"You been on one of these tours before?" Shirl asks.

"First one," Ian answers.

Shirl's eyes widen. "Wow. Adult tour for first timers. Very brave." She shakes her head and plops back down in her seat. "Good luck."

Ian glances at me. I shrug. I have no idea what Shirl is talking about. I did sign up for an adult tour. *Because we're adults.* Why would I sign up for anything else?

I put Shirl's comment out of my mind and lean back. Ian pulls out his phone and a pair of earbuds. He hands one to me. I plug it in my ear; he uses the other. We spend the remainder of the ride listening to Ian's country guitar playlist, one he'd made that features easy guitar solos. He insists I'll be able to play a ton of these in a few weeks. I'm not so sure.

The bus lurches around a corner and I fall into him, my body against his. His torso is more muscular than I would have guessed. I stay for a beat longer than necessary then shift back away from him, inches between us.

Eventually, the bus turns wide into a parking lot and pulls to an abrupt stop. Tour participants erupt into whoops and cheers. A man catcalls. I peer out the window. Waves roll on the Atlantic Ocean in the distance.

What the heck? All this excitement for the beach?

Our guide, a smiley woman named Daisy, steps to the front. "Full day at the beach." She pulls a bunch of slim papers from a bag and holds them up. "Get your lunch vouchers on your way off, be back to the bus at four, and wear *plenty* of sunscreen." She winks as she says the last part. More catcalls. A rowdy group, I guess.

The driver pushes the lever to open the door. I sling the sack over my shoulder; Ian does the same with his duffel. We get off the bus and I nod toward and octagon-shaped wooden struc-ture. "Let's change in the bathrooms."

Ian agrees and I step into the women's room. As soon as I'm inside, I take a step back. Something is not right. The women in here are…naked. And not locker-room naked—like women putting on actual clothes in a hurry. No one is in a hurry. Clus-ters of nude women stand around talking. No clothes are in sight. Not on the floors or on the benches or on the women. It's just skin and boobs and—what *is* this?

"Rebecca?"

I whip my head around. It's Kimmy. But for a towel around her neck, she's naked. I cross my arms over my chest, which is ridiculous since I'm the one wearing clothes.

"What are you doing here?" she asks.

"I—" I look around. "I don't know." I lean forward. "What is this?"

She laughs. "It's a nude beach, sweetie. Did you not know that?"

"I came on the mystery bus tour?" I say this like a question.

Kimmy nods. "Oh, yeah. They come here a lot."

"Do *you* come here a lot?" I can't conceal my surprise. Not that clothing-optional beaches wouldn't be totally on brand for Kimmy.

"Sure. No tan lines."

She waves an arm down her body, and yup, she's right. No tan lines. Not that I needed to know that. Or wanted to. I look around the room. I am way more uncomfortable with this than I ever would have expected. I lean forward. "I took Ian here," I whisper.

Kimmy's eyebrows shoot up. "Ian. From work?"

"Yes. I didn't know we were going to a nude beach. It was a mystery."

She laughs.

"It's not funny."

"It is, actually."

She must take in my unamused expression because she changes tack. "Rebecca. You're young and beautiful with a gorgeous figure."

I roll my eyes.

She puts a hand on my shoulder. "Gorgeous figure," she repeats. "Just lean into today. Have fun and don't worry about what anyone else thinks. That's what I always do." She kisses the top of my head and trots off.

I'm frozen in place. I can't visualize myself walking out of this bathroom naked, no matter what Kimmy says. Even the most free-spirited version of myself wouldn't do that. And how would the day go with Ian if we were both nude? Do we just have normal conversations with my boobs hanging out and his junk on display? Do we eat nude? Walk on the beach?

No.

No way.

The scenarios that could ensue are way too embarrassing.

We'll just find another beach and hang out until the bus leaves. Yes. That's it. There's no way Ian would parade around naked for the day, fun lesson or not. I visualize him in his polo, buttoned to the tippy top. Yeah. No way. He's probably back on the bus already, hyperventilating.

I breathe a sigh of relief and move into a remote corner of the changing area, no longer surprised that there are no curtains or stalls or privacy whatsoever. I whip off my clothes, put on my suit and cover up. Surrounded by naked women, I feel silly, like I'm in an evening gown at a backyard barbeque. Whatever. I'll find Ian and explain. We'll have a good laugh. It will be fine.

I step out of the bathroom, feeling self-conscious in spite of the fact that I'm fully dressed. Maybe because of it? Either way, I am supremely uncomfortable. I jerk my head around, looking for Ian. I don't see him. A hand on my shoulder. I whirl around.

It's Ian, arms outstretched, a smile on his face. I glance down. Full frontal.

CHAPTER 18

I*an*

"Did it." I hold my arms out and smile.

Rebecca says nothing. She looks everywhere but at me, a shell-shocked expression on her features. Plus, she's in a bathing suit. And a cover up.

Okay.

Feeling dumb. And exposed. I feel like the Adam to her Eve, in desperate need of a fig leaf. But there's nothing to cover up with. I'm just standing there. Buck naked. The momentary pride I felt in the locker room at my rare "why the hell not" decision to bare all morphs into acute embarrassment. It's like one of those dreams where you're naked in a crowd, but this time, it's real.

I edge toward the men's room, hoping the shadow of the overhang will shade my junk. I grab my duffel, my shorts and T-shirt inside. "Did you not want to—" I start. It hadn't occurred to me that Rebecca would not be up for this. I'd assumed she was teasing when she said she didn't know what we'd be doing.

She shakes her head. "No. I'm up for it. Definitely." She takes a few steps toward the entrance of the beach. "I'll just, you know, do it on the beach."

She turns but not before I catch the red in her cheeks. Maybe she really didn't know.

"You don't have to do this," I call after her.

She strides faster. "I want to," she says over her shoulder. She sounds very much like it's the last thing she wants to do.

"Really, Rebecca. It's fine."

"I want to," she says in a tone I've heard her use with the Music All Around kids. It's her don't-question-me tone.

I follow her onto the pathway toward the beach, over grass-covered dunes, and onto fine, white sand. Just about everyone is naked or half-naked. All types of bodies inhabit the beach—big, small, shaved, hairy, tall, petite, old, young, pierced, plain, black, brown, white. There's a group of men playing paddleball in nothing but cowboy hats. Topless women surf. One man is covered in tattoos. *Everywhere.*

It's strange.

But, also, not. Everyone seems to accept everyone else's choice. Full frontal, topless, suited. It's all okay. The vibe is the same as I get from Brenda and her friends: come as you are. You're welcome here. I kind of like it.

"Ian, Rebecca."

I turn. It's Kimmy. She runs up to us, sand kicking behind her feet as she moves. She holds up a green Frisbee. "Wanna join?"

I do not know how to react or where to put my eyes. Kimmy is my pseudo boss. I'm the sensitivity trainer. Surely, both of us standing feet apart naked on a beach is outside any appropriate protocol. I step back. I feel horrified. I must look it.

She waves at me. "We're all good, Ian. I won't tell if you don't." She holds up the Frisbee again. "We got a group going." She points to a cluster of naked individuals down the beach.

I look at Rebecca. There's a big fat no in every inch of her expression. I know that look. I won't subject Rebecca to forced participation. "Maybe later."

"Okay." Kimmy looks me up and down with a smile. Definitely an etiquette no-no. "Remember that sunscreen, Ian." She winks and dashes off.

I look at Rebecca after.

"I didn't know she'd be here," she says quickly.

"It's so weird."

"It is. Really weird."

She laughs and it's like her discomfort uncorks. "There's a remote spot," she says and points to a place toward the back of the beach. "Let's go there."

We reach the spot and Rebecca spreads out two thick terry towels. I set up a small umbrella between them. After, I lie on my stomach, turn my head to the side, away from Rebecca, to give her privacy.

Clothing rustles. I smell suntan lotion. I feel Rebecca moving, her warmth beside me. The hot sun beats down on my bare skin. A vision of Audrey pops in my head. I think about her less now, with the guitar lessons and the outings with Rebecca. I wonder what she would think if she knew I was lying on a beach naked next to a pretty woman. She'd be happy I put myself out there, that much I can guarantee. But I don't think she'd like Rebecca.

I turn my head and Rebecca's face, flushed from the sun, is a foot from my own, her hair splayed out over her back. She's on her stomach, a bikini top untied at the back, part of an ample breast visible from the side. *If* she were my girlfriend, I'd be pretty worked up right now.

"Audrey would be surprised by this," I say. "For sure."

I know the comment is random, but I'm struggling to keep Audrey in my mind right now, what with the sunscreen on Rebecca's bare skin glinting in the sun. I don't want to be that pervert kind of guy who can't lie on a beach naked with a girl without thinking about sex.

Yeah, right.

All I can think about is sex.

"Tell me about Audrey." Rebecca opens her eyes and looks in my direction.

"What do you want to know?"

"What she's like. Where you met. What you fell in love with."

"I took her to the senior prom, but we didn't start dating seriously until a few years ago."

Rebecca props herself up on her elbows, more of her breasts visible now. I try not to look.

"She's sweet," I continue. "She likes to garden. And she's a receptionist." I search for more things to say, but despite my best efforts, I can't think of anything. How is that possible? It's like every possible interesting thing about Audrey has vanished from my memory. "She has two cats," I blurt finally. "Oreo and Midnight."

Rebecca's lips tug at the corners. "Please tell me the names are ironic."

I smile. "They're not. I pushed for Bono and Jagger. But Audrey wanted names that matched their fur."

Rebecca guffaws. "Sorry," she says.

A laugh bursts from my gut. "It's all right. The names *are* stupid." I'd always thought that. I'd just never admitted it to Audrey. I pause. "How about you? Anyone in your life?"

She shakes her head. "Nope. Not since college."

"Really?"

She lays her head down on the towel. "You sound surprised."

"You strike me as the kind of person that would have parties to go to every night and lots of boyfriends."

A seagull lands in front of us and hops on the sand.

"So, a slut?" She gives a wicked smile.

"No, not a slut. Fun."

She's quiet a moment; the seagull continues to hop. She traces a circle in the sand with her index finger. "I'm different from who you think I am. At least I used to be. I was super shy in high school, and I had zero self-confidence. All I wanted was to blend in."

I try and fail to picture this. I put my head on the towel so it's parallel to hers. "Rebecca, how can that be? When I met you, you didn't even have shoes on?"

She laughs and it lights up her face. "My brothers were perfect. Straight-A students, varsity crew athletes, officers in all sorts of school clubs. I'm pretty sure Mark was an altar boy for a while—I lost track." She lets out a breath. "I struggled in school. And I hate to sweat, let alone compete. I was an outsider in my own family, unfavorably compared to Mark and John, and a huge disappointment to my parents." She shoos a horsefly with her hand. "Living with that kind of unstated disapproval? It eats away at you."

"I'm sorry."

"Eh. I figured things out. Maybe went too far in the other direction." She smiles.

"Definitely not. I like you just as you are."

"I like you too, Oxford." She winks. "Way more than I thought I would."

She shuts her eyes, and I stare at her a moment. Soft skin, thick unruly hair, pink pouty lips. I can't believe she hasn't had a boyfriend since college. Or that she lacked confidence for so long.

"Ian," she says, eyes still closed.

"Yeah."

"I have a confession to make."

My first thought is that she has feelings for me. The feeling of elation in my gut at this potential revelation is unmistakable. Rebecca *likes* me.

"I didn't know we were coming to a nude beach."

Or that. I tamp down my misplaced happiness. "I kind of got that vibe when I came out of the men's room."

"Was I that obvious?"

"You looked like you wanted to crawl into a hole."

"I did, and I was going to tell you the truth, but then you marched out being exhibitionist and all that."

I glance at her, a bit of red creeping into my cheeks. "Bit of a surprise, eh?"

"Ian, you button your shirts to the top. I didn't think there was any way you would do this."

"Me either. Then I was in the locker room and I thought, what the hell? If not now, when?"

"Well, it's progress, that's for sure. No one could accuse you of being uptight today."

"I know, right?" I pat myself on the back. "Kudos to me."

"Kudos to you."

She checks her phone. "It's almost noon. Should we get some lunch?"

I sit up. Her hand shoots out.

"Wait. First, you are going to tie my bikini top because I'm not parading around topless. Then put on your shorts. *Please.* I'm not eating lunch with all that"—she waves her hand toward my groin—"out on display."

She closes her eyes and I move over her. I push her hair, thick and soft, to one side and grab the tiny strings of her bikini. I tie them. Her skin glistens; it's soft and warm under my hands. I stare glance at the dip of her back, the rise her buttocks. She smells good, sunscreen infused with the light floral scent she normally wears.

"Done yet?"

I shift away from her. I've taken too long. Way too long. "Yeah." I grab at my duffel. "Sorry. Let me get my shorts on."

I tug them on, fast, and try to the put the sensuality of the previous moment from my mind.

Rebecca and I are friends.

Friends.

FRIENDS.

She pushes up. "Hey E." She twists in my direction and points at me with her index finger. "Let's go."

CHAPTER 19

ebecca

R   Amanda, our server at The Ocean Kitchen, seats us at a small wooden table under a huge green and white awning. Lazy fans with thick straw blades circle overhead; massive ferns hang around the perimeter. The space smells like salt and sea and sunscreen.

Ian is dressed now, thank God.

He looks good without clothes. Trim with visible ab muscles, just the right amount of chest hair. Unexpectedly large biceps, a firm rear end that I tried hard not to look at. He's got stubble now, an addition since our bus encounter. I like it.

I still can't believe he bared all. I would have bet my life savings on the opposite. Possibly my soul.

Ian holds up the vouchers we got on the bus to Amanda. "Are these good here?"

She takes them from his hand. "Sure are. But you can only get the bus special."

"We'll take two," I say.

"You got it." Amanda bustles away.

Ian looks at me. "You don't want to know what the bus special is?"

"Nope. It's free. That's all I need to know."

He shrugs. "Okay. Could be gross though."

"I'll eat it if you will."

He juts his hand over the table and we shake. "You're on."

Amanda returns twenty minutes later with drinks and two plates featuring the biggest hot dogs I have ever seen next to two mounds—one coleslaw, one potato salad. Centered on each of the mounds is a small cherry. A few small tomatoes sit at the top of each dog.

"Enjoy!" Amanda sings out.

Ian stares at the plate. "Do you think—" he starts.

I stare at the food, obviously intended to look suggestive. "Yes."

He looks at the plate a moment longer, and a laugh bursts from him. Deep and guttural, the kind of laugh reserved for truly funny events. The sound is contagious, and I laugh too, more so than is justified by a suggestive food arrangement. But it feels good to let loose after yesterday's parental luncheon, after today's nude beach fiasco.

Still laughing, Ian whips out his phone. "I've got to take a picture for Audrey."

Audrey. Her name, said twice today now, immediately douses the hilarity of the moment, and my breath immediately calms. "Right," I manage. "Are you guys talking again?" I hate that my voice goes up an octave with the question.

"No," he says, centering his phone over the plate, "but it will be good to share with her later." He snaps the picture, checks it, then puts his phone on the table. "She won't believe I was naked on a public beach." He picks up a fork and points at me with it. "You may have to vouch for me."

"Sure. Of course." Jealousy twists in my chest. I'm not sure why. It's not like I like Ian romantically. And, even if there was a sliver of a chance that I could, I know about Audrey. She's the entire reason we're here today. To help Ian meet *her* objective that he be more loose.

He stuffs a forkful of coleslaw in his mouth, seemingly unaware of the temporary impact Audrey's name has had on me. He swallows. "Good."

We spend the next few minutes inhaling our food in the same manner as athletes after an arduous workout. We gulp down our iced teas and order hot fudge sundaes. Both of us guess how they might be made to look evocative. Two scoops, definitely. Probably a banana for good measure.

They end up being regular old sundaes.

"Biggest accomplishment?" Ian asks, a spoonful of ice cream poised on his spoon.

"Me?" I put my hand on my chest.

He bugs his eyes out. "Yes, you."

"What is this? Ice breaker hour?"

He smiles. "Just trying to get to know you better."

I slice a bit of whipped cream with my spoon, pop it in my mouth, and swallow. "Fine. My biggest accomplishment is qualifying to try out for *Country Clash*. You?"

"Employee of the month, Mr. Steak."

I tip my head. "Come on."

"It's very competitive, Rebecca," he says, his expression deadpan. "There are only twelve months a year."

"Right, right, right. I hadn't thought about that."

A glob of Ian's ice cream, a chocolaty mess with big slivers of M&M pieces, slides down the side of his bowl. Without thinking, I scoop it off with my own spoon and put it in my mouth. "Sorry," I say after swallowing, "it was dripping."

"Considering we spent the last several hours next to each other naked, I don't think we can realistically bar eating off each other's plates. In fact," he takes an enormous spoonful of ice cream from my bowl and shovels it in his mouth, "we're even."

"You took way more." I take another spoonful of his. He does the same. The pattern continues until we're both laughing again, spooning off each other's ice cream piles at rapid speeds, our utensils clashing in the middle. It's extraordinarily juvenile, something I might have done with Lily in elementary school.

"I surrender," Ian finally says. He waves a white napkin in defeat.

I hold up my spoon. "Victorious." We both laugh; I set down my spoon. "For someone who claims to be uptight, you are killing it today, Ian Ledger."

He shrugs. "I'm not uptight around people I'm comfortable with."

The meaning of the statement is immediately clear. *I* am someone he feels comfortable with. The knowledge makes me feel warm.

"Biggest regret," he says.

"Back to the ice breaker questions, I see."

"Again, just want to get to know you better. I used to ask these kinds of questions on all my dates." He holds out his hand. "Not that this is a date."

"Of course not. And good thing because if you peppered me with inane questions on a date, zero chance I'd put out."

"Good to know. Also explains a lot about the lack of romance in my youth." He gives a sheepish smile.

"You didn't really ask those questions on dates, did you?"

"I did."

I smack my forehead with an open palm. "Ian. No."

"I'm awkward. What can I say?" He shrugs. "The least you can do is answer my question."

"Okay, fine. My biggest regret is not getting my driver's license."

He's quiet a moment, almost like he's digesting what I just said. "Wait. You don't have a driver's license?"

"No. That's why I don't have a car."

He shakes his head, brows furrowed like he can't wrap his head around this fact. "Why wouldn't you just get a license?"

My first instinct is to say something pithy; I tell him the truth instead. That I learned to physically drive a car fine, but I couldn't pass the written test.

Ian looks at me intently. "You can still take the test, you know. It doesn't have to be a regret."

"I won't pass."

A flash of astonishment crosses his features. "Why would you say that? You're quick, Rebecca. I've never seen someone learn music as fast as you do." He pauses. "You can pass that test."

He makes the final statement with such conviction; I think about it. Could I pass? Maybe? I am a different person than I was at seventeen.

"I'll consider it," I say, "but not until after the audition."

Ian nods, seemingly satisfied. "Fair enough."

We check out of the restaurant, which consists of Amanda marking our vouchers with smiley faces. There's an hour before the bus leaves. In lieu of going back to the beach, we walk through the town, a strange mix of upscale shops and ones crammed with cheap beach-themed gear. There's a fair number of restaurants and candy shops. The scents of pizza, baked goods, and hot dogs fill the air.

Sandy Toes souvenir shop sits between a store featuring gold-framed beach prints and one called Hats Off to You that sells nothing but hats. Sandy Toes is crammed with everything you might envision could be a beach souvenir: glasses, towels, keychains, earrings. Tiny bikinis hang from ceiling rafters, and giant metal bins of flip-flops, sand toys, and towels are scattered throughout the space. Backpack beach chairs line both sides of the store. It's all cheap but in the best possible way.

Inside the store, I buy Ian a T-shirt with the caption "I Beared It ALL at Califon Beach." There's a cartoon bear on a beach towel in the center. I'm positive it's something Ian will never, ever wear, but when I give it to him, he rips off his own shirt and puts it on. The bear stretches out across his chest, the result even more ridiculous than I'd imagined.

"Hot." I wink at him.

He holds up a small brown bag stamped with the Sandy Toes logo. "I got something for you too."

"Yeah?"

He hands me the bag. I reach in and pull out a keychain featuring a giant turtle in a sun hat, Califon Beach on its brim. I look up at him.

"For your car keys," he says and winks. "Don't make the license thing a regret."

I stare at the keychain a long moment before looking up and meeting Ian's eyes. "Thank you."

"You're very welcome."

We start back to the bus, and I turn to him. "Hey," I say, turtle keychain gripped in my hand. "You never did tell me. What's your biggest regret?"

We take a bunch of steps before he answers. "I think I haven't made it yet."

CHAPTER 20

I an
I think I haven't made it yet.

It's been two weeks since I made the comment, and Rebecca and I are in her half of the duplex practicing guitar. I'd passed the remark off as silly, but the truth is, I was thinking about Rebecca when I said it. It's strange how my feelings for her have changed—contempt to intrigue to friendship. And now —what? Possibility. That, as little time as I've known her, I feel something.

I think she does too.

Technically, I'm on a break with Audrey. Technically, I'm *supposed* to see other people. But if I act on these feelings for Rebecca, they might not be reciprocated. And, if they are, what then? Ditch Audrey? Who, weeks ago, I was one hundred percent certain was my person? Or just have a casual fling with Rebecca? Could I even do that? I'm not really a casual fling kind of guy.

Rebecca brings me back to the moment with a guitar riff. She looks up after. "Good?"

"Better."

She swipes a piece of sweet and sour chicken from a carton of Chinese food on the coffee table. She's dramatically increased her practice time, a fact I know from the sound of her singing and playing at all hours through our shared wall. Sometimes, I yell advice from my side, but most nights, we meet on one side of the duplex or the other, an unwritten rule that the owner provide dinner. Rebecca always heats up frozen meals. Her mantra: "Stouffer's has a team of professionals working on these recipes. Who am I to question them?" Typically, she doesn't microwave the meals long enough, and halfway through, we hit blocks of food-ice and have to put the food in to cook for extra time. Eating like this should be something I hate, especially having grown up with my mother and Brenda, both fantastic cooks. But I look forward to the company and the meals. I've even got some ideas for Brenda if she ever does launch that frozen food line.

Rebecca eats another piece of chicken. Her guitar hangs from her neck. "Do you think I should go an octave lower for the refrain? Maybe an E3?"

I consider. Rebecca decided to sing a country version of Elvis's "Jailhouse Rock." The song is a fantastic fit for her voice, but an octave lower, if she can pull it off, would really show off her range. "Try it."

From my seat on the floor, I grab an eggroll from the table and bite into it. Rebecca sings the refrain in the new octave. I nod. "Yeah. That works." I grab the carton of fried rice and spoon some on a plate. "Do it from the top."

She salutes me. "Yes, sir."

I roll my eyes.

She plays the song, then again, then a third time. I swear we'll both have earworms of "Jailhouse Rock" forever. After singing it the fourth time, Rebecca pulls the guitar off her neck and sets it near the table. "I think that's it for now," she says. "I think I'm getting it."

"Me too."

She moves next to me in front of the couch, and we lean against it, legs outstretched, the edges of our bare feet touching. The silence is congenial.

"I've got another fun lesson for you Saturday night," she says finally.

"Another one? I'm not fun enough yet? Even after the beach?"

She slaps my thigh. "The beach was clearly an outlier, Ian. No way are you *that* fun. Plus, we're running out of time. Three weeks to the wedding, right?"

I sit up straighter and angle my face so I can see her better. "Yup. Three weeks." Saying it out loud makes the time seem excessively short.

She pulls her knees to her chest. "We've got to squeeze in as much fun as we can."

"Agreed. So," I say, genuinely curious, "what have you got for me this time?"

"You"—she points an index finger at my chest—"are going speed dating."

The lightness of the moment evaporates instantly. Speed dating. Small talk in timed two-minute intervals. AKA my worst nightmare. "Rebecca, no."

"Ian, come on. You're handsome and charming—"

"Said no one ever."

"You're handsome and charming," she says again. "All you need is confidence. You can talk to people, even strangers, and do just fine. You'll see."

I say nothing, the speed dating scenario clear in my mind:
Me: "Hello."
Speed dating partner: "Hello."
Awkward chatter.
Repeat.

She scooches back on the floor and sits opposite me. "Ian,

how is it possible you can walk around a beach buck naked and be this afraid to talk to strangers?"

"Easy. I don't have to talk to people naked. In fact, my being naked likely is repelling enough to keep people away. Win-win."

"You're crazy." She shakes her head. "And, believe me, there's nothing repelling about how you look naked."

I meet her eyes a moment, then look down. A flush creeps across my cheeks. Did Rebecca just compliment my nudity?

"I mean—" she starts, her face pink like I imagine mine is.

"There's nothing repelling about how you look naked either," I say, trying to right the moment for her. "Not that I was looking."

"Of course not."

I pull at my T-shirt collar. She looks at the floor. There's a palpable sexual tension in the room now. Probably because we're both picturing each other naked.

"Glad we settled that," Rebecca says finally.

"Always good for friends to agree on how they look naked."

She swallows. "Yes. I'm surprised we haven't talked about it until now."

I smile, she laughs, and whatever tense moment we had appears to be over. Mostly.

"Now that that's out of the way, what about you?"

"What about me?"

"You're charming and pretty, and unlike me, a master of conversation. Maybe you should speed date?"

She shakes her head. "No. No. No. No. No. This is a you thing. It's a fun lesson."

"What if it's a music lesson too? Then you have to do it."

She raises an eyebrow. "What could speed dating possibly have to do with music?"

"You need confidence to play. Speed dating will give it to you." As preposterous as the connection is, now that I've said it out loud, it makes sense. Rebecca does need confidence. Validation from a room full of single guys could give it to her.

She bites her lip, traces a circle on the carpet with her index finger. I try to read her expression. Why is she hesitating? She's the one who's graceful in social situations. And she's the one who's actually single. Still, I have enough social discomfort on my own, I won't force it on others. "If you don't want to—" I start.

"No," she says, looking suddenly decisive. "I'll do it."

CHAPTER 21

R ebecca

Ian rented a car for a few days—the getaway car, he keeps calling it. On the night of the speed dating event, I slip into the passenger seat. The scent inside is heavy with cologne. Ian's cologne? He's never worn it before.

"Got yourself some new cologne," I tease.

Ian starts the car. "Too much?"

It is absolutely too much. It was probably too much when he bought the bottle.

"You can tell me." His tone is vulnerable; I can't tease him.

"Just the right amount," I say. "And you look good too."

This part is true. He does look good. Blue T-shirt instead of a golf shirt, nice-fitting jeans, his hair a little spiky, like he used gel.

"Thanks." He nods his head toward me. "Nice dress."

Moronically, I look down. Yup. Same dress I had on when I walked out of the duplex. Short and red with little white polka dots. "Thank you."

"I made a list of questions," Ian volunteers. "It's there. On the console."

I look down. There's an index card with Ian's neat penmanship on one side. I pick it up and scan: What topic are you most knowledgeable about? What would be the name of your biography? What era in history would you love to visit and why?

I put the card down after that one. "Ian, no."

"What?"

"What era in history would you love to visit? Come on, E."

"It's a good question. Personally, I'd like to go back to the times of cavemen."

I swing my head so I can see his face. "Cavemen? Why?"

"I'm not telling you now. Since you made fun of the question."

"Oh my God." I move and lean my head back on the seat. "You are such a child."

He drums the steering wheel. "Well, what are you going to ask? Since it won't be about favorite historical eras."

I pull at the hem of my dress. "I don't know. Where are you from? What do you do? That kind of thing."

"That's pretty boring, Rebecca." He glances at me then back at the road. "How are you the one giving the fun lessons?"

"Okay, fine. I'll ask one of your questions."

"Really?"

"Yup. The biography one. That's not all that bad." I check my phone. "It's a left here, by the way."

Ian maneuvers the car to the street on the left. "So. What's your biography name?" he asks.

"Right now? *Rebecca Chapman: Irked.*" I wave my hands like an underscore.

He pulls into a parking space near the bar. "Ha. Mine is *Ian Ledger: Scared to Talk.*"

I put my hand on his forearm. "Don't be scared to talk, Ian."

He meets my eyes. "I'll do my best."

He averts his gaze, opens the door, and steps out. I get out and stand next to him. With both of us dressed up, it feels more like a date, like we're a couple, instead of two friends on a speed dating excursion. I pretend for a moment that's the reality: Ian and me on a date. A long, lazy dinner sharing appetizers, sipping drinks, and finding out why the heck he wants to go back to caveman times. We'd take a walk on the beach, Ian yammering on about different constellations. Maybe get ice cream. And after?

Rebecca, no. No after.

I can't let myself think about it. Okay. I already think about it. When Ian's close to me. When he inspects my fingers to make sure the callouses aren't too bad. When he pretends my horrible heated-up dinners are good. His lopsided smile, the way he walks, when he rakes his hair and it sticks up all over. His nervousness in social situations, the ridiculous questions he asks, his debate team clothes. Endearing. All of it. In a way I never would have expected.

My growing feelings for Ian are why I signed him up for speed dating to begin with. I need to see Ian with other girls. As much time as we've spent together, as much as I enjoy his company, he's not mine. I need to get used to that fact real fast. The wedding is right around the corner. So's the reunion with Audrey.

We reach the door. Ian angles his head toward me, the contours of his face illuminated by the moon. "So we're doing this?"

"Absolutely." I give a bright smile, put my hand on the doorknob, and pull.

It's chaos inside. People, presumably single, are crammed around the edges of a dark space that smells like a combination of perfume, cologne, and spilled beer. Long tables with chairs on either side are laid out in the center like it's a massive dining area. Music blasts from a DJ in the corner. An older woman with coiffed blond hair and red lipstick puts her hand on Ian's arm. She's in a black T-shirt which says "Go or

No Dating Service" in neon green letters. "Speed dating?" she asks.

"Yes."

Ian's response is barely audible.

"We're both here for the speed dating," I say.

"Signed up?"

"Yes." I give her our names and she hands me a stack of cards.

"Event starts in five minutes. Good luck."

Ian and I move away from her, and he pulls one of the cards out of my hand. His eyes pop. "They're scorecards."

I glance at a card, titled "Rate Your Date." A bunch of numbers line one side, each followed by a line with the denotation "One Word Description." Next to this are two words: "Go" or "No." Circle Go if you want to see your date again, No if you don't. That simple. Except—

"I'm going to get all No's," Ian says.

Except that.

He could get all No's. Ian, trying his best in his casual jeans, spiked hair, and too strong cologne, the index card of inane questions tucked in his pocket. I inspect the women standing in clusters in their tight dresses, tall drinks in their hands, easy laughs on their mouths. One slaps the shoulder of the guy next to her. Another reapplies lipstick with a smacking sound. Two of them sway to the music. I know these women.

I'm one of them.

What would I think if some guy asked me my favorite era? If he took painstakingly long pauses between questions? Or broke out into random facts about constellations? What if he told me he was a sensitivity consultant? That he was from Nebraska?

Two minutes. That's all I would have. It wouldn't be enough time to learn the good parts—Ian's sly humor, his insane musical talent, the tenderness with which he talks about his sister. I wouldn't notice his dimple in the dark; I wouldn't know what makes him laugh.

I stare at the scorecard, at the words: No or Go.

What word would I circle if I'd met Ian here tonight? No or Go?

I know the answer and grab Ian's hand. "Let's get out of here."

CHAPTER 22

I *an*
Rebecca places her hand over mine. She drags me out the door and down the sidewalk like she's on a mission. When she deems we're far enough away, she stops, drops my hand, and faces me. "I didn't like the look of the people in there."

"Really?" I lift an eyebrow.

"No."

"Because I think you chickened out."

"I did *not* chicken out."

"Seems like you did. I was totally ready. Gel in my hair, questions in my pocket." I hit my jeans where I'd put the list. "Plus, I have my scorecards." I hold out the cards like a fan. "I was stoked."

She puts a hand on one hip and juts her chin out. "Stoked?"

"Yeah."

She makes a finger gun at me. "You're so full of it. Come on. Let's get drinks."

She strides down the sidewalk toward another bar and swings open the door. I step inside a space with dark rugs and booths, the seats covered in green vinyl. A Bing Crosby song blares. Everyone in the place looks like they were born in the 1930s. Maybe before. White hair. Bald heads. Walkers. I lean my head toward Rebecca and whisper, "Do you like the look of these people?"

"Ian, I swear—"

I put my hand on my heart. "I'm kidding. I love it here." I take another step inside. "I really, really love it." I lean toward her. "I am stoked to be here with you, Rebecca Chapman."

She smiles, steps inside, and swats me with her scorecards. "I try to do something nice and get you out of the speed dating—"

I put my hand on her shoulder. "And I am eternally grateful. Come on, drinks are on me."

The hostess seats us at a booth and we order beers. Rebecca sets her scorecards on the table. I swipe one and hold it up. "So how do you think this thing works? What do you put on the lines?" I point to the tiny lines after each number.

She grabs the card from me, puts it on the table, and inspects it. Her hair falls in front of her face, a wild mane of color. She looks up. "You're supposed to use a one-word description." She points to small print at the bottom. "That's what the lines are for."

"One word." I shake my head. "That's rough."

"It's not like you're getting graded on it."

The server sets down our beers, both in frosty old-style mugs. I thank her, pick mine up, and look again at the tiny lines on the card. "How do you get the essence of somebody with just one word?"

Rebecca shakes her head, a "you are impossible, but I love you anyway" kind of shake. "I don't think people at that event are looking for the essence of anyone, Ian."

"Okay. Fine." I take a gulp of beer, my hand gripped around the thick handle. "But one word? Come on. That's hard."

"Hard. Now there's a word. That could be one." She winks.

The innuendo dawns on me. "I can't believe you went there."

"That's what she said."

I shake my head. "Only you." I look down at the card, then back up at her. "So what would be your word for me?"

She laughs. "For you? That's easy. 'Uptight.'"

"Uptight? Come on. I was nude on a beach. I played tag in foam."

She waves at me. "Fine. Fair. That was before. That was debate team Ian." She pauses. "If my first word for you was uptight, what's your first word for me? When we met on the bus."

I take another sip of beer. "On the bus, my word for you would have been 'questionable.'"

She slaps the table. "Questionable?"

"You were on a public bus without shoes, Rebecca."

"Details, schmeetails." Her mouth twists into a grin. "And what would your word be now?"

"Now?" I rap my fingers on the table. Words tumble through my brain—charismatic, beautiful, funny, talented, humble.

I take too long, I guess.

"Never mind. Never mind." She waves her hand in the direction of the card.

I look up. Her face is pink.

"I have words," I say, realizing that she might think I drew a blank. "Just too many. I want to pick the perfect one." I pause. "What's your word for me now, anyway? Still 'uptight'?"

"No." She picks up a cocktail napkin and rips a piece off the corner. She tears it in her fingers then finally says, "Surprising."

Surprising. I turn the word around in my head.

"You surprise me," she says. "In a good way. You're different than I expected you'd be."

Surprising. I like it. I'm better than she thought I'd be, more than the uptight guy on the bus.

She pushes a scorecard across the table toward me. "Write

your word for me down." She fishes through her purse and produces a pen. "I'll look at it later."

I'm not sure why she wants to look at it later, but I'm okay with that. If I say the word out loud, my facial expression, my body language—just the way that I say it—might expose my shifting feelings for her.

I twist the pen in my hand and she stares at it, her nose scrunched, an index finger curled around a lock of her hair. I'm not thinking about her word anymore. I'm thinking about her.

"Fine." I write a word, the perfect one, fold up the paper, and hand it to her.

* * *

WE DON'T HAVE another fun lesson. The next two weeks are jampacked with getting Rebecca getting ready for the audition. Scratch that. The next two weeks are spent convincing Rebecca that she *is* ready for the audition. Nerves—hers—are going to kill her. And there's no convincing her that the audition isn't life or death. To her, not making *Country Clash* is the death of her dream.

Today, three days before "A" day, she bangs on the joint wall, a habit we've both gotten into the past weeks. Easier than texting. Faster than calling. Her muffled voice comes through the wall. "It's here."

It. I know what she's talking about. Rebecca had an audition outfit she didn't like when she modeled it for Brenda over Face-Time. After, Brenda insisted on getting involved. She sent "the perfect" audition outfit, and apparently, it's here. I can only hope the outfit is everything it was billed to be. Rebecca's already frayed.

"Come over," she yells through the wall.

I can't read her tone, and wimpy as it sounds, I don't want to go over there. Have I mentioned she's been very erratic? Still,

I'm her guitar coach and pseudo mentor and friend. I leave my side of the duplex, push open the door.

"Ta da!" She holds her hands up.

My mouth hangs open.

She's in *the outfit.*

And she looks fabulous.

"Wow."

"I know, right?"

She's in form-fitting jeans and a cowboy shirt covered in black sequins and an ample amount of fringe. Her waist is wrapped in a belt, the kind with the big buckle in the front. The cowboy boots are red, a bit of color. A mess of curls peek out from an authentic looking black cowboy hat.

"Look at you."

"I know!" She does a quick spin. "We've got to FaceTime Brenda."

Rebecca presses a button on her phone. Brenda's been a "contact" of hers since the nude beach day, the day she became, in Brenda's own words, "a national hero." "You got that prick to bare it all?" she'd said.

Yeah. They love me.

Brenda's face is on the screen. Rebecca thrusts the phone at me and stands back.

Screaming. Fan girl, crazy screaming.

"Shit, my queen," Brenda says, "you look like a star. Julian," she calls, "get in here. You have to see this."

Julian appears; both his head and Brenda's compete for space on the tiny screen.

"Star power," Julian enthuses.

"Thank you." A blush creeps up her cheeks.

"Any time you have an audition or show, I'm your girl," Brenda says. "By the way, we'd like you to come to the Vineyard for the weekend after the audition. We'll celebrate."

Rebecca tilts her head. "Isn't the weekend after the audition your wedding?"

"You're invited, doll." She slaps Julian on the shoulder. "Right?"

"Of course. Country music's biggest future star at our day? We'd be honored."

Rebecca squints at the phone. "Are you sure?"

"Positive. Ian will bring you."

She looks at me. I nod. I have to, right? I can't say "don't come." And the truth is, I *want* Rebecca to come. That's the problem. I won't be able to sort my feelings for Audrey when Rebecca's a few steps away.

"Okay. I'll be there!" Rebecca says. Her face erupts into a grin, and she gives me a thumbs up.

I guess I'll have to figure it out.

CHAPTER 23

R ebecca
Audition day.
Audition Day.
AUDITION DAY.
That's how it feels in my mind. Like:
No big deal.
A little bit of a big deal.
The biggest, friggin' deal.

I'm not sure how Ian is dealing with me. We're seated at the Good Morning Café, a restaurant inside the New York Marriott, the place of the audition. Ian and I paid way more than either of us could afford to stay over last night.

I'd thought I wouldn't want him here, that his presence would make me nervous like it always did when my brothers and parents were around. But it doesn't. He's been a steadying force. He stayed with me during rehearsal yesterday, a walk-through of how things would look today. During it, he didn't pepper me with questions or give advice, which honestly, is exactly what I needed. He's allowed me to be silent most of the time.

Because I just can't talk.

My life is on the line.

At least that's how it feels. Like my life's entire direction will be decided this afternoon:

Path one: Dream come true and a chance at fame. The opportunity to prove to my family that I am a musician with a viable career.

Or path two: Return to my starter job, tail between my legs. End up working as a real estate paralegal for John.

Ugh.

No.

I have to get these best-and-worst-case scenarios out of my head. They're making me crazy.

The server appears. Ian eyes me, and when I don't speak, he orders my performance meal: peanut butter toast with banana, fruit, and room temperature water with a dash of honey. He orders the same for himself. I'm pretty sure it's because he knows I'd be jealous of his usual omelet, even sans potato chips.

After breakfast, I try to relax in my room, and when I can't, I walk next door and knock on Ian's. He swings it open. I enter the space and collapse on his bed, arms across my stomach, hands clasped.

Ian sits at a small table, scrolling through his phone.

My stomach flip-flops. Like performance anxiety. But without the performance. I try mindful breathing.

Inhale, 1-2-3.

Exhale, 1-2-3.

Inhale, 1-2-3.

Exhale, 1-2-3.

My breathing gets more rapid with this effort, not less, and I sit up.

I have to do something about my nerves.

Ian moves in front of me, tips my head up with his index

finger. "You're ready, Rebecca. It's going to be fine." He sits down beside me. "Let me massage your neck."

I teasingly push at his shoulder. "Are you trying to pick me up? Because you're timing sucks."

He smiles. "No, I'm not trying to pick you up. I just heard massages are good for nerves." He gestures to the chair he was just sitting in. "It's probably easier if you're in the chair."

I move to the chair. It sits in front of a window overlooking Forty-Sixth Street. We're on the fourth floor, low enough that I can easily make out the crush of pedestrians hurrying along the sidewalk. The crowds, the noise, the busyness of Times Square. It would seem exciting if I was here for a different reason; today, the atmosphere just makes me tense.

I close my eyes. Ian grips my shoulders and kneads with capable hands. He rubs deep circles on my muscles with his index fingers—first the shoulders, then my neck. My muscles go soft under his touch. "That's good," I say after a few moments. I open my eyes.

Ian's phone is face up on the table, an article on the screen: "Top Five Ways to Help a Loved One Calm Pre-Audition Jitters." The first tip advises reassuring the person that they are prepared, and that the audition will go fine. The second is to offer a massage. The article goes on to explain the benefits, but I don't read further. I'm incredibly touched.

"What is blue and smells like red paint?" he asks.

I narrow my eyes.

"What's blue and smells like red paint?" he repeats.

I glance at the article. Tip number three: tell a joke to lighten the mood. I smile. "I don't know," I say, "what's blue and smells like red paint?"

"Blue paint."

I pause a moment, turning the words in my head, then I burst out with a laugh. "Is that supposed to be a joke?"

"It's an anti-joke," he says, his expression deadpan. "Anyway, are you looking forward to Martha's Vineyard? Brenda and Julian will keep you well fed."

I glance down. Tip number four: bring up subjects other than the audition.

A surge of warmth rushes through me. I twist to look at him, his earnest face, his genuine desire to help me. It's hard to imagine how much I'd disliked him. Without speaking, I stand and wrap my arms around him in a tight hug. He waits a moment, almost as if trying to figure out what *this* is, then envelops me back in strong arms. "Thank you," I say into his chest. "Thank you for caring."

"Of course I care. This is your dream."

My eyes fill. For the first time, I feel like someone, other than me, believes my dream is valid and worthy of pursuing. Lily supports me, but as an engineer with a high-paying job, she doesn't really get it. Kimmy is great for high fives and pats on the back. Beyond that, she hasn't shown interest. And my immediate family has been a lost cause.

I pull back. "I'm lucky to have met you on the bus."

He looks in my eyes and gives me the broad Ian smile. "Ditto."

* * *

TWO HOURS LATER, I step out of the elevator on the top floor of the Marriott Marquis, Ian behind me. It's a zoo. Girls with long spiral curls and short denim skirts; men in big-buckled belts and bolo ties. Families with signs. Cameras and reporters with microphones. Officials bustle around in black polos featuring the *Country Clash* insignia.

I'm not sure what I'm supposed to do.

Ian takes my shoulder and guides me toward a tiny woman

with a clipboard. "I've got Rebecca Chapman to audition," he says.

She pulls a long red fingernail down a page printed with names and stops at mine. "You're number thirty-eight," she says without looking up. "Welcome to the Clash." I see my name on the page, the word "alto" next to it.

Rebecca Chapman. Alto. That's it. It's ludicrous. The fate of my life is in the hands of people who know me only as: Rebecca Chapman. Alto. A surge of hysteria surges through me. I put my hand over my mouth to stifle a laugh. The three words run over and over in my head: Rebecca Chapman. Alto. Rebecca Chapman. Alto. Rebecca Chapman. Alto.

I'm not *just* an alto. I've got a full range. Should I tell them that? I open my mouth in the direction of the woman with the clipboard. Ian grabs my arm, his face a mask of concern.

"Let's sit down."

I open my mouth just as what I was going to say leaves my mind. Ian commandeers me into a seat in the back corner. It's a good spot. Far enough away to be somewhat private but still in the room. I nod at him; he reads my thoughts.

"The advantage of being friends with an introvert. I can immediately flesh out the best quiet spots." He winks. "I'll get you some water." He takes a few steps then looks back. "I know. Room temperature."

I lean back and look around the space, at the other contestants. My competition. There are two kinds of looks. The first is over-the-top country—all fringe and boots and sequins. The second is plain—jeans and T-shirts. One T-shirted guy looks visibly nervous, like he might throw up. He catches my eye; I give him a thumbs up.

Ian returns, hands me my room temperature water, and takes the seat next to mine. He doesn't speak or scroll through his phone or fidget. He's just there. A fortress of support. His ability to just sit is an underappreciated skill, I realize. Were the situation reversed, I'm sure I'd be chattering away, asking inane things like how many people sat in these very same chairs before us. His unusual prowess for calm and quiet makes me think the premise of the fun lessons is flawed. Maybe it's not Ian who needs to be different. Maybe it's the rest of us.

As the number snakes closer to thirty-eight and the seats fill with more and more people, it seems a whole lot less special that I got granted an audition. There are a ton of people here, a ton of people to compete against, and my nerves, already at a breaking point, ratchet up. Ian, maybe sensing this or maybe just having perfect timing, puts his hand over mine. Its warmth, the knowledge that he cares, that he supports me, calms my nerves.

"Thirty-eight," the clipboard woman yells.

Ian squeezes my hand.

I don't move.

She holds up a finger. "Thirty-eight."

"Go get 'em, tiger," Ian whispers.

I stand, grab my guitar, and follow clipboard woman down a long hall. Big glossy photographs of country stars stand on easels every few feet. We get to the end of the hall and I'm directed to stand behind a huge divider. I peek around the side and see the judges and the poor guy standing in front them, getting who knows what feedback.

I reach in my pocket, finger the scorecard from Ian, from the aborted speed dating event. In an unusual demonstration of restraint, I haven't looked at it yet. I tucked it in my pocket—a bit of Ian for good luck—and intended to look at it after the audition or later. Or maybe never. I'm not sure I really want to know what Ian thinks of me. Or I do. But only if it's good.

I twist the edge of the paper, and like I'm possessed by some divine force, I pull it out, unfold it, and stare at the singular word in Ian's neat scrawl. "Marvelous."

I smile, fold the paper, and tuck it in my pocket. Marvelous.

Ian thinks I'm marvelous.

Nerves drain from my body. A guy in a *Country Clash* shirt gestures for me to come forward. I walk toward the judges calm and courageous.

Someone marvelous.

CHAPTER 24

I *an*

The clipboard woman strides ahead. I follow.

"Post-audition area is here." She swings open a door. "Make yourself at home. Auditions are usually twenty minutes."

I step into the room. It's all shades of beige—tan, sand, oat, camel, buff. Soft chairs and couches fill the space. Kleenex boxes sit on every table surface. They don't give the best vibe. Why would there be a need for that many Kleenex?

I'm the only person in the room. Thank God because I'm nervous as hell. And not in the mood for singer-supportive small talk—What's your loved one singing? What voice part is he/she? Any musical credits?

My mouth is dry; my hands are clammy. I'm nauseous. Jeez. I feel this way and I'm not even auditioning. How is Rebecca possibly doing?

Please do well.

I'm not the most spiritual person in the world, but I look upward as I think this, beaming my thoughts into the sky. I haven't wished for divine intervention this fervently since I prayed for Brenda to change her mind—to have things go back to "normal"—when I was sixteen.

I move to the wall, put my ear against it. I strain to hear "Jailhouse Rock," a song that, after listening to it hundreds of times, I swore I'd never want to hear again.

Nothing.

I pace from one end of the room to the other. Again and again. Like a tiger in a zoo. I check my watch. Five minutes have passed. I put my ear to the wall again. Nothing.

I finally sit, pull out my phone, and mindlessly scroll through social media. I still follow Audrey, of course. She's got a new photo on her feed—her and her mother at lunch at the country club. She's wearing the yellow dress I love; her crystal blue eyes meet mine through the phone. I stare at the image a moment, but not with the zap of longing I'd had a few weeks back. I don't know what to make of that change, but I don't have time to dwell on it because the door flies open.

My head jolts up, but it's not Rebecca. It's an older man, here to support his musician I presume. Neither of us speaks, but a look passes between us, quiet keepers of someone else's dream.

We sit on the tan couch in silence. I close my eyes and visualize Rebecca singing not just with her voice but her soul. Lots of people can sing notes. Musicians feel them. I picture her, hear her, so vividly that when she bursts through the door, it takes me a minute to reconcile that the flesh and blood Rebecca is before me and not in my mind.

I stand. "Well?"

She squeals and catapults into my arms, legs wrapped around me. "Good?" I confirm.

She drops her body down, sliding against me, and steps back. "Ian, it was perfect. Keith Church called my riff insane. Moira said I reinvented Elvis."

I throw my head back. "Yes!"

Our hands meet in a double high five.

She exhales. "I can't believe it's over."

"I'm so happy for you." I envelop her in a tight hug. I see the man, still waiting for his singer, and nod at him over Rebecca's shoulder. He nods back. There's an unspoken solidarity between waiting loved ones. Nothing is in our control.

Rebecca and I exit the room, walk toward the elevator. She chatters about the judges, the process, how she did with the different parts of the song we'd worked on. She bounces as she walks, grabs my arms as we move, her excitement seemingly uncontainable.

"Just don't forget me when you're a big star," I say, half kidding.

The silver elevator doors slide open and we step inside.

Rebecca looks at me. "Ian, you can't be serious."

I am serious, but I don't say that.

The doors slide closed. It's just the two of us in the elevator. The privacy in the small space makes the moment feel more intense.

"I'll never forget you. Not just what you did to help me prepare," she continues, "but for all your support today and yesterday. You being here. That made the difference."

"Rebecca, no—" I shake my head. I don't want any credit. This is her.

Her hand juts out over mine. "No, really. You have no idea how much it meant to me." She reaches in her pocket and pulls out the scorecard. "How much this means to me."

I stare at the paper, feel a blush creeping into my cheeks.

"Thank you, Ian."

The elevator slides open and I step out, a lump in my throat. I'm happy for Rebecca. But it's more than that. This small exchange feels like a precursor to the inevitable goodbye. This unexpected pit stop in my life—meeting someone like Rebecca, doing things way out of my comfort zone—is almost over.

We move down the hall, stand in front of our side-by-side

rooms. Rebecca rubs her hands down her pant legs. "I guess we should pack."

"Yeah," I say, but leaving now, after Rebecca's success, feels anticlimactic. Who leaves New York City when you have something to celebrate?

I grab her hand. "Let's stay another night."

Her eyes widen. "You think?"

"You slayed that audition. We should celebrate."

She looks up, then nods. "Yes. Let's do it."

We move toward our rooms. "I'll book us the rooms again," I tell her.

We agree to meet in front of our doors at seven and I slip inside mine. I call the front desk, but when I try to rebook, there's just one room available. Mine.

I call Rebecca and tell her. I'm thinking she's going to call it off or suggest we look at another hotel. Instead, she laughs. "No problem. We'll bunk up together. It'll be like a slumber party. I'll get my stuff together and be right over."

She clicks off and I turn her words over in my mind. A slumber party. One room. Both of us. Of course. Not a big deal.

Unless you're super attracted to the person you're sharing a room with.

I take a deep breath. I need to get a handle on my feelings for Rebecca. She sees me as a friend. The I-like-you-like-a-brother vibe emanates from her loud and clear. Case in point: I'm a mass of sexual tension just thinking of sharing the room together and she's what? Thinking it's a *slumber party*. Pillow fights and pedicures and late-night sundaes.

She knocks and I exhale.

I can do this. Two friends, sharing a room. No big deal.

"It's me, E."

I pull open the door and throw out my hand. "Welcome to my humble abode."

Rebecca steps inside and hurls her half-open suitcase on the nearest bed. A mass of stuff—clothes, toiletries, delicates —spill out.

I lift an eyebrow. "Still a neat freak, I see."

She plucks a shirt from the mess on the bed and throws it on top of the suitcase. "Oh my God, don't tell me." She strides to the hotel room closet and pulls opens the door. My shirts hang in a neat row, pants folded on the shelf on top. At the bottom of the closet are two pairs of shoes, side by side, a balled pair of socks inside each. She looks back toward me. "Only you."

"Only me what?"

"Only you would unpack for one night."

"What does the length of time have to do with it? Just because it's one night is no reason to be a slob."

She smiles at me—the exasperated-but-I-still-like-you one— and shakes her head. "I'm getting a shower." She swipes items from the pile on the bed and steps into the bathroom. A moment later, the water turns on.

And my mind goes there.

To her. In the shower. With soap and lathering and the whole bit.

Crap.

It's going to be a long night.

* * *

AN HOUR LATER, we step out of the hotel into the center of Times Square. Rebecca still looks like a star in dark jeans, high heels, and a swingy lavender tank that ties at the neck. Her hair is pulled up and wisps of it frame her face. I'm in my standard debate team clothes.

The night is dark. The city is not. It's lit up by marquee and store fronts and billboards, a patchwork of illuminated squares. Sound pulses. People crowd the streets. From my vantage point, there's a same-sex couple holding hands, a woman with bright pink hair and nose rings, a man with tattoos up and down his arms. A woman with a hijab, a man with an Afro. A couple dressed as superheroes.

No one gives anyone else a second look or a discrediting glance, and walking in the midst of it all, it strikes me: The stereotype of New Yorkers as cold is blatantly false. Manhattan brims with a kind of acceptance almost impossible to find in other places.

I wonder, briefly, how it would have been for Brenda to have transitioned in a place like this. In this no big deal, you-do-you, melting pot of a city. I can only imagine it would have been easier. And why shouldn't it have been? Brenda's gender identity, her pronouns, all of it, belong to her. The opinions of others as to them are misplaced.

We walk a few blocks. Rebecca pulls at my arm. "Let's try here."

It's a small restaurant with a green awning. Jake's. Through the windows I see small tables with candles. The atmosphere is dark and cozy, with a celebratory ambiance. The kind of place that will induce "remember when" moments. It'll probably be a fortune. I can treat. It's our last weekend before the wedding, after all. "Let's do it."

She tips her head, her eyes on the menu out front. "Are you sure?"

"Absolutely. My treat." She opens her mouth. "My treat," I repeat before she can protest.

I push open the door, buoyed by the decision, anticipating the kind of night worthy of a celebration. I step up to the hostess stand. "Table for two."

"Do you have a reservation?"

"No."

She scans down a long list of names, then looks up. "Sorry. We can't seat you now. Earliest I have is 9:50. Shall I take your name?" She says this like eating dinner at 9:50 at night is a normal thing. It's 7:10 right now.

Rebecca steps up. "That's too late. Let's keep looking," she whispers.

"I—" I wanted to do this. I wanted to eat here. But she's right. It is too late.

We step into the mass of people on the sidewalk.

"Is Mr. Steak a chain?" she asks. "If there's one in Manhattan, maybe you could get us a table."

I fall into step beside her. "I *was* employee of the month. Status like that? It still holds considerable weight." I pause. "Unfortunately, they don't have a location in New York."

"Bummer."

We walk another block. Rebecca throws her arm across my chest. "There."

I follow her gaze. It's a diner. It's actually called "Diner."

I look in the front window. The space *looks* like a diner. Black and white floors, spacious booths with laminate tables and vinyl-covered seats. A long, chrome-edged counter with black twisty stools in front. Covered glass cases feature baked goods and pies.

"Bec, no. We should eat somewhere special." I look at the diner and back at her.

"It's just us, Ian. Let's not put pressure on ourselves to have 'an experience.'" She makes quotation marks with her fingers as she says the last phrase. "We like diners. It's kind of our thing."

Our thing. I like that. And, as much as I wanted to treat Rebecca to something more elegant, I like us having a thing more. "All right."

The server seats us at a table in the front, a few feet from the busy street on the other side of the glass. We order our usual from Della's—burgers, fries, milkshakes. The food comes immediately.

"It's like they beamed it," Rebecca says.

I laugh. And we eat. The food's great. The conversation flows but not in a way that's forced. It's a perfect night. My feelings are a crush of happiness twinged with melancholy. I feel like a star high school athlete at his last home game. It's all been great, but it will be over soon.

She taps my hand. "What's up. Why are you quiet?"

I look up. I didn't realize I'd been quiet, and while I could explain to Rebecca what I'm feeling, I don't know that she feels the same way—that she's sad our time together is nearing an end. So...

I make an obnoxious slurp with my milkshake straw. It's so loud, the people at the next table look over.

Juvenile behavior 101: ignore feelings; do dumb shit.

"Seriously, Ian." Rebecca leans forward.

"What? It's good." I place the heavy glass on the table with an emphatic thump, pull two twenties from my wallet and throw them on our bill. "My treat, by the way."

Rebecca clasps her hands over her chest. "My knight in shining armor."

"Any time, Lady Rebecca."

We leave the diner and move through the crowd. There's a night club a block away, but the line is so long it snakes around the building. "No," we say in unison.

I look at her. "Crowded night clubs aren't really us."

"No. We're more nude beach kind of people."

"Exactly."

"Go back to the hotel?"

"Of course," I say and grab her hand. "Our slumber party awaits."

CHAPTER 25

Rebecca

R I'm on the bed in the hotel room in sweat clothes, my face stripped clean of make-up. I look like the sad "before" picture in a magazine makeover spread.

Ian's in the other bed. His covers are pulled up to his chin, and he's got the TV remote in his hand. He points it at the television. "This?"

I glance at the screen. A detective show. One of the *CSIs*, I think. "Nah."

"This?"

A rerun of *Friends*. "Nah."

"This?"

A cooking show. "Nope."

He slings the remote across the few feet that separate our beds. And us. "Okay, Lady Rebecca, you choose."

I flip through the channels. Ian picks up the hotel phone and presses a button. "I'd like to order a pizza for room service. Room 408." He holds his hand over the receiver. "Want anything?" he mouths.

I shake my head.

"Also, two waters, please. Thanks." He hangs up.

I swing my head toward him, point the remote in his direction. "Did you seriously just order pizza?"

He looks at me like I'm nuts. "It's room service." He says this like no other explanation is required.

"Aren't you full?"

"Of course. But if a hotel has room service, you have to order something. It's part of the experience."

I think back to all my hotel experiences with my family. I can't remember getting room service a single time.

"Okay," he says when I don't speak, "maybe it's just a me-and-Brenda thing, but once we were old enough, my parents put us in our own room if we traveled. We *always* got room service. It's tradition."

"Room service as a tradition." I nod in his direction. "I like it. I may adopt that myself." I adjust my pillows, lean back, and find my favorite HGTV show—*Love It or List It.* Almost immediately, I become more invested than I should in whether the couple will keep their house or move into a new one. Ian watches too; the pizza arrives.

It feels exactly like what I said it would be: a slumber party.

I regret calling it that a little.

I also regret the sweats and makeup-free face.

It's not that I expected something romantic to happen.

I didn't even want anything romantic to happen until today, with Ian being so perfectly Ian, and knowing all the right things to do to make me feel better. And just what to say to make me laugh. Kindness and humor: the real way to a girl's heart. At least to mine.

I glance at Ian, his pizza folded over like a taco. What would he do if I moved to his bed? If I kissed him?

I think about it a moment, my lips on his, then blink. He'd probably push me away. He has *his Audrey* and he's way too much of a gentleman to cheat on her. Even for just one night. Even if they're on a break.

I lean into the fluff of the pillow. The couple on the television show decided to "love it."

"Knew it," Ian says.

"They always love it," I tell him.

"Why do you watch it then?"

"You never know, right? This couple could be the one that defies the odds."

"You're nuts." He says it in such an affectionate tone it makes me feel warm. After, he gets up, puts the pizza box on the dresser, and heads to the bathroom. The whir of his electronic toothbrush fills the room. He brushes for a full two minutes. His dedication to oral hygiene tracks so closely with the Ian I know that I smile. It seems, somehow, adorable.

I'm still smiling when he emerges from the bathroom in the "I Beared It ALL at Califon Beach" T-shirt I got him. I stare at him, my smile wider.

"What?"

"The shirt. You're wearing it."

"Of course, I'm wearing it. You gave it to me."

"Oh."

"I like it. This bear is a badass." He points to the cartoonish bear on the shirt, which of course, looks nothing like a badass. "Are you good if I turn out the light?"

"Yeah, sure." I try not to think about his endearing teeth-brushing habits. Or how the ridiculous T-shirt pulls across his surprisingly broad chest. I put out of my mind his disheveled hair, the five-o'clock shadow, and the lopsided smile.

"Night, Rebecca."

"Night," I say too quickly. "Don't let the bed bugs bite and all."

"And don't let the ceiling cave in," he deadpans.

I think a moment, then remember his mishap at Shelly's by

the Sea. That ceiling fiasco is the whole reason he came to stay in the other half of the duplex. "I forgot about that."

"Not me. Waking up in the middle of the night and seeing Lou at the foot of my bed with a headlamp on—not something I'll ever forget."

I sit up in bed, make out his frame in the darkness. "No," I hiss.

"Yup. He and Sue were both there."

"Oh my God." I clamp my hand over my mouth. "How did you end up in their bedroom anyway?" I ask, remembering the rest of this story.

"Sue told me it was a spare. It wasn't until I woke up and saw pictures of them and their family and some very unfortunately placed undergarments that I realized."

"Ian. No!"

"Hey. It's not like I *wanted* to see them."

I collapse back onto the bed. "Weird that, had that whole thing not happened, we might not have become friends."

He turns toward me. "So, you admit we're friends then?"

"I'm pretty sure we crossed the friendship barrier when I saw your junk on Califon Beach."

He snorts laughter—a signal, I've come to learn, that he thinks something is especially funny.

"Seriously, Ian. Of course we're friends."

I close my eyes. I'm giddy-happy on the surface; poignancy pulses underneath. I'm not ready to hand Ian over to Audrey, the woman who so callously told him he had to change. Says who? Ian's fine just how he is.

Not going to lie. The closer we get to the wedding, the more I kind of hate her.

"So, friend, would you ever come visit me in Nebraska?"

And see you and Audrey and your 2.5 perfect children? No thanks.

"Of course," I lie. "I'll stop in during my famous-country-music-person tour. Just look for the bus with my face on it."

"You joke, but it will probably happen."

I don't say it won't for fear of summoning a karmic force, one that links my thoughts to reality. I need to stay positive.

I change the subject. "Are you looking forward to going home?"

"Somewhat," he says. "I'll miss some things about Cape May."

"Me?"

"Mainly you. And fresh seafood." He pauses. "I'll probably miss the fresh seafood the most."

"Jerk."

"Hey. Don't criticize until you've eaten seafood in Nebraska. There's a reason there's no Mr. Fish, you know."

I smile, but the joke makes my heart hurt. I don't want to lose this. Or him.

"I'll miss you too, Ian."

CHAPTER 26

I *an*

It's Thursday. My last day at Mrs. Fishes. Kimmy smiles and lifts a glass of champagne. "Here's a big thanks to Ian Ledger."

The Mrs. Fishes employees gathered in the conference room, by force I'm pretty sure, hold up their glasses. There's a lackluster "to Ian," except from Rebecca, who says the phrase so loudly, it's comical.

I don't blame people for not caring that today is my last day. I didn't try to bond with any of them. Random social connections are not my strength to begin with, and since I had such a strong comfort level with Rebecca, it was too easy to lean on her for everything. I'm not sure I made much of a difference in the culture here either. Kimmy said she'd consider a man for the next executive position, but I don't think she meant it. She did alter her Fisherman of the Month program, renaming it Fisher*person* of the Month. I guess it's a win.

Kimmy cuts generous slices of a sheet cake that says "Best Wishes Ian" in green icing. She sets them on floral paper plates. The group stands with plates of cake and plastic forks. I can practically hear the collective question: how long do I have to stay so as not to look rude?

I make small talk with a few women. I use the tip Rebecca gave me: just turn the last thing they say into a question. Example: Marge, a quality control professional says, "We're repainting our kitchen this weekend." I say: "So you're repainting your kitchen this weekend?" Marge goes on to tell me more about the task. It's amazing how well it works.

Though I'm more comfortable with idle conversation than I was before, I still don't like it. I'd rather talk to Rebecca about virtually anything than hear about Marge's house-painting job. She's painting the kitchen yellow, by the way. And she's thinking about stenciling the top with a heart pattern.

Yeah. No one cares, Marge.

The party ends quickly, probably because people care even less about saying goodbye than they do about Marge's kitchen color. Kimmy boxes up the cake in record speed, and fifteen minutes later, Rebecca and I are standing outside my rented car. She throws a floral duffel into the back seat. "Are you sure Brenda and Julian won't mind that we're coming early? Don't they have a lot to do?"

I pull open the driver's-side door. "They're caterers, remember? They thrive on two things: cooking and feeding people their cooking." I glance over at her, her brows knitted with concern. "Honestly, Rebecca, it's fine."

It is fine. Consummate entertainers, Julian and Brenda take the adage "the more the merrier" to an entirely new level. Their home vibrates with the energy of the myriad personalities passing through at any given time.

Rebecca plugs her phone into the USB port. "Sorry. Growing up, my parents hardly ever entertained. And when they did, there was so much pressure for everything to be perfect that it took all the fun out of it. I used to dread parties."

I start the car and back out of the parking lot. "Brenda's

always thought perfection is overrated. Her catering mantra is: Give people good food and make them feel at home. Everything will flow from there."

Rebecca tips her head. "She isn't wrong."

"Brenda seldom is."

I punch the Steamship Authority address—the place where we'll catch the ferry to the Vineyard—into the navigation system. Rebecca starts a country playlist and pulls a bag of Munchos from a Wawa bag. "Can't have a road trip without Munchos."

She angles the bag toward me. I dip my hand inside, pull out a bunch of chips, and stuff them in my mouth. My phone pings with a text message. "Can you see what that is?" I ask, my voice garbled from the chips. "It's on the floor."

Rebecca reaches down and grabs my phone. As soon as she does, I wish I hadn't asked. The text is probably from Audrey. We've been communicating the past few days. The texts started out transactional—what time she'll be in; yes, she'll bring my suit and tie; and, no, no need for her to pick up a gift. They morphed from there. Nothing intensely personal, just more friendly. *What have you been up to? Want to go to the beach in Martha's Vineyard?* That kind of thing. But Audrey's last text said: *Can't wait to see you.* She punctuated it with a heart emoji.

Rebecca types in the phone password I'd told her weeks ago and glances at the screen. "It's from Audrey," she says in a neutral tone. "She took off from work tomorrow. She'll be here a day early."

"Oh."

It's all I can manage to say. I should be ecstatic. I'll see Audrey in less than forty-eight hours, and given her texts, it doesn't seem as if the end of the relationship is imminent.

But I wanted these last two days with just Rebecca. Everything will change once Audrey arrives.

"That's exciting," Rebecca says. She sounds happy for me. Really happy.

I'm stupid.

Rebecca doesn't need to revel in our final days together. Of course she doesn't. She'll hear from *Country Clash* any day. On to bigger and better things. Just like we'd planned.

"Pretty exciting," I agree. "Haven't seen her in eight weeks."

The phone pings with a text notification a second time. Rebecca scans the screen. "Audrey's parents are flying in Saturday for the wedding."

"What?" The word bursts from my mouth.

Rebecca swings her head in my direction. "Is that bad?"

"They weren't supportive of Brenda's transition."

She pauses. "Do you think they've changed?"

"I doubt it." I press on the gas pedal; the car speeds up.

"Whoa there, cowboy." Rebecca puts her hand on the steering wheel. "Slow down."

"Sorry." I shake my head. "It's just that, after Brenda announced her transition, I'd been so angry. I moved out and stayed at Audrey's. I was trying to make a point; I don't know to who."

I pause, temporarily feeling exactly as I did then. Sixteen and confused and desperately wanting the brother I knew. Not the sister I had yet to accept.

"Audrey's parents outright told me that Brenda and my parents were sinners. It was the last thing I needed to hear. Even after I came to understand Brenda's decision, they never acknowledged it. Always asked me how my brother was, you know."

Rebecca grabs a handful of Munchos. "Why would Brenda invite them?"

"For me."

I know this is why. Invitations went out pre-Rebecca and before my break with Audrey. Brenda, being the forgiving and lovely human being that she is, wanted to send me a message with the invite: I accept your probable future family no matter what. Just like you accept mine.

So Brenda. I understand her intent with the invitation. But I still wish the Montgomerys weren't coming. Even if they are trying to make amends or understand, they don't deserve to be there.

Rebecca places my phone on the console between us. "Why would Brenda invite them for you?"

"Everyone thought Audrey and I would get married. So not inviting them would be kind of like not inviting my in-laws."

It's silent a moment. And not the kind of silence that peppers normal conversation. It's a heavy one. "Oh," Rebecca says finally, "I didn't realize."

She sounds hurt. I shouldn't have dropped the "M" word so cavalierly. I assumed she knew Audrey and I were that serious.

"It's not like I have a ring or anything," I say quickly.

"Right." She shakes her head, almost like she's resetting herself. "Of course. You two have been dating a long time. That would be the expected next step."

"That it would," I agree.

An upbeat Kenny Chesney song blares from the car speakers.

"So," I say, changing the subject, "is my last fun lesson still tomorrow?"

In my peripheral vision, I see Rebecca's lips curl into a smile. "It is. Brenda helped me with it."

"Brenda?" This is news to me. "That can't be good."

"You'll like it, Ian," she says. "It's a good one."

CHAPTER 27

R*ebecca*

It's after midnight when Ian and I arrive at Brenda and Julian's house. The house is tucked deep inside thick woods off a dirt path. This is a surprise. Jersey beach towns are not typically woodsy. Just sidewalks and houses and the beach.

The home is well lit, and as we approach, I make out a big front porch with ferns and rockers, a giant picture window, and a shingled exterior. There's a massive perennial garden with lights in front of the porch, a white picket fence in front of it. Despite the late hour, music and conversation hum from inside.

We make our way over a cobblestone walk, duffels slung over our shoulders. Ian carries a giant bottle of wine because, as he says, Brenda will NOT tolerate guests cooking or bringing food. I've got a bouquet of flowers.

Ian grabs my hand. "Sorry," he says immediately, "there's a surprise step here."

As soon as he says it, I hit my foot on the stair he's talking about. He steadies me. "Thanks." I look in his direction, see his profile in the moonlight. He's relaxed and cheerful, like a little kid about to open a gift. His happy demeanor might be because he's about to see Brenda. But it's just as likely he's looking forward to seeing Audrey the day after tomorrow. Ever since the "we're probably going to get married" conversation in the car, I've been steeling myself against feeling hurt by his affection for her. Of course, he loves her. Of course, they've thought about marriage. They've been dating for years.

I've known him for eight weeks.

So, as much as I like him and as much as I cherish our friendship, our dynamic is about to change. I know this. I have to be ready.

We reach the front door. I look down and see it. My hand nestled inside Ian's.

Oh.

I drop it, and he slides his gaze toward me. "My hand on fire or something?"

"No," I say in the quippish tone I use when trying to suppress my feelings. "I just don't want you ruining my rap with the other guys. I am single, you know."

He nods, his hand on the doorknob. "Single, right. Do you want a wingman?"

"You?"

"Sure."

"No way. You would be the worst wingman ever."

He widens his eyes. "Why?"

I stop and lean on one leg, hand on my hip. "You don't like to talk to people, remember?"

He gives a playful push at my shoulder. "Hey. I'm improving."

"Not enough to be *my* wingman."

"Ouch." He pushes open the door to the house. "Let me know if you change your mind."

I follow him inside, marvel at the fact he didn't feel a need to knock. That's something I have never, ever done at either

Mark's or John's home. I even knock at my parents' house, and I grew up there.

I wonder how it would feel to have that kind of comfort level with your family—no big deal to barge right in after midnight. But, of course, I do have a comfort level like that. With Ian. We walk right into each other's duplex halves all the time. If we're not in each other's homes, we yell at each other through the wall.

We walk through the foyer, past an eclectic family room. We move into a massive, state-of-the-art kitchen with sliding glass doors that open to a patio outside. There are people inside and out, the hum of music a steady drumbeat in the background. Every conceivable flat surface has some type of food on it—dips, veggies, crocks of meatballs. There are pots on the stove, dishes in the sink, and so many ingredients on the counters, it looks like something exploded. Everyone has a cocktail or wine or beer, and bottles of all of them compete for space with the food. There's conversation, laughter, people dancing on the outdoor patio.

It's completely chaotic.

And equally perfect.

For me, anyway.

But it's not the kind of party that would be Ian's jam. The mess alone might kill him, let alone the crowd and the noise and the strangers. But he's smiling, heading toward a woman with a purple sarong and a black tank top who I immediately recognize as Brenda. They embrace, arms tight around each other. Brenda, head on Ian's shoulder, opens her eyes.

"Rebecca!"

She lets Ian go, takes both of my hands in hers and squeezes. "I am so glad you came." Her eyes meet mine. They're kind. Like Ian's.

"Julian," she yells, "Ian and Rebecca are here."

A tall man with curly black hair, dark eyes, and tanned skin moves through the crowd toward us. He hugs us each as if we'd met a dozen times before. "Welcome, mates," he says. "What can I get you to drink?"

Ian asks for a beer; I ask for a surprise.

Julian moves toward the fridge; Brenda grabs a glass and a spoon off the nearest table. She clinks them together. "Everyone," she says, "my extraordinarily shy brother, Ian, and his beautiful friend, Rebecca, are here." She sweeps her arm over us in a way that would make Vanna White proud. "Please make them feel at home."

I swing my head toward Ian, thinking he'll be mortified, but he just shakes his head and smiles. He's used to this from Brenda, I guess.

A woman moves over on a bench at a long kitchen table and taps on the seat. She gives us a wide smile. "Come. Sit."

Ian and I sit, thighs and shoulders mashed together due to lack of space. Our feet touch under the table and our faces are inches apart. I love being near him like this. His scent, his skin, the closeness. I try to shake off the feeling.

He's not yours, Rebecca.

Julian sets a craft beer in front of Ian, one I know he'll love because it's locally brewed. My drink comes next, served in a margarita glass rimmed with the kind of colored sprinkles normally seen on ice cream cones. The drink itself is pink with a cherry garnish. The ice cubes have bits of strawberries inside.

"This looks spectacular!" I burst out, because honestly, it's the only reaction you can have to a cocktail like this.

Julian nods. "Something sweet for the sweetheart."

"Hey Jules," a woman at the end of the table yells, "why didn't I get one of those?"

He gives her a wide smile. "Because you're a bloody freeloader."

The woman laughs, and Julian dips his head between mine

and Ian's. "Ignore her," he says teasingly, "she's our neighbor but she practically lives here."

Brenda moves behind Julian, two giant dinner plates in her hands. She sets them in front of us. Lasagna. Salad. Rolls. "I *know* Ian didn't feed you appropriately," she says.

"Hey," Ian protests in a little-brotherish way, "we got food."

"Hmm." She looks to me. "Some type of burger masquerading as a meal, yes?"

I laugh; she's right.

"Please," she says with a mock eyeroll, "enjoy some real food. And Ian"—she puts her arms on Ian's shoulders—"the offer to run a frozen food service company for us is still open."

Ian shakes his head. "When are you ever going to stop asking me to do that?"

"When you say yes."

She moves back to the kitchen, and Ian and I scarf the food down like we haven't eaten in months. And if this is what meals are supposed to taste like, we probably haven't. We join in the conversation at the table, a smattering of local friends and relatives. The group makes it easy to join in, and soon, Ian is recruited for some ongoing cornhole tournament on the deck. There's a max exodus of cornholers (their word, not mine) to the outside area. I stay back with Brenda. We're alone.

My nerves tingle. Brenda's important to Ian, and I want desperately for her to like me. I bite my lip, scrape my hand through my hair. My normally busy mind—the one that never fails to find *something* to chatter about—is blank.

Brenda picks up a tray of brownies from an adjacent counter and slaps them in front of me. "Do you like caramel?"

"Yeah."

"Caramel swirls in those." She nods at the plate. "Have one. Let me know what you think."

I pick one up and bite off a piece. The taste explodes in my mouth. I nod and swallow. "Amazing."

"Right?" She picks one up and bites it. "It's my mom's recipe. Ian probably told you she's a party planner."

I swallow my second, massive bite of brownie. "He did. In fact, he made me a seahorse out of balloons. He said he used to make balloon animals for your mom's parties."

Brenda rolls her eyes, her affection for Ian clear in the gesture. "He's such a dork."

I laugh. "But a sweet dork."

"Definitely a sweet dork." She touches my shoulder. "I give you credit for sticking with him long enough to get to know him. Most people don't get that far with him, you know."

I smile. I like talking about Ian with someone who knows him so well. Who loves him.

"But for those lucky few people he's comfortable with," Brenda continues, "Ian's a gold star among humans. Kind, funny, loyal. He's one in a million, my brother."

I swallow a lump in my throat.

Brenda meets my eyes. "You've been good for him, Rebecca."

"He's been good for me, too." Ridiculously, my eyes well when I say this. I blink hard. I don't want Brenda to see.

"I like you for him, Rebecca. I know it's not my place, but he's happy when he's with you. He's himself in a way he's not with other girls."

"Audrey?"

She sips her wine. "Not my place, but what the hell." She lifts her glass, then drains it. "Audrey was Ian's first girlfriend, his first and only—you know." She lifts her eyebrows, the inference clear. "He's never been confident with girls—or people, as you know. He's got a comfort level with Audrey just because she's been in his life so long. I think he's afraid to let that go."

"You don't think he loves her?" My voice catches.

"I'm sure he thinks he does. But she doesn't make him laugh. And she doesn't—" She stops. "She doesn't appreciate him, you know? She doesn't accept the shy parts of him. Like this break."

She rolls her eyes. "Ian has to jump through hoops to prove something to her—I don't even know what." She shakes her body like she's removing a bad thought. "Sorry. It just makes me mad."

"Me too," I say but the words come out soft, and I'm not sure Brenda hears. We're interrupted by rowdy cornholers charging through the open sliding glass door.

She leans toward me. "I don't want to presume," she whispers, "but I think you care about Ian as more than a friend."

I don't respond, but I'm sure the answer, the resounding YES, is clear on my face.

Brenda taps my shoulder. "If I were you, Rebecca, I'd go for it."

CHAPTER 28

I *an*
"Night skinny-dipping?"

Rebecca swings her head toward me on the beach path, sunglasses pushed up on her head. "No."

"Karaoke?"

"Nope."

"A food eating contest?"

"Good idea, but no." Rebecca snaps me with her towel. "You have to wait for tonight."

"Fine." I exhale, a pretend frustrated breath. All day, I've been teasing Rebecca, trying to get her to tell me about the final fun lesson. She won't budge.

Rebecca stops where the sandy path meets asphalt and puts on a pair of bright blue flip-flops with tiny dancing flamingos all over them. She has a variety of flip-flops, I've learned on this trip, all of them a little crazy. Yesterday's looked like lobsters.

She points her towel in the direction of a bike rack. "There they are."

We head toward the beach bikes Brenda lent us. Big pastel-colored ones with fat tires and wide seats. We load our beach gear in the oversized front baskets and start the two-mile trek from South Beach to Brenda and Julian's house.

It's been a good day.

We'd slept in, me on the couch downstairs, Rebecca in Brenda's favorite guest room—painted pink with the ceiling the color of the sky, clouds and birds and all. For breakfast, Julian made us crepes with fresh strawberries and homemade whipped cream. We'd eaten, the four of us, in a cozy seating area on the back patio. After, Brenda prepared picnic lunches for Rebecca and me because, as she put it, my packed lunches are "crap."

We'd spent the day at South Beach, the beach with my favorite kind of waves: big easy swells. Both Rebecca and I like to swim, and we spent considerable time in the water. Between ocean runs, we read books (non-fiction for me; thriller for her) and took naps on an oversized beach blanket, sporadically picking at the food Brenda had packed. Occasionally, one of us would point out a seal head bobbing in the distance or mention something we'd just read. But mostly we were quiet.

Back at the house, showered and good-tired from the sun, we pick at a hodgepodge of food. Slowly, the scene starts to unfold as it did the night before, with guests appearing at random, the house morphing from quiet to one humming with life and music and laughter.

Rebecca passes my line of vision. She winks and points at her watch.

I shake my head. She's been doing that all night, making it seem as if the fun lesson—whatever the heck it is this time—is imminent. But it's almost ten o'clock and I'm starting to think she's teasing me, that there is no lesson. Surprisingly, I'm disappointed. Not that I *want* to be made to do something ridiculous. I just like seeing what she comes up with. And I like the look on her face right before she tells me what the lesson is, like the details of the task are about to burst out of her. And I want one more memory with just Rebecca before Audrey arrives, one more thing we could look back on and laugh, even if the joke is on me.

I bend down to get another beer from a cooler when someone slips a cloth over my eyes.

"It's time, Sir Ian," Rebecca says. She ties the cloth.

"A blindfold? Seriously?"

"Yes, a blindfold. This is a surprise." She puts her hands on my shoulders and guides me around the outside of the house.

There's a smattering of "goodbye, Ian" and "good luck, Ian" from the assembled guests. Rebecca leads me to what I'm pretty sure is the driveway. She opens a car door and pushes me toward it.

"Are you taking me to a remote location to kill me?" I ask.

She pushes my head down, presumably so I don't hit it on the car doorframe. "Only if you get on my nerves."

Once I'm in the car, she slides in next to me. Her bare thighs touch mine. I inhale her perfume. It's different today. Lilac?

The door slams. "Okay, Brenda," Rebecca says.

The car starts. "Brenda?" I say through a smile. "This can't be good."

"You'll like it, Ian," she says.

We take a twisty, five-minute ride and the car stops. The door opens. I'm expecting to hear people or see store lights through the blindfold. Instead, it's pitch black, the only sound that of birds and cicadas and very distant ocean swells. Rebecca pulls at my arm, and I scooch across the seat. She helps me stand.

"Text me," Brenda calls. The car rattles off.

Okay. We're in a remote location with, as far as I can tell, no people around. "Rebecca Chapman," I say, "what in the world are we doing?"

She grips my shoulders and whispers in my ear. "How many times do I have to tell you it's a surprise?"

I smile; then it vanishes. Maybe the surprise has to do with Audrey. Has she come early? Has Rebecca arranged a meeting?

My heart drops. I feel guilty that it does. It's not that I don't want to see Audrey. I just don't want to see her tonight. Tonight is the last hoorah, the final solo memory of this unexpected friendship.

"Just us?" I ask.

"Maybe."

She says it in a teasing tone which makes me think that, no, we are not alone. My mind spins with how to play it if Audrey is here. I mean, I can't exactly tell her to go to a hotel so I have one last night with my buddy.

Rebecca guides me up several flights of stairs. She pushes open what I imagine is a gate. I step onto a flat landing; we're still outside. Rebecca removes the blindfold.

"Ta-da!"

It's just us. That's the first thing I notice. The second: we are on an extraordinary rooftop deck with a view of South Beach. Custom lighting, deep-cushioned couches, and a blazing gas fireplace create the kind of ambiance usually reserved for the movies. On a large table between the couches, an ice bucket of champagne sits alongside a charcuterie board.

"What this?" I ask, trying to figure out the catch. "Am I going to be a waiter later on or something?"

"Nope," Rebecca says, a satisfied look on her face. "No lesson tonight. We're going to watch the Perseid meteor shower."

I digest her words. The Perseid meteor shower? It's one of the best meteor showers to observe. I knew its height was in August, but I'd been too distracted to figure out a time to see it. I swallow a lump in my throat, touched. "How did you know?"

"You mentioned it at our first dinner. At The Lobster House, remember?"

I think back and I do remember it, Rebecca trying to guess

my hobbies, me telling her about my interest in astronomy. We barely knew each other back then.

I look around the incredible space. "What is this place?"

"Julian and Brenda rented it for the week. They're going to stay here after the wedding, but she said we could use it tonight." She holds her hands out in an expansive gesture. "It's the best place on the island for stargazing."

I look at the sky, inky black with a crescent moon; bright stars dot the background. "This is a perfect place to watch." I meet her eyes. "Thank you."

"You're welcome."

"And there's no catch?" I grab the bottle of champagne. "I don't have to watch naked or anything?"

She swipes two flutes from a nearby bar. "You can watch naked if you want, Ian. This night is for you."

I pop the champagne cork; bits of frothy liquid pour out onto my hands. "For me? Why?"

"It's a thanks. For being such a good friend, for helping me with my audition. It's just—"

She gets choked up, and my own eyes well. I look away. I don't want to get emotional. If I do, I'll blabber. And for me, blabbering never ends well.

"Just thanks, Ian," she spits out.

I swallow my emotions. "You're welcome." I hand her a flute then hold up my own. "To friendship."

"To friendship."

We clink our glasses and drink to friendship.

But it feels like a lot more than that.

CHAPTER 29

R ebecca
We stand, staring at each other, champagne
glasses in our hands. His jaw is chiseled with that
five-o'clock shadow he grows every weekend. His eyes, probably my favorite feature of Ian Ledger, are earnest.

I think about Brenda's words: "If I were you, I'd go for it."

I want to.

I can't.

What if he doesn't feel the same way?

I move to the couch and sit. "Shall we watch?"

Ian grabs an oversized woolly blanket from an adjacent
chair, sits next to me, and places it over our bare legs. It's cozy
under the blanket, our skin warmed by the fire. I snuggle back
in the couch, my body touching Ian's. I sip my champagne and
the whole of it—the atmosphere, the night, the proximity to Ian
—feels decadent.

A meteor shoots through the sky, a streak of bright light in
the darkness. Before I can comment, a second blasts across the
inky black, then two more.

"There they go," Ian says and holds up his glass. "To the Perseids."

"To the Perseids." I clink my glass against his, unable to avert my eyes from the spectacular nighttime show. Meteor after meteor projects across the sky in succession.

"Is it always like this?"

Ian grabs a cracker and layers it with cheese and meat. "It depends on the moon. If the moon is bright, you can't see them as well." He nods toward the sliver of a moon. "Tonight is the perfect night for it."

I stare at the sky, bright streaks moving through it like celestial fireworks. It's astounding. This meteor shower happens every year, each night for several weeks. And I've never seen it. I didn't even know it existed until Ian mentioned it. "How do people not know about this?"

Ian shrugs. "Too busy, I guess. Too many earthly concerns to take a break." He pours us more champagne. "Stillness, stopping —way underrated, in my opinion."

I look at him, his eyes still fixed on the night sky. "Don't change, Ian." The words come out soft.

"What?" He shifts his gaze from the sky to me.

"Don't change." I move to face him. "The fun lessons. You trying to be different from who you are. Don't. You should stay exactly the same."

"An uptight, unfriendly prick?"

I set my champagne flute on the table. "A sensitive man who prefers to observe rather than be the center of things. A man who can sit and be still and do nothing." I put my hand on his. "That day at the audition, you were so present. You didn't scroll through your phone or try to fill my head with a bunch of platitudes. You were just there, not trying to change anything, not having to do anything." I pause. "That's rare, Ian."

He looks contemplative, and in Ian style, he waits a few beats before responding. "Thank you," he says, "that's one of the nicest things anyone has ever said to me."

"I mean it."

"I liked the fun lessons though. It felt good to let loose. You helped me with that. So," he continues, "you shouldn't change either. You're perfect just as you are."

His voice catches and we're silent a moment, eyes fixed on each other, meteors cascading over our heads.

Go for it.

Audrey's coming tomorrow.

Tonight is my chance.

I inch closer to him, put my hands on his face, and draw him toward me.

"We shouldn't—" he starts.

"We should," I whisper. "Just this once."

His heart hammers against my chest. Or maybe it's mine. I can't tell.

"I want to be with you, Ian. Not as a friend." Vulnerability pools out of me with the words.

"I want to be with you too." He shakes his head. "So much, you have no idea. But—"

I kiss him, then pull back. "No buts. One night. No strings. Back to being friends tomorrow."

He looks unsure. "It's not that I don't want to—"

I reach out and put my hand on his mouth. "This is the last chance, right? The last night before your break is done?"

He nods then pulls me toward him, his hand tangled in my hair, his breathing heavy. "Are you sure about this? Because I can't lose you."

A bright meteor shoots over our heads.

"You won't."

* * *

We wake up the next morning in one of the bedrooms at the rented beach house, our naked bodies tangled under thick blankets. It's early and bits of sunlight streak through the clouds, the beginning of the day's heat. My head rests on Ian's chest; he strokes my hair.

"I loved last night," he says.

"Me too." I lift my head, look at him.

He kisses the top of my head. "Shall I make us breakfast?"

"By make, do you mean go and buy donuts?"

"No. By make, I mean go and see what Brenda has already stocked this place with."

I sit up at the mention of Brenda, pull the blanket over my chest. "I never texted her. I was supposed to text her to get us." I scramble and push discarded clothes from the side table. I find my phone underneath and whip it around. There's a text from Brenda from around 2:00 a.m. *Guess you don't need a ride….* She included a winking emoji.

Ian takes the phone from my hand, reaches over, and puts it on the table. "Don't worry about it."

I sink back against the pillow, pull the blanket up to my chin, and close my eyes. I sigh, a contented one, and shift my body to the side, Ian's arms round me. I refuse to think about anything other than this moment (i.e., the impending arrival of Audrey) and drift off. I wake up to the smell of coffee. I open my eyes and see Ian at a small desk in the room, reading the same book he'd had on the beach yesterday.

"Good morning again," he says. "I made coffee. And there's stuff for breakfast too." He leaves and comes back with a tray, two steaming cups of coffee, and Danishes with thick white icing and pecans on top. He puts the tray on my lap, takes off his shirt and shorts, and slips in next to me. His bare skin is warm against mine.

"I've never had breakfast in bed," I admit. I pull off a piece of Danish.

He picks up his coffee mug. "Me neither."

"To us, then," I pick up my coffee cup and clink it against his. It would be perfect.

But.

I know I said I was okay with this being just a one-time thing. I was kidding myself. I'd thought the sex would be a one-off, probably awkward. A crazy bon voyage to cap off a most unexpected eight weeks together. But it was more than that.

At least for me.

CHAPTER 30

Ian

I kiss Rebecca—again because I can't stop—when my phone pings with a text message. I ignore it. She pulls back. "You should get that."

"It can wait." I ignore the message and kiss her again. We repeat our lovemaking in a way that feels like we are making up for lost time. I lie with her after, my hand tangled in her hair.

"Mate. Ian?"

I pull back. The voice, the accent, is unmistakable. It's Julian. My mind flies to Brenda and I swing back the covers. "Julian," I call, "everything all right?"

"Sort of."

He sounds closer. Like he's on the stairs. Rebecca scrambles for her underwear. I pull on my clothes from last night and bolt downstairs. "What's wrong?"

He holds up a hand. "No one's hurt. But Audrey and her parents are at our house. Your parents too."

"Audrey and our parents are at the house?" I repeat this like it's a hard concept to understand, like I wasn't expecting them later today. Still, I can't get my head around it. They're here. Not in a few weeks or a few days or a few hours. They're here now.

"They're early." I state the obvious.

"I know," Julian says. "Getting here early was a surprise. We texted you. You didn't answer."

I hear footsteps on the stairs and turn to see Rebecca at the bottom, her expression unreadable.

Shit. I thought we'd have more time to—I don't know. Figure things out. Talk about—what? I don't even know. Would she want a relationship with me if it were possible? She'd said this would be a one-off. A madcap, final goodbye. Did she mean it?

"Rebecca—" I start, but the words lodge in my mouth.

"You need to go," she says, her voice commanding.

"I—"

"You need to go," she says more forcefully. Her tone is different, almost cold. It's like a boundary extemporaneously sprouted between us.

I scrub my hand over my face. I hate that I've done this. I'm *not* a cheater. Yet here I am. A cheater. Not that I regret last night. As complicated as our night together has made things, it was perfect. I can't—won't—regret it.

"I'll stay here." She makes a shooing motion with her hands. "We knew what this was."

Julian looks from me to Rebecca and steps to the door. He pulls it open. "I'll be outside, mate."

The door slams behind him. "Last night—" I start.

Rebecca runs a hand through her hair, still tousled. "Ian please. You've got to go."

"Come back with me."

"We can't. We look like the morning after."

I glance at my reflection in the oven. I've got major bedhead. My clothes are wrinkled.

"I can't just leave you here."

"You can't leave me in this multi-million-dollar beach house? I think I'll be fine, Ian."

Her tone seems more caustic than teasing, so I leave it. We'll talk later. I need to know what she's thinking. Hell. I need to know what *I'm* thinking. This is all so messed up. I spring forward and kiss her on the cheek, but the effort feels flat. Almost unwanted. "Talk later?"

"Sure."

I swing open the door, my body like lead. I don't want to leave. But I can't stay. I have to at least see Audrey.

I get in the passenger side of Julian's car and pull down the passenger-side mirror. I look awful. I push my hair to flatten it, pull at my shirt in an effort to get the wrinkles out. Do I smell like sex? Probably. I might even smell like Rebecca's perfume. "I should shower," I blurt.

Julian gives me a sideways glance and pulls into the driveway. "No kidding. You're totally whiffy." He stops the car partway up the driveway. "Brenda told them you were running. Use the back stairs, shower, and come down. They'll expect that." He pauses. "I'll go back for Rebecca."

Rebecca. My heart cliffdives at the sound of her name. For all she's meant to me—for all that we've meant to each other—she shouldn't be sitting alone like a discard. "I should go back with you."

Julian looks at me. "Then what?"

He's right. Then what? Introduce her to Audrey?

My head drops. I hold it in my hands and take a deep breath. "All right."

I push open the door. I sneak up the back stairs feeling every bit like a caricature of the cheating man that I am.

I shower and shave my five-o'clock shadow. I've become a more casual dresser since Rebecca—T-shirts and sport shorts and slides—but I dress in the clothes Audrey's used to. A navy polo and khaki shorts. I slip on boat shoes, ones I recall Rebecca had made fun of.

I head downstairs, and when I reach the bottom, they're all

plainly in view: my parents, the Montgomerys, Audrey, Julian, and Brenda. They sit as a group around a heavy rectangular table, a plate of scones and a pitcher of icy lemonade in the center. Mr. Montgomery says something; they all laugh. Brenda passes him another scone. It looks natural. Warm. Like everyone gets along perfectly.

It's exactly what I've always wanted.

CHAPTER 31

R*ebecca*

I move to the insane deck where, less than twenty-four hours ago, Ian and I kissed. I feel his arms around me, hear his voice in my ear. "You're marvelous, Rebecca."

Marvelous. That word. That perfect word. Ian Ledger is the only person who has ever made me feel worthy of it.

Remnants of the night are strewn across the space: champagne flutes with bits of liquid still at the bottom, a discarded blanket on the ground, disheveled couch cushions. I've already cleaned up inside. It was a frantic effort, the "I don't know what to do with my hands and thoughts so I'll just scrub the bathroom sink" kind. I start cleaning up here now. I replace the pillows, refold the blanket, grab the empty flutes and bring them to the kitchen. I fill the sink with soapy water and immerse them under it.

I try to convince myself that pushing Ian in Audrey's direction was the right decision. Brenda might not think she's right for him, but I know I'm not. I can't offer him something concrete—the steady family, 2.5 kids kind of life he always wanted. *When* I make *Country Clash*, my life will change. I'll be in Nashville. There'll be taping and concerts and tours. I have no idea how the dynamics will unfold or how Ian could possibly fit inside them.

Still. This, the aftermath of last night, hurts. Like crazy.

I set the flutes on a paper towel to dry and shake out my hands. Julian's car, visible in the kitchen window, rattles up the drive. I step outside with just my purse; I don't have any belongings here. As much as it seemed like I lured Ian to this house with the intent of sleeping with him, that hadn't been the plan. The incredible atmosphere, the champagne, and the lingering attraction I'd had for weeks collided in one extraordinary, incredible night. ONE being the operative word.

Julian waves and I get in the passenger side of the car. Absent a few niceties, he's silent. I'm sure he's just trying to give me space; still, I feel like the shunned mistress, Julian playing clean up so my identity will remain a secret. And, though I *know* that's not what last night was—it was too special, too intimate, to be that—the feeling smarts.

Julian pulls the car to a stop at the top of the drive. "They're on the patio," he says.

I nod and open the door. As soon as I step out, I'm assaulted by laughter. The normal, happy laughter of people glad to see each other.

I sneak into the house and skulk up the stairs. There's a window at the top that overlooks the patio and I peek out. I see Ian right away. He's in his standard debate team wear; he shaved the five-o'clock shadow. I look to his left and my breath catches. Audrey. She's more beautiful in person than in the photographs I've seen. Long strawberry-blond hair, delicate features, pale skin. She looks fragile, like a rare bird. Her hand is over the top of Ian's.

To their right is a couple I assume are Audrey's parents. Mr. Montgomery is heavyset, Mrs. Montgomery slender like

Audrey. Ian's mom is exactly how she looks in pictures: chic and confident. The kind of woman that would say: "Yes, my child's trans. Do you have an issue with that?" Ian's dad looks like him.

Julian arrives with a plate of cookies and sets them on the table. Mr. Montgomery grabs one and holds it up; there's some laughter. I'm not sure why it's funny, but one thing is clear: the reunion is going well.

AUDREY LOOKS UP; our eyes meet for an instant. I duck, panicked, then realize she's never met me. To her, I'm just another wedding guest staying at the house. She doesn't know about my feelings for Ian. About our friendship. About last night.

I move away from the window and step into my room. I shut the door, lean against it. My chest burns. Feelings of jealousy, anger, and hurt swirl in my gut. They're misplaced, I know. This —Ian and Audrey reuniting at the wedding—had always been the endgame. But seeing him with her? Awful. I feel an uncharacteristic and intense hatred toward her. It floors me. I mean, I don't even *know* her.

I need to get a grip.

I fish inside my purse for my phone. If there's an email from *Country Clash*, a yes, it will be a salve to this torrent of emotions and maybe, just maybe, I can think sensibly. I pull up my emails and scan down.

Kohls.

Yankee Candle.

Bath and Body Works.

DSW Shoes.

If I've never noticed it before, I notice it now. Nearly all of my emails are from store lists, ones I'd signed up for to get some discount. It's incredibly annoying, scrolling through this endless list. *Unsubscribe already, Rebecca.* I reach the end. There's nothing from *Country Clash*. There is an email from Olivia at Music All Around. I open that one.

Bec,

Want to confirm you'll be back next Saturday for your class. Kids miss you. Also, any interest in doing a Tuesday-night class? More kids have signed up, even ones from the mainland. MAA is trending. Who knew?

O

I STARE AT THE MESSAGE, conjure my kids. Charity with her pigtails and earnest face. Robert, an energetic kid who listens. Sam, an energetic kid who does *not* listen. I've found, with Sam, if you give him a job, he's awesome. He's my go-to for passing out instruments. I miss them.

I email that I'll be back for class Saturday and that I'll think about Tuesday. If I get *Country Clash*, I can't do that, obviously. And if I don't?

I can't think about that right now.

I turn on the shower, turn the dial toward "H" until it's nearly scalding. Something about hot water, really hot water, has always felt cleansing. I slip under the shower head, let the water cascade over my body. I lather myself up with soap and shampoo; the bubbles slide down my body. After, I step out and pluck a plush pink towel from a pile of perfectly folded ones. It smells like lavender. I wrap it around myself, move into the bedroom, and check for a *Country Clash* email again. Nothing.

My phone pings. Ian. *Can we talk later?*

I grip the phone. I can't fathom talking to Ian right now. I can't imagine staying. If I'm here, I'll eventually have to talk to Audrey. A lot. At the rehearsal dinner, at the wedding. If I pass her in the hall of the house on her way to *Ian's room*. I'll watch her and Ian dance and sit together and tell the kind of inside jokes inevitable after so many years. And before my eyes, Ian will again become more hers than mine, clean-shaven and proper. The kind of guy that wears boat shoes unironically.

I can't do it.

I'd told Ian that one night together wouldn't change things. I was wrong.

I pull out my duffel, haphazardly throw my belongings inside. I make ferry reservations, figure out the bus routes back to Cape May, and call an Uber. I'll text Ian and Brenda once I'm off island, too far away to be coaxed back. I am genuinely sad I'll miss the wedding. I like Brenda and Julian.

When the Uber arrives. I give a final glance to the house. I recall the giddiness I'd felt when Ian and I had gotten here, when our friendship seemed invincible. Everything is different now.

Once on the ferry, I take a seat on the top level, as far away from any other person as I can reasonably get. Salt air fills my nostrils; ocean waves curl toward the shore. I pull out my phone to check my email. I don't expect to see anything. But it's there. *Country Clash* Audition Results.

My breath catches. My hands shake. My heart beats in my chest.

They're here.

The results.

I hover my finger over the email, close my eyes, and press.

At first, I can barely comprehend the big block of text. I take a deep breath and read, word for word, slowly, so I don't miss anything. There's an extra audition for the people on the list. And if you're not on it? Better luck next time.

I scan down the list of names.

Oh God.

Please let my name be there.

Please.

It's there. The last one. Rebecca Chapman, vocalist, alto.

I exhale. Thank God. Though I dread the idea of another

audition, I needed this. Something to hold on to while I adjust to my Ian-free reality.

I pull up my texts. The audition is the perfect excuse for my early departure. I start a joint one to Ian and Brenda, less personal that way. *Hey guys. Sorry I had to run suddenly but exciting news! I've made it to another round of Country Clash auditions. I have only a few days to prepare. I hope you understand. Love to you all.*

I press send, a trace of guilt in my gut. A joint text with his sister is a bit cold, given everything that transpired between Ian and me. But moving on means closing off.

It's the only way I'll get over him.

CHAPTER 32

I *an*

Guilt is heavy. I know this because, as I walk with Audrey on the beach, my body feels like it's weighed down with lead. My phone pings; I glance at the screen. A text from Rebecca. And boom. The lead gets heavier.

As much as I want to, I don't pull it up. I can't. Audrey will ask questions. Plus, I'll need time to answer it. Or, better yet, talk to Rebecca in person. The way I'd left her was awful.

Audrey grabs my hand, snakes her fingers through mine. She squeezes. "I'm so glad to be here." She looks up at me with those blue eyes, the ones that invaded my dreams the first few weeks we'd been apart. An ocean breeze blows at her hair.

She lets go of my hand and pushes at my chest. "That's when you say, 'I'm glad you're here too.'"

"Right," I say, shaking my head, "of course."

She stops, faces me, and grips both my hands. "I know this is weird."

My throat is jammed. Probably from all the guilt-laden lead packed inside my body.

"Eight weeks is a long time." She looks at the sand, then up at

me again. "Can we just—" She stops and squishes her facial
features in a way that makes it seem like she's about to sneeze.
I'd always found it adorable. "Can we just start over?" she
finishes. "I don't need to know if you, you know, saw anyone."

My heart dips. I'm an asshole. *She knows.*

"I dated," she continues. "You dated, probably. It's in the past.
Nothing we should get into, I think."

Oh.

The don't-ask-don't-tell mantra isn't about me. It's
about her.

Weeks ago, I'd have been consumed with jealous, unasked
questions. Instead, I'm relieved. Sort of. It's clear Audrey had
other relationships. She's given me a free pass not to feel guilty
about anything, even last night.

And yet.

Rebecca. She's in my thoughts. Ironically, more than Audrey.

"I've missed you." She lets go of my hands, puts her arms
around my neck, and pulls my face toward hers. She kisses me.
That familiar kiss I'd ached for, one I thought I'd trade my soul
to have back. But now, inexplicably, I'm comparing kissing
Audrey to how I felt with Rebecca last night.

I don't mean to. It happens anyway.

I pull back. "Let's walk."

A quizzical look crosses her features. "Sure," she agrees after
a beat.

We take a few steps, and for the second time on this very
short walk, she grabs my hand. I've never been a handholding
kind of person. Audrey and I have different heights, different
gaits, but now, we're moored together through some romantic
social convention. It's hard to walk naturally.

"Any highlights of the past weeks?" I ask finally.

"Oreo's pregnant."

At the mention of Oreo, I recall Rebecca's reaction to
Audrey's cats: *Please tell me the names are ironic.*

I smile, then register Audrey's words. "Wait. Oreo's pregnant?"

"Yup. Due in two weeks."

I shake my head. "Didn't you have her fixed?"

She shrugs. "I thought I did."

"Wow. That'll be fun."

I'm not sure it will. I mean, I like kittens as much as the next guy. But Audrey's a little crazy with the cats. She *makes* their food, like from scratch. I'm not sure how she'll be with kittens.

"You're going to give them away, right? The kittens."

"Some," she says. "My parents are going to take at least one."

How many kittens are in a typical litter? I rack my brain, but before I can make a guess,

Audrey squeals. She lets go of my hand, runs to the surf, and swipes a conch shell from the beach. She races back, holds it to her ear. "You can hear the ocean waves in this, you know."

She holds it to my ear. I cannot hear the ocean waves. I can smell what I think might be a dead sea creature inside the shell.

"Can you hear it?" she asks, the smelly, sandy rock still uncomfortably close to my ear.

"Yeah," I lie, "I can."

"I'm going to keep it," she says triumphantly.

I'm not sure if she's allowed to keep conchs, and even she is, it smells. I open my mouth to say this, then shut it. Audrey will just turn it into an example of me being uptight. Because *fun* people like having rancid and possibly illegal sea life in their possession.

"So how about you?" she asks. "Any highlights from your break?"

My break. I nearly laugh. She makes it sound like the past weeks were part of a summer vacation instead of a forced romantic hiatus.

"I went to a nude beach." For some inexplicable reason, I'm proud to say this.

"Like," she tilts her head, "the kind where people don't wear clothes?"

We walk a few steps. "Yup."

"Did *you* not wear anything?"

"I did not."

"Like everything was out?" She moves the conch around her groin area.

"Everything."

"Oh." She's quiet a beat. "That seems inappropriate, Ian."

I stop. "I thought that's the kind of thing you wanted me to do."

She turns to face me. "I wanted you to be more friendly, do some more interesting things—"

"That's not interesting? A nude beach?"

"Right. Sorry." She exhales. "Didn't mean to overreact." A seagull screeches overhead. She pokes me playfully on the arm. "Guess I didn't want a bunch of other girls seeing The Ambassador."

I laugh, a genuine one. "The Ambassador" has been her nickname for my penis for years; I'm not sure how it got started.

"Who'd you even go with anyway?" she asks.

The smile leaves my face. "People from work," I say neutrally.

"Work? Weren't you there to calm down the culture?"

"They had this planned ahead of time," I say, like the nude beach outing was a company excursion. Worst liar ever. My tombstone epitaph for sure.

The path to the house comes into view, a giant yellow cat in its center.

"Kitty!" Audrey dodges toward the cat. It runs into the brush and Audrey returns to my side.

"I played in a foam pit," I volunteer. "And I reenacted a sword fight at a Renaissance Faire."

"Really?"

"Yeah."

I fill her in on the details of both. It's a funny conversation, but of course, both of those things remind me of Rebecca, so it's not actually all that funny. We approach the house and slip inside. No one's around.

I hold up my phone. "I've got to return some work emails." I start up the stairs.

Audrey follows me because, of course, we're sharing a room. I'd forgotten that.

"I'll just rest on the bed," she says.

"Of course."

As soon as we get into the room, I head to the bathroom, sit on the toilet seat, and pull up the text from Rebecca. It's to me and Brenda.

Hey guys. Sorry I had to run suddenly but exciting news! I've made it to another round of Country Clash auditions. I have only a few days to prepare. I hope you understand. Love to you all.

I reread it.

Sorry I had to run. She's gone. Rebecca's gone. It's inconceivable that she's not two doors down, or walking the beach, or buying another pair of ridiculous flip-flops for her collection. I won't get to talk to her face-to-face. My head drops; I rake my hair.

I stare at my phone, start a text back.

Good news.

No.

Great news about the Country Clash callback. When is it? Do you need help?

No.

Miss you. So sorry you left. Happy about the callback.

No.

Wow. I start the next text draft. What should it say? Wow, great news? Wow, good for you? Wow, so happy for you, Rebecca.

"Are you okay in there, Ian?"

I glance at the closed door. "I'm okay."

I start again. The bathroom door swings open, Audrey in its frame. She's wearing white lingerie with tons of lace. Super sexy.

"I'm looking for The Ambassador," she says, a lilt in her voice. "Have you seen him?"

I look at my draft text then back at her. "Umm."

It's the wrong thing to say. Obviously. She stares at me a long moment. "Umm? Seriously? Eight weeks and this is the reception I get?"

"The eight weeks was your idea," I retort. "Sorry if I can't just jump back into things like nothing happened."

She storms out of the bathroom. I follow, phone still in my hand. She swipes her dress off the floor, pulls it over her head. "Do you not want to be with me anymore? Is that it?"

It's the million-dollar question. Because I don't know what I want. A few weeks ago, I'd have jumped on the chance to be with Audrey. But things feel different now. I wouldn't feel right about sleeping with Audrey just yet, not after last night. Despite my actions, I'd like to think I've got enough integrity for at least that.

I don't know what to say so I don't speak.

Wrong.

Again.

"Okay. Wow." She wedges her feet into a pair of sandals. "I'll see you later then, Ian." She pulls open the door and steps through. It slams behind her.

I sit on the bed, toss my phone. Which is when I realize my draft text to Rebecca accidentally went through. It says: *Wow.*

CHAPTER 33

R*ebecca*
The phone pings with a text. I pull it out of my
bag, hold my breath as I click. Ian.
Wow.

I stare at the word.

Wow.

Wow? It's sarcastic in its singularity. And confusing. Wow
that I left? Or wow about the audition? Or both? It's impossible
to know because it's ONE WORD. I turn the phone over then
inexplicably turn it back and look at the text again. Like I could
have missed something. Nope. Still just *Wow.*

Okay. I try to spin the response into something better. I
can't. I thought I meant something to Ian. Maybe not a forever
thing, like he clearly has with Audrey, but something more than
a single word.

Wow.

I pick up my phone and start texting the same word back to
him. It's as succinct a description of how I feel as I can think of.
My thumb hovers over the send button, the word "wow" in the
text box.

No.

I switch off the phone without sending. I *did* just leave without a real goodbye. Ian might be pissed. I would be.

I lean back and the foghorn blares. BLARES. I jump. It's directly over my head. Which explains why no one is sitting here but me. It trumpets again and I move toward the exit, duffel slung over one shoulder, giant guitar case gripped in one hand. It's cumbersome to move at all, let alone quickly, and the horn roars for the third time. Honestly, ferry operator. People know you're here. The boat is massive.

It takes me forever to navigate down the stairs and off the ferry. I start to sweat from the heat. I bump into at least a dozen people with the guitar case.

"Do you need help?"

I turn. A guy, my age, with long hair, a black T-shirt, and sunglasses that can best be described as *shades* stares at me.

He's my type. Or what I thought was my type before Ian.

"Sure. Thanks."

He grabs the guitar and duffel like they're nothing. "Where to?" He looks around the lot, expecting, I guess, that I'd have a car.

"Bus stop." I nod my head in its direction, a trickle of sweat slides down my face.

Shade guy squints. "Need a ride?"

I laugh. "Don't think you're going to Jersey, so no thanks."

He sets my belongings down next to the bench at the stop. "Jersey? Who the heck goes to Jersey when you could be here?"

"People who live there," I deadpan.

"Touché." He laughs. "When does your bus leave? Have time for an iced coffee?" He gestures toward a coffee shop literally twenty feet from where we're sitting.

My bus does not arrive for over an hour; I definitely have time. There's no harm. No reason not to say yes. Plus having a coffee with shade guy would get my mind off of Ian. Still. I don't want to.

"No thanks."

He shrugs. "Okay then. Best." He holds up a hand, heads into the coffee shop, and steps behind the bar. He works there. Or owns it. Either way, I now have to sit for over an hour in his direct line of vision. I can't maneuver my things and go somewhere else, not without making an even bigger scene. I'm stuck in the sweltering heat.

I pull out my phone. It's almost dead.

I'm stuck in the sweltering heat with an almost dead phone and no way to charge it.

Great, Rebecca.

* * *

IT'S NEARLY nine at night when Lily picks me up at the Trenton bus terminal, the whole ordeal home taking more than twice as long as it would have had I just had a license and driven. I'm hot. Sweaty. Hangry. Irritated. With myself, for not being able to drive. With Ian. With Audrey. With the *Country Clash* audition panel who didn't just pick me straight off. I'm even irritated with stupid shade guy.

I collapse into Lily's passenger seat.

Lily opens the driver's-side door and glances at me. "You look like hell."

"Thanks?"

"Seriously. What happened to you?"

I open my mouth with the intention of saying something pithy. But I'm bone-tired, and I miss Ian, and I'm angry that I have to go through the stress of a second audition. "Everything sucks; that's what happened."

She slides across the seat, wraps her arms around me, and squeezes. "What is it?"

I open my mouth. A mess of gibberish comes out.

She tilts her head. "I'm getting you food first." She starts the car and begins to drive. I lean back and close my eyes, relieved to let her take over. The car rumbles on for a good ten minutes before Lily pulls to a stop and shuts off the engine. I open my eyes. We're in the parking lot of a small bar we've been to a bunch of times.

Once we're seated, Lily orders appetizers—nachos, mozzarella sticks, wings—and two beers. The beers arrive first; we sip them in silence. The food comes not that long after, and I pile up a plate and shovel it in my mouth. As Lily guessed, a full stomach calms my emotions.

"I had sex with Ian," I blurt.

The corners of her mouth tug into a smile.

"It's not a good thing."

She bangs the table. "Yeah it is. How did that happen?"

"It was me." I lean back in the chair. It moves and the legs scrape across the floor. "I wanted to, Lil. I knew Audrey was coming and we wouldn't get another chance. It was my idea. I thought it—" I shake my head. "I don't know what I thought. That it would get him out of my system maybe?" I look at the floor. I don't admit that, after, I'd hoped he would change his mind. That he'd pick me over her. I look up. "I think I love him, Lil."

"Oh, Bec." She shoots her hand out and puts it over mine. "Does he know?"

I shake my head. "Audrey's there now. She's adorable and perfect and can give him everything he wants."

"Which is?"

"Normalcy."

Lily retrieves her hand and takes a sip from her beer bottle. "How do you know he wants normalcy?"

"Because he's Ian and that's how Ian operates. He actually put his clothes away for a one-night stay in a hotel, hangers and all."

"John—"

I hold up my hand. "*Do not* compare him to John."

"Fine. But you don't know. Maybe you've changed him."

"No." I grab a nacho and load it with a ton of crap. "You should have seen them together with their families. It was like a reunion of the happiest people on earth." I shovel the nacho in my mouth, chew, and swallow. "Oh, and then there's this." I explain about my text and show her Ian's single word text response.

"Wow. That's it?"

I shove my phone back in my purse. "Doesn't exactly give the vibe that he's pining over me, does it?" I feel the torrent of emotions again—love, jealousy, loss.

Lily pushes the plate with the last mozzarella stick toward me. "You need to move on."

"You think?" I bug my eyes out.

"I mean," she says, "delete his contact." She grabs my phone and waves it. "Go cold turkey on this."

I take a bite of the mozzarella stick, swipe the stretch of cheese with my finger. I don't want to cut Ian out of my life. But where can our relationship possibly go? Continued contact under these circumstances would be painful.

I extricate the phone from Lily's hands.

"I'll think about it."

CHAPTER 34

I*an*

It's the wedding. I'm at the altar, waiting for Brenda, her man of honor. Audrey waves at me from the second pew, all smiles. She forgave me for dissing her overture, said she "totally understood." We spent last night sleeping fully clothed, side by side, like siblings on a family vacation. Right now, she's buttressed between her parents. Both Mr. and Mrs. Montgomery have been surprisingly supportive of the wedding. Strangely so, almost like they'd never told me Brenda*n* was going against God's will and that they, magnanimous as they were, were going to pray for *him*. Like they hadn't shunned my parents for years.

Audrey meets my eyes and it's there, that warm feeling I used to get whenever I even thought about her. Then zap. It's gone.

Flashes of love.

It's the best way I can characterize how I feel. Nothing steady or overwhelming. Just bursts of feeling, little hints of how it once was between us.

And in between the bursts?

I think about Rebecca.

I followed up on the accidental *wow* text, or tried to anyway. Two messages I spent forever crafting were unable to send due to the sketchy internet at the house. Just as well. I'm hopeless with texts. I tried to call, twice, but I got interrupted both times. And this won't be a hey-what's-up conversation. I need to *really* talk to Rebecca. I don't know where her head's at after the other night. All I know is that I'm here with my steady girlfriend of forever, and practically all I can think about is her.

My thoughts are interrupted by the appearance of Brenda at the end of the church aisle.

Oh.

Wow.

I'd seen the wedding dress in pictures she'd sent to Rebecca via text. When Rebecca showed me the photos, I recall thinking the dress looked exactly like what it was, a wedding dress—white and long and no big deal. Now? Brenda's stunning. Absolutely beautiful. And it's not just the dress. It's the way she wears it—with confidence and elegance and poise. Likes she owns it. And the body inside.

Growing up, I never thought I'd be standing at my sister's wedding, but now, seeing her happy and whole, makes me glad she persevered with her choice. Even if I'd been unable to see it at the time.

Julian's breath catches as Brenda approaches; he looks at her like she's a gift. During the ceremony, each recite such personal, heartfelt vows to the other, listening to them is like watching their love unfurl, overpowering and vulnerable.

The minister declares them man and wife to thunderous applause. My sister and Julian kiss, link hands, and march back down the aisle of a church so crowded, it's standing room only. I follow them down the aisle. Audrey catches my eye and winks.

I wink back. The small moment feels weird, like I'm playing the part of her boyfriend.

I reach the end of the aisle, stand with the other members of the bridal party for a receiving line, aka my worst nightmare.

"Do I have to?" I mouth to Brenda.

We've had this conversation numerous times since I found out greeting dozens of strangers in a post-ceremony line is mandatory for the man of honor.

"Yes." She points to my place in line with a smile.

Ugh. The things I'll do for my sister.

I feel incredibly awkward at first but figure out a routine a few people in. Half hugs for the women—the kind where you don't really touch; handshakes for the guys. My standard phrase: "Thanks for coming." It's kind of a dumb phrase considering I'd invited no one and planned nothing. Still, it works.

A woman in a fuchsia dress, floral hat, and bright pink lipstick approaches. I go for my standard air hug, and mid-movement, she grabs my shoulders and pulls me against her. Her hand skims my butt and she doesn't let go. It's so over the top that I almost laugh, and when she finally releases me, I think of Rebecca. She would find the whole thing hilarious. I file the memory away to share.

I've filed quite a few memories for her. Like Brenda and Julian's exchange of vows. The woman I saw on the beach with flip-flops that looked like tacos. A Mrs. Fishes truck, right here, on the island. I guess I've been doing that the whole time I've known her, taking note of things I'd like to tell her about. Difference is, I used to see her every day. Now I have no plans to see her at all.

"Ian!!"

Audrey, in a short navy dress, flings her arms around me. Her long hair slips across my shoulder, and she smells like she always has, like gardenias. Her body feels familiar.

She steps back and adjusts my tie. "You look incredible."

"So do you." It's true. She does.

She brushes her hands down the front of her dress and smiles. "Thanks."

Mr. Montgomery raps me on the shoulder; Mrs. Montgomery gives me a tight hug.

After the receiving line, there's a marathon photography session. I'm pretty sure more pictures are taken of me that one hour than in my entire life so far. After, I find Audrey at the reception. She's sipping a glass of champagne and talking to a group of people I'm fairly certain she's never met. She's always been good in these situations, able to break into groups in a way I'd never been able to manage.

I move to her side. She glances up. Happiness flashes across her face and she twists her arm around mine. "This is Ian," she announces, "brother of the bride."

There's a general fuss. Audrey grabs a bottle and a plate from a nearby table and holds them in my direction. "Thought you might need these after that receiving line," she whispers.

I take the items from her hands. A craft beer, locally brewed, and a plate of food that includes all my favorites: bacon-wrapped scallops, crabcakes, and pigs-in-a-blanket. A pile of veggies too. I stare at the food. Fixing a plate is admittedly a small gesture, but kind. She's trying.

We take the food to our table, and I spend a blissful ten minutes with no conversation. Even Audrey doesn't talk. And she hates silence. I soften at her effort to give me space.

"You seem different," she says finally.

"Yeah?" I shift my seat and look at her. "Good or bad?"

"Good," she says without hesitation. She squeezes my hand and smiles. "Definitely good."

I wait for more, wanting to know what makes me good-different, but before I can ask, Audrey's parents approach our table. Mrs. Montgomery takes the seat next to Audrey. Mr.

Montgomery puts a hand on my shoulder, his face near my ear. "Cigar?"

I angle my face. Cigars are huge to Mr. Montgomery. He's an avid collector, stores his extensive offering in a glass-case humidor. I've only seen him smoke on a handful of occasions; he's never asked me to join.

As a rule, I'm not a fan of cigar smoking. It seems an extension of the good old boys club. Even now, it's clear Mr. Montgomery intends it to be a man thing. Audrey and her mom are to stay back while we—*the men*—inhale deadly tobacco and discuss weighty matters.

Audrey squeezes my thigh, low key thrilled, apparently, that I've been offered the opportunity to *smoke cigars* with her dad. Mr. Montgomery opens his suit jacket to reveal that, yes, the cigars are in there. And, though I want to say no on principle, I'm curious. I've always felt Mr. Montgomery merely tolerated me as a "she could do worse" choice for Audrey. I'd assumed he'd held out hope that she'd find someone else, a manly man, instead of me, a sensitivity consultant with liberal parents and a trans sibling. I have no idea what's put me in the inner, cigar-smoking circle. I'm too curious not to find out.

"Sure." I stand and glance at Audrey. She looks like she might clap.

Mr. Montgomery raps me on the back as we walk outside. We find a spot on the small patch of grass dedicated for smoking. A woman's there already, a lit cigarette between her fingers. Mr. Montgomery ignores her, pulls out two fat cigars and a cutter and chops off the ends. Next, he pulls out a lighter, holds his cigar in front of the flame. He twists it like he's toasting a marshmallow, and once it's lit, he nods in my direction.

I take the lighter and follow his protocol. After, we stand with our lit cigars in silence, puffing in the light of the moon.

"So, your brother is married," he says.

I stiffen.

He holds out a hand. "Sorry. Your sister." He gives a sheepish look. "I'm still learning. It can be hard for us old folks, sometimes. All this new age stuff."

It's not hard for my parents. And it's not "stuff." I want to articulate this, but Mr. Montgomery speaks before I get a chance.

"Do you love Audrey, Ian?"

I step back, the question so forthright I forget about the prior thread of our conversation. Do I love Audrey? I did. I do. But my feelings have shifted. My love feels different now. Or maybe I'm not in my right mind at the moment, given what's transpired in the past forty-eight hours.

He puts his hand on my shoulder. "Sorry. Of course, you do." He looks me in the eyes.

"You've been dating my Audrey for some time now."

"On and off." I look down then up again. "She wanted a break this summer."

"Right." He looks up at the moon, exhales a long breath. "She needs a commitment, Ian." He looks me in the eye. "A real one. Not this on-again-off-again girlfriend-boyfriend bull crap."

I freeze, the cigar dormant in my hand.

He pulls a small box from his suit jacket, thrusts it toward me. "Go on." He nods in my direction.

I take the box and flip the top. It's a ring.

"It's my grandmother's. That ring has been in my family for generations."

"It's beautiful," I manage. And it is. Platinum with a sapphire in the center circled by diamonds.

He blows smoke from his cigar, meets my eyes. "You have my permission, son. Ask her."

CHAPTER 35

R*ebecca*

Ian and I spoke the day after Brenda's wedding. He explained he hadn't meant to send the "wow" message, that the Wi-Fi had been sketchy, and both of these details track. Since then, he's talked me through some audition points and made me laugh over his travails in the receiving line. He's sent at least six pictures of flip-flops. He's never mentioned Audrey. And we've never discussed "the night." I can't begin to wrap my head around how I feel about it all. I have an audition to crush.

Today is *the* day, the day of *Country Clash* audition number two. I clutch my cell to one ear, hold my hand over the other to deafen the cars and people and general noise of Times Square.

"Just breathe. You'll be fine." Ian's voice is calm and solid. Like him.

"Thanks, Ian."

I switch off the phone.

Lily pulls on my arm. "We should go back. You need to get dressed." She puts her hands on my shoulders. "IT'S. ALMOST.

TIME." She says it like that, loud and with a space between each word. She jumps too.

I know she means well.

She's driving me crazy.

When she offered to come to the audition, I thought it would be a good idea. Lily's typically calm. Not Ian-level calm, but still, level-headed. She's been the opposite since we arrived in New York, almost manic in her desperation to hype me up.

"Time to glam up!" She claps. "You got this. You got this."

I stare at her.

She grips my shoulders and steers me toward the hotel door.

Once in our shared room, I dress in the bathroom. I inspect myself in a giant mirror with flowers etched around the rim. The outfit, the same one I'd worn for the first audition, feels different this time around. Or maybe it's me that feels different. I don't know. I sit on the toilet seat and put my head in my hands.

Come on, Rebecca. Get it together.

Just breathe.

I take a deep breath, stand, and push open the door. Lily leaps off the bed. "Bec, you look amazing!" She circles me like a predator. "A—MAZE—ZING. Like, wow."

"Thanks." I grab my cowboy hat from the closet and place it on my head.

"No way," she says, pushing at my shoulders. "You look like a friggin' star. Wait." She grabs her phone and snaps a picture. "I have to show John."

I open my mouth to protest. I haven't discussed the audition process with my family much. And I don't want John, or any of them, seeing me in my costume. I know they wouldn't mock me; they're family. But still, country music and all that goes with it is a huge contrast to their medical and legal worlds, and I can't help but feel I'll be judged. It's the last thing I need.

"Wait—" I jut my hand out toward her phone.

The swish sound from the sent text fills the room. Lily looks up, oblivious to my concern. "Sent it, superstar. Let's go." She moves to the door and claps. *Again.* "Let's go. Let's go. Let's go."

Lily strides down the hall toward the elevator. I practically run to keep up—the heavy guitar case bumps against my leg, my sack of supplies shifts on my back. So different from when Ian was here. He carried my guitar, walked with an easy gate I could keep pace with.

Lily punches the up button for the elevator. Punch. Punch. Punch. Punch. Punch.

Honestly.

It's not like the elevator will move faster if she keeps pressing the button. I open my mouth to say this just as the silver doors slide open.

Lily jumps in an elevator filled with grim-faced men and women in business suits. I get a bad vibe. I want to wait for the next elevator. I try to catch Lily's attention, but she grabs my arm and pulls me forward. "Get on in here, superstar." The doors slide closed.

Lily puts her hands on my shoulders. "This is country music's next big star," she announces to our serious elevator companions.

No one says anything, the quiet amplified in the small space. My cheeks burn. Finally, the woman next to me says, "Nice hat."

Oh my God.

Lily babbles on, about me presumably. I don't know. I've blocked her out.

Every second on the elevator feels like an hour, so it seems like several days have elapsed by the time I finally step off.

The audition is on the same floor as before, same hotel, but it looks different now. Fewer people, fewer chairs. No *Country Clash* signs. There's a check-in guy with a clipboard instead of a check-in girl. The differences shouldn't matter; they rattle me anyway.

I check in and we sit in two of the few chairs available. I sip my room temperature water and try to get in a good headspace. Lily talks about nonsense until clipboard guy approaches. "Rebecca Chapman?"

Lily shoots out of her seat. "Right here."

I stand, pick up my guitar, and follow the guy. Lily claps behind me. "Go get 'em, Bec! You got it. You got it, girl."

I don't feel like I got it. In fact, I feel decidedly like I do not "got it." I'm nauseous, I'm tight. My mouth is dry.

I inhale a breath, try to convince myself that this is no different than last time. I was nervous then too, right? I'd calmed down after I'd seen Ian's word for me: marvelous. I say the word in the head. *Marvelous. I'm marvelous.* I whisper it: "Marvelous."

I don't feel marvelous. I feel like I might be sick.

"Rebecca Chapman." A woman waves at me from the space on the stage. I step forward and peer at the judges. They're different this time. I hadn't expected that.

I smile but it doesn't feel right. I'm pretty sure it's a cross between a smirk and a grimace. I put the guitar around my neck, stand, and wait. Last time, the judges asked me a few questions, told me when to start.

The only female judge checks her watch. My stomach plummets.

I guess I'm supposed to just start. Maybe? "Should I just start?" My tone is meek. Timidness I haven't felt since high school courses through me. I play a chord on the guitar, the wrong one. I start my song but it's off. I stop.

"Sorry." I pause. "Can I start over?"

The woman judge leans back in a black swivel chair, hands behind her head. "Sure."

I start again. The guitar chord is right, but when I sing, I'm off pitch. I hear it; my mind races. Should I ask to start over again? Should I keep going? How bad is it? Bad. I feel it.

I finish the song. "That wasn't my best," I offer. "Can I—" I pause. "Try again?"

One of the male judges leans forward. "We've got what we need."

The guitar hangs from my neck. I stand there, unable to accept what happened.

"Bobby Axler," the woman, the one who'd called my name, calls the next person. A guy with longish hair moves onto the stage, next to where I'm standing.

I'm dismissed. Obviously. I wait another second, hoping desperately one of the judges might call out that I should take another shot. A second go-around would take less than three minutes.

No one says anything, and my continued presence on the stage is increasingly awkward. Finally, I move off the stage, down the hall, and to the "loved ones" waiting room. Lily charges at me as soon as I open the door. "How did it go?"

"Marvelous," I lie.

CHAPTER 36

I *an*

I pull out my phone and check for a message from Rebecca. She hasn't contacted me since telling me her audition went "great" a few days ago. I keep thinking maybe she's heard from *Country Clash* but there's no message. I want to call and ask but don't. Things have been weird between us since I got back to Nebraska.

During our last call, I'd made the mistake of bringing up "the night" because we never talked about it, and honestly, I can't get her, that night, any of it, out of my head.

Forget it, Ian.

Rebecca's exact words.

I'd protested. Or tried to.

We knew what it was. A one-time thing. We need to move on.

And that was it. She'd ended the conversation; we haven't spoken since. And I've spent the past four days trying to recapture the certainty I'd felt about Audrey, when I'd been agonized by the separation. I know the change in my feelings doesn't make sense. It's only been eight weeks. It was only one night. It would be nonsensical to change my life plan, especially when it's clear Rebecca sees our relationship as nothing more than a fling.

I've taken the ring out twice. I visualize how it would look—me down on one knee, flipping the box, asking the question. But I stop short of making an actual plan—this date, this place, this time.

Right now, my lunch hour, I'm with Audrey in her apartment. She's hovering over the nesting box—a giant cardboard box lined with blankets in her laundry room—the place where Oreo is to give birth. "Thanks for coming, Ian. I think she's in labor."

I glance at the cat. She's sitting in the middle of the box, her tail curled around her body. She looks the same—exactly—as she has every time I've seen her. "Are you sure?"

Audrey's head shoots up. "She has all the signs. A decrease in appetite, her temperature's down. And she keeps running away from me."

"She's running away from you because she's in labor. No other reason?"

I mean this as a joke. Audrey puts her hand on her hip. "Lack of affection is *a sign*, Ian." She resumes staring at Oreo. The cat blinks and hops out of the box.

Audrey flails her arms. "See?"

"I stand corrected. Labor is imminent."

"Right?"

"No. I'm kidding." I lean against the dryer. "You're thinking way too much about this. Cats give birth without human intervention every day. You don't have to do anything."

"I need to be there for her." She bends down and adjusts towels in the box.

Good Lord. "She'll be fine. Really." I glance at my watch. "Look, I've got to get back to work."

She stands and smooths out her shorts. "You're still good to eat with my parents tonight, right? For Mom's birthday?"

"Of course. Looking forward to it."

Not!

I haven't seen Mr. Montgomery since the wedding weekend, haven't spoken to him since "the talk." I'm afraid I'll be pulled aside for another cigar-smoking you-better-ask-my-daughter-to-marry-you fest. And I'm not ready to ask. Today's conversation about "being there" for Oreo did not move the dial.

She pecks my cheek. "Six good?"

"That works." I turn toward the door.

"I'll call you right away if Oreo goes into labor."

I swing my head around, expecting a smile or some indication she's joking. Nope. "Sure. Thanks."

I walk to my car. Was Audrey always like this, kind of devoid of humor? I flood my brain with memories, and no, she's laughed plenty of times. And she's made jokes.

Apparently, it's just my sense of humor she doesn't get.

Not like Rebecca did.

My heart ricochets. I tamp it down. I have to get used to the fact that Rebecca does not feel about me the way I feel about her.

I swing my car into the parking lot of LCR, shut it off, and stare at the nondescript tan building. It's not just Audrey I'm unclear on, it's the job too. It feels more and more like my role as a sensitivity consultant is less about enlightening people and more about helping companies *look* progressive. But it's an illusion. I'm not changing underlying beliefs. I'm just helping to cover up the bad ones with politically correct lingo.

I walk into the building and move straight to my office. My computer is already on. My half-done project, the modernization of the copy on the website for Toytopia, is on the screen. I stare at the last thing I'd written: "Toytopia is an innovative company with an unbridled commitment to diversity and inclusion." Is it? I have no idea.

I backspace over the sentence, character by character. In its place, I type: "Toytopia hired me to write politically correct text in order to expand their customer base and quiet objections from historically underrepresented groups." I lean back when I'm done. That text is probably the truest thing I've written since I started this job.

I'm not sure I can do this anymore.

What would I do instead?

Sales? No. The small talk would kill me.

Teaching? No. I'm not the best with kids.

Some other kind of consulting? Maybe?

I swivel in my chair, and it comes to me—the obvious. Brenda's half-joke, half-serious idea of me helping her and Julian start a frozen food meal service for their catering company. I bolt up in the chair; it reverberates behind me.

I click off the Toytopia project and type "how to create frozen meals" verbatim into the search bar. Hundreds of ideas for homemade frozen meals fill my screen. Duh. I search "how to make frozen meals for commercial sale." Warmer. Lots of relevant sites for this one. I click on one site, then another, until I'm lost in logistics like ice packs and Styrofoam boxes and shipping costs. It's a lot. I open a new document and start listing items—things I make, things Brenda and Julian make, that would be good as frozen meals. I list ten, then realize the time. 6:01. Crap. I have to go. I text Audrey with a work-related excuse, grab my bag, and drive straight to her house. I text her when I get there.

"Sorry." I blurt out the word as soon as she gets in the car.

She puts her hand over mine. "It's okay. Mom wants to eat at the country club now, so dinner won't be until seven."

"Should we wait a bit then?" I want to spend as little time with Mr. Montgomery as possible.

"They want us to join them for cocktails."

Of course they do.

"Super."

I force a smile, clutch the steering wheel with one hand, rub the back of my neck with the other. I'm thirsty. My stomach churns. I don't want to see Mr. Montgomery. I'm sure the expectation was that I would have asked Audrey to marry me already. Or at least have a plan to.

My phone pings in my work bag, and for no rational reason, I automatically think it's a message from Rebecca. Maybe an explanation as to how she feels. Finally. I don't want Audrey to read it, so I wave at the bag. "Don't worry about getting it."

Too late. Audrey's hand is deep in the bag, fishing.

"Really, Aud. It's okay. I can get it later."

It's silent a moment; I hear an intake of breath. I'm thinking this is it, the moment of truth. There's something incriminating on the phone. She knows how I feel about Rebecca. I'm almost relieved.

I shift my head and look at her. She's looking at something. But it's not my phone.

It's the ring.

CHAPTER 37

R ebecca
It's dusk on a Saturday, and I stop a block before
Kimmy's. I perch at the edge of an empty bench, in
view of the ocean, a smattering of families still on the sand,
taking in the last gasp of summer.

I pull my phone from my purse and switch it on. A photo of
Ian and me in New York at the first *Country Clash* audition—my
wallpaper—stares back at me. I know I should change it. Every
time I see Ian's face, it's a reminder that he, and his sheepish,
heartwarming smile, is fifteen hundred miles away with another
woman. But the picture feels lucky, and I don't want to change
anything before I get the official *Country Clash* results. A bit of
superstition, I guess.

They're releasing the name of the final contestants today,
and though my audition was disastrous, I'm holding out hope I
did enough.

I pull up my emails (again). My heart beats wildly; I hold my
breath.

Nothing.

I scroll down ridiculously far to make sure I didn't miss

anything, some rogue email that slipped my notice. I check the spam, refresh.

Nope. Nothing.

I exhale, relieved. As long as I don't know the answer for sure, I can live in the world of possibility, one where I am a smash hit on *Country Clash*. I fantasize about it, more now that Ian's gone. I'm okay to stay in the realm of maybe a bit longer.

I stand and smooth out my shorts, continue the walk toward Kimmy's. She insisted that I come for dinner to discuss a new campaign for Mrs. Fishes. I don't know what it's for, but I'm glad for the invitation. I need a diversion.

I reach her front steps and lift a gold knocker shaped like a lobster. It connects with the door with a thud. I hear footsteps, but no one comes, and I lift the knocker again. The door swings open.

"Surprise!"

I step back.

My parents, brothers, Lily, and Kimmy are crowded around the door. My heart jolts. Did I make it? Did they know something? Is a television crew in the back, ready to film my reaction to getting on the show? I smile wide and crane my neck. I half expect a big black lens to be trained on my face. There's nothing.

Dad touches my shoulder. "Are you surprised, sweetheart?"

"Yes." I smile and wait for the punchline. When none is offered, I ask, "What's it for?"

"It's for you, dummy." John pushes at my shoulder with rare brotherly affection. "The results come out today, right?"

"Yes." The word comes out slowly; I'm trying to process.

"We thought it would be good to have family around when you get them," Mom interjects. She's smiling wide, like having a non-professional daughter who sings country music was her dream all along.

"You'll make it," Lily calls.

I look around, reality sinking in. My family is here, gathered to celebrate my music and a future career. I'm being taken seriously. My music is being taken seriously. A lump forms in the center of my throat. Happiness and pride flood my body. And fear.

What if I don't get it?

Kimmy grabs my hand. "Come on. Party's back here."

She leads me to her great room, the one where she has all her parties. An image of the foam party, of being here with Ian, pops into my head, a hit to the gut. I wish, viscerally wish, he were here right now. He would be so happy for me.

But he's not here. And, even if he were, he'd have Audrey with him. Seeing them together would be much, much worse than being alone.

"Enjoy!" Kimmy waves her hand over the kind of buffet only she can put together, complete with the lobster tails my parents can never get enough of. There's a fully stocked bar, a bartender behind it. Tristan. The super-built guy who'd been here for the foam party.

I angle my head back toward the buffet and spy the cake, centered on its own table. I inhale a breath. A photo of me in my audition outfit, the one Lily took and sent to John, is overlaid on the icing. I'd been so nervous at the time, I hadn't really looked at myself. I stare at my image now. I look good. Like I belong on a stage. Like I could, in fact, be a star.

Mark grabs a plate. "So, Rebecca, are you going to have a stage name? Something like"—he taps a finger on his chin—"Sky Gold?"

"Sky Gold?" Lily shakes her head. "No. You should go by Lily." She underscores the air. "Just Lily."

"Maybe Little Sister?" offers John. "Or Lil' Sis? That's catchy, right?"

I can't tell if he's serious.

"I think I'll keep Rebecca Chapman for now."

"It's a beautiful name," Mom volunteers.

"Says the person who picked it," Mark taps her shoulder good-naturedly.

We laugh, all of us, a rare moment of frivolity for the ever-professional Chapman family.

Tristan steps into the center of the circle with an ornate silver tray of champagne flutes.

Kimmy grabs one. "Time for a toast." She waits as everyone gets a glass, then lifts hers over her head. "To Rebecca, our own shining star."

"To Rebecca." The clinking of glass fills the air. I feel almost giddy, convinced that, yes, this is some cosmic sign, and I'm certain to get on the show. I visualize clicking on the email, seeing "Congratulations" written out in the standard Times New Roman default text. There will be details. Where to go, what to bring, names of band members. Exciting days ahead. But I won't worry about any of that tonight. Tonight, I'll bask in the approval of my family.

I stack my plate with crab cakes, shrimp, salad, and thick slices of bread slathered with butter. I join my family at an exquisitely set table on Kimmy's upper deck, panoramic ocean views around us. I inhale salt air. Soft music pipes out from speakers. Rays from the setting sun warm my skin.

"Tell us about the audition," Dad says, fork poised midair. "What was it like?"

"Well," I start, and I tell them all about the first audition. I omit from the story, and my mind, any details about the second, horrid one.

"Ian Ledger went with you, right?" Kimmy asks.

I freeze at the sound of his name. "The first audition, yes," I manage. "Ian taught me guitar," I say by way of explanation. "He's the one who came with us to lunch that time, after the showcase."

My parents and John nod. None of them mention the lunch

conversation, the efforts to convince me that my life would be more "on track" if I were a paralegal at John's firm. But the night is too perfect for me to hold any continued resentment. I let it go.

"Wait." Mark slaps the table. "You can play the guitar?"

He says it like playing the guitar is the most badass thing on earth, and I smile. "Yes, I can play the guitar."

"Can you right now?" he asks.

"I could, but I don't have a guitar."

Mark slaps his forehead. "Right."

Kimmy looks at Tristan, who nods. "I have a guitar," he says. "Gibson?"

"Sure." Gibson is *the* brand for guitars.

Tristan goes into the house, to get the guitar, I assume. It's clear that he's not just the bartender but that he's staying here with Kimmy. I shake my head. Only her.

Tristan returns with a beautiful Gibson Sweetwater. He bends down and sets it next to my chair with an appreciative nod. One musician to another.

I don't know what it is—the free-flowing alcohol, the sea air, this unexpected outpouring of love from my family—but I'm not nervous. Instead, I'm charged up. I *want* to show my family what I can do.

I push my chair back and grip the guitar in a way that's become familiar after hours (and hours and hours) of practice. "I'll play my audition song." I play the first few chords, start to sing. I concentrate on those first few measures and verses, eyes fixed on the ground. Once I'm sure I'm in it, the right pitch and the right rhythm, I look up. No one is eating or drinking, every set of eyes fixed on me, admiration in their expressions. I'm buoyed by their support. I lose myself in the moment, singing as the sun sets, basking in the familial approval that has escaped me for so long.

I finish, rest the guitar on my knees.

John stands and starts to clap. Kimmy stands—my parents, everyone. They're all clapping. A standing ovation.

I feel my throat; the lump is back. I brush my eyes with the back of my hand.

"Absolutely perfect," Mom says.

"Amazing," Dad agrees.

A smattering of compliments unlike I've ever received follows. We finish our meals and cut the "Rebecca cake." Tristan hands me a slice. "Beautiful playing," he whispers.

After cake, we sit with after-dinner cocktails in the moonlight, and I realize the obvious. I've been so busy with my family, so busy savoring their approval, I haven't checked the results.

I grab my purse and excuse myself to the bathroom. I lean against the sink, pull out my phone. I'm almost not nervous. I'm expecting a yes. It's a yes. It has to be a yes. The karmic gods wouldn't be so cruel as to take this from me now, would they?

I pull up my emails. It's there, one from *Country Clash*. I close my eyes and click.

CHAPTER 38

I *an*
Audrey's in the passenger seat, staring at the ring.
I cross a lane of traffic, pull into the parking lot of a strip mall that has seen better days. I look at her.

The sun, beating through the car glass, hits the diamond. Light sparks.

"Is this," she pauses, "my grandmother's ring?"

"Yes."

She stares at it a long moment, then pulls her eyes toward me. "Were you—" she starts, then shakes her head. "Never mind." She places it back in the box, closes the lid, and tucks it into my bag. There's a hint of a smile on her face.

"I—" I start.

She shakes her hands over the bag. "I shouldn't have looked. Don't worry. Consider it unseen." She smiles again, takes my hand, and squeezes it. She nods toward the road. "We should go, Ian."

I drive in silence and a slideshow of married life with Audrey clicks through my mind. We'd have kids. Two, three maybe. We'd move to one of those houses in suburbs, the kind with block parties and neighborhood watches and kids that catch fireflies on warm summer nights. We'd attend the events we grew up with—the Fourth of July parade, the Christmas tree lighting, Springfest. Celebrations at Mr. Steak. Sunday dinners with parents. Growing old with my first and only girlfriend, a woman I've known all my life.

It's what I always envisioned.

It's what I always wanted.

Life with Audrey checks every box.

I swing the car into the country club parking lot, pull into a space. I look at Audrey.

"I know it's been weird," she starts. "And I know I was harsh, with the forced separation and all. And keeping you at a distance sometimes." She clutches both my hands in hers. "I just wanted to be sure, you know. And I am sure. I'm sure I love you, Ian Ledger. We're meant to be together. So," she continues, a teasing lilt in her voice, "if you do have a question for me, just know, the answer is yes."

This is it. Mr. Montgomery's approval. A certain yes from Audrey. Both roadblocks to a proposal, lifted.

But it doesn't feel right.

I love Audrey, but it's a childish kind of love. A "my first girl-friend" kind of love that, until the past few weeks, I hadn't realized was lacking in depth. We talk about the cats, she does anyway, and our jobs and our parents and all the dozens of people we both know. But we never discuss anything of substance. It's like the old cliché: We love each other. We're not in love with each other.

I think she knows this too, deep down. Why else would she keep the idea of a proposal at a distance for so long? Or insist on a total, see-other-people, break?

I'm not sure what's changed for her, why this relationship, the one she didn't want a few months ago, she's certain about now. Maybe lack of better options. Or anxiousness to move on and start a family. I don't think it's because she's come to the conclusion that we're soulmates.

It doesn't matter. Because I know in my gut. I do love someone.

And it isn't Audrey.

CHAPTER 39

Rebecca

Still in Kimmy's powder room, I open my eyes and read the email.

Dear Ms. Chapman.

Good.

Your audition was outstanding.

Yes!

You are a talented vocalist with a bright future.

Yeah, yeah. Keep going....

Unfortunately.

No.

My eyes fixate on the word. Never, in the history of time, has any good news followed the word "unfortunately." Unfortunately, you're sick. Unfortunately, the company downsized. Unfortunately, someone else got the house.

Unfortunately, we cast you on the show?

It's not going to say that.

I'm frozen, staring at the word, suspending time for the final moments I can live in blissful ignorance. I shut my eyes, open them, and read the rest of the sentence.

Unfortunately, we have cast other singers for the available slots. Best wishes in your future endeavors.

I feel nothing for a moment. Like it won't be that bad. Like the news won't rip open my soul. Like I won't be destined to a boring desk job *forever.*

I pull up the email and read it a second time. Still no. It's a no. After my endless fantasies, the hours upon hours of rehearsal, the New York trips and the nerves and the waiting, it's a no.

NO.

I didn't make it. There won't be rehearsals to go to or music to learn. I won't get fitted for costumes or pose for photo shoots. I won't travel. No bonding with band members between shows. No live audience. No judges. No chance for a stage name, even one as dumb as Sky Gold.

Sky Gold. Mark. God. I'll have to tell my family. Imminently. *This* is why they're gathered after all. I can't not tell them.

My phone rings. I jolt at the sound, press Accept without thinking.

"Rebecca."

It's Ian. His voice low and comforting and familiar.

"Ian. To what do I owe the pleasure?" I try to sound flip and fun; it comes out caustic instead.

"Um, it's uh—" he pauses.

"Cat got your tongue? Is it Oreo?" I intend it to be a joke.

He doesn't laugh. There's a long pause.

"It's Audrey."

Audrey. Her name pierces through me and the thought of her and Ian together tears the emotional wound from the audition results so wide, it's a giant, ugly gash full of every negative mental state under the sun. I cannot give advice to Ian on his love life. Or hear about how great things are going. Or, God, be told they're tying the knot. Maybe if I'd made the show, I could handle it. Right now, having just gotten the news, my family right outside the door—I can't handle anything about Audrey.

"I made it," I blurt out. "I made *Country Clash.*"

I don't know why I lie. I think I just wanted to know how it would feel to say it: "Yes. I made it." Even if it's not true.

I open my mouth to correct the statement but Ian's happy-screaming and there's an unrecognizable squeal outside the bathroom door. Phone still on my ear, Ian's congratulatory words flowing through the plastic, I push the door open and peek my head out the crack.

The girlish squeal came from *my mother.* She's standing outside the door, that look of pride I'd seen on her face a gazillion times for Mark and John clear on her face.

"Did I hear that right? You made the show?"

"Mom—" I start.

"Oh," Ian says, "your family is there. Oh, that is great, perfect. Enjoy this moment, enjoy every bit of it." He pauses. "I am so, so happy for you, Rebecca. And proud too. I'll catch you later." He disconnects. A lump lodges in my throat. I wish so badly I'd actually made the show that it physically hurts.

Mom grabs my elbow. "Come on. Tell everyone the news." She puts a hand on my shoulder, guides me toward the great room. "So exciting, Rebecca. And after hearing you sing, well," she pauses, "no wonder."

I want to point out that she has heard me sing, and notwithstanding that, she wanted me to take a paralegal job. She never believed I would make it as a singer, make the show, any of it. This I-knew-it-all-along attitude? It's hypocritical.

But of course, I *didn't* get cast on the show.

So.

I guess Mom was right the first time.

Once we're in the great room, Mom grabs a glass and spoon off the bar. She taps it and steps back, the signal clear. I'm supposed to share the news now.

My family members stop talking. I'd felt equal to them earlier. Now, as before, their degrees and positions stand tall in my mind.

Mark Chapman, MD.

John Chapman, JD.

The Honorable Helene Chapman.

Richard Chapman, MD.

Kimberly Chapman, CEO, Mrs. Fishes.

Lily Chapman, environmental engineer.

At least I'm on par with Tristan, the bartender. Then again, Tristan is incredibly hot. And he might have some secret degree I don't know about. Plus, his guitar is way nicer than mine. So, yeah, Tristan trumps me too.

"Rebecca," Mom prompts.

"I made it," I say. "I made the show."

CHAPTER 40

T hree months later
   Ian
   "I'm *obsessed* with this drink." Jessica, my date,
holds some fruity concoction across the small table. It's inches
from my face. I eye the drink. Am I meant to taste it? Drink out
of her straw? We barely know each other.

"Looks good," I say. "Enjoy."

She pulls it back, takes a deep, cheek-sucking sip. "So good.
Really. I'm obsessed."

"Glad you like it." I'm not sure what else to say. I think we've
covered what we can about the drink.

"Like it? I'm obsessed."

Right.

I stand. "If you'll excuse me a minute." I gesture towards the
men's room.

"Obsessed," Jessica yells after me.

I escape inside the bathroom, take refuge in a stall. I call
Brenda.

I've been living with her and Julian for a solid month. Days after I broke up with Audrey, I quit my job in spectacular fashion, telling Daniel, my boss, his company was a sham.

And after this life-changing one-two punch, I ran into either Daniel or Audrey *everywhere*. The grocery store, the bakery, a Target two towns away. The day before I left, my barber seated me next to Mr. Montgomery for a twenty-minute haircut that seemed to take hours.

It would be fine, or at least better, if I was talking to Rebecca. But she's busy. With rehearsal and fittings and a whole new exciting life that has nothing to do with me. We've only had a handful a conversations, all short, and none conducive to the news: I broke up with my girlfriend of forever because I'm in love with you.

She doesn't know anything.

Not that I left my job, not that I broke up with Audrey. And I can't tell her. I realized that after I called the night of the breakup, the night she told me she'd made the show. I mean, what kind of emotional pressure would that put on her? *I know you're chasing your dream and all, but just so you know, I've completely altered my life because I secretly love you.* I can't do that.

The predictable staples of my life in Carlisle shattered, I'd been miserable. And embarrassed. In a small town, everyone knows everything, and I felt like I was walking around with a big fat sign across my forehead: "Man in Throes of Emotional Chaos."

Brenda took pity on me. She extended an invitation for me to "get away" and I jumped on it. Casper and I (one of Oreo's kittens, don't ask) arrived two days later. I'm supposed to be researching frozen food options for the catering company, but I haven't done anything except create an elaborate folder system.

I've been just as unmoored here as I'd been in Carlisle. So, in an effort to "cheer me up," Julian set me up with Jessica, a friend of a friend of a friend, also using Martha's Vineyard as a refuge from real life.

"She's horrible," I whisper into the phone.

"You're horrible," Brenda quips back.

"No. Seriously. She's obsessed with everything. The restaurant, Martha's Vineyard, her drink."

"She's enthusiastic."

"She's overusing the word."

"Seriously, Ian."

"She is," I insist, though I realize, out of context, how petty the complaint sounds.

"You have to stay for dinner. You don't have to go out with her again."

She sounds exactly like Mom did during my teen years:

Ian, you have to go to the party.

Ian, you can't hide in your room.

Ian, just say hello.

Somehow, with Rebecca, I'd forgotten my hatred of social events, of dating, of most people, if I'm honest. I don't regret breaking up with Audrey—she deserves someone who truly loves her—but I do miss her.

"It's one dinner," Brenda says.

"Fine."

"Love you, brother." She clicks off the call.

Okay.

I can do this. I have to do this. Feigning an excuse would be rude and hurtful. And it would solidify my hermit-like tendencies. I have to take small steps, or I'll never do anything. It'll be me, Casper, and Netflix. *Forever.*

I step toward the table. Jessica's got a lock of wavy brown hair wrapped around her index finger. She's studying the menu. I look at her a moment. She *is* pretty. And—what did Brenda call it?—enthusiastic. I mean, at least she liked the drink. She wasn't complaining about it. Right?

"Hey." I slide into my seat.

She flips the menu around. "Oh my God. There are so many good choices. I'm *obsessed* with this place."

* * *

I WAKE THE NEXT MORNING, Casper curled up in the crook of my knees. He's still little and predominantly white. Audrey named him because he's white like the ghost, of course. As ridiculous as the name is, it felt disloyal to change it.

I brush my teeth, rake my hair with my fingers, and decide not to shave (again). Still wearing the sweats I slept in, I grab Casper and carry him downstairs.

Brenda and Julian are at the kitchen table with plates of croissants, fruit, and steaming coffee cups. They glance up at Casper and me as we enter. Brenda clears her throat. I get the distinct feeling I'm about to get a "talking to."

"Your life is off track," she says.

"Jeez." I set Casper down and pull out a can of his cat food.

"Sorry, but it's true."

I open the can, and the scent of warm croissants and freshly brewed coffee is immediately overpowered by the distinct, and not all that pleasant, smell of wet cat food. I scoop some into a dish and set it on the floor.

"Is this about Jessica? Because we just didn't hit it off." I move to the coffee pot.

"It's not about Jessica." Brenda takes a sip of coffee. "It's about you, moping around, sleeping half the day, acting like you lost your best friend."

I did lose my best friend. But I don't say that.

"You need direction, Ian."

I pour coffee into a mug. I want to say it's too early for this conversation, but it's almost noon. I perch on one of the stools that line the kitchen island. "Sorry."

Her eyes soften. "I don't mean for you to be sorry. I get it. And you know I'm supportive."

She has been. I mean, she was happy about the breakup with Audrey. No surprise there. She'd understood about the job. I didn't tell her I'm in love with Rebecca, but I think she knows.

Julian puts his hand over mine. "What she's trying to say, mate, is we'd really like you to dig into the frozen food part of the business. Treat it like a real job."

Oof. That statement smarts in its truth. I hadn't been taking the opportunity seriously.

Brenda gets up, retrieves a manila folder, and sets it in front of me. "We'll start with half a dozen entrées or so in local stores. It will help annualize our income."

Brenda has complained about the seasonal nature of Martha's Vineyard before. How, with the exception of Christmas, the catering business dries up when it gets cold. "Frozen food is complicated," I admit. If my research illustrated anything, it was this point.

"You've got a business degree. That's more than we have." Brenda holds up the now noticeably thin manila folder. "Everything we know, the few contacts we have, are in here."

I open the folder, blankly scan the few pages in there. But my mind, my non-dreamer, reality-based mind, is swimming with potential issues. There would need to be licenses. FDA guidelines we'd have to adhere to. Plus freezing and packaging and distribution. It's a lot.

Julian meets my eyes. "We know it might not be feasible, but if it is, frozen food is a billion-dollar industry."

Billion-dollar? I stare at the pages.

Brenda puts a reassuring hand on my shoulder. "We don't expect you to launch it alone. We just want you to take the first steps, see what we need to really do this."

"Why me?" I spit out the question because, as much as a job on a beautiful island appeals to me, I don't want a pity position.

"Why not you?" Brenda says. "I love you. I trust you. And it's not like there are dozens of people with food service knowledge on the island."

I smile. "So. I'm kind of a last resort?"

"You are *absolutely* a last resort," she teases.

I sip my coffee. It's a good offer. And it's not like there are other, more attractive options. Moving back to Carlisle is a big no. I could move somewhere else, somewhere random. But I know myself. I'd never go out. And if I did, I wouldn't speak to anyone.

"So?" Brenda asks. "Are you in?"

Why not?

I hold up my coffee cup in a toast-like gesture. "You bet."

CHAPTER 41

R*ebecca*
"You have to tell them. They'll all be here in two weeks." Kimmy, stretching for a morning run, bends down and touches her toes.

She's the only one who knows about my lie. I had to tell her. I work for her. And I live in her property. But I didn't tell anyone else. As far as my family and Ian are concerned, I'm cast on the show, living my best life as a budding country music star.

I peer at her from my vantage point on the circular stairs. "I know."

Truthfully, I *could* hide out at the duplex. It's not like my family would expect me to be at Kimmy's pre-Thanksgiving Thanksgiving. And I could make an excuse not to come home for the real Thanksgiving. That would give me until Christmas to work up the courage to tell the truth. The show airs in January.

Kimmy seems to sense my trepidation. "They'll understand."

"Yeah." I say the word noncommittally because I'm not sure they will. I've been *very* detailed in my description of my life as a *Country Clash* star. I've made up names of band members, described my varied costumes. I sang a score of a song I wrote and passed it off as one for the show. I do the same for Ian, just shorter versions. I try not to stay on the phone too long with him, afraid he'll make the inevitable announcement: "I'm getting married." And that news? *That* would be the straw that breaks me.

I feel guilty about the fabrication. Most days, I convince myself that the stories are a cathartic exercise. But they're not. I'm using them to grasp at a lost fantasy I should have come to terms with months ago.

Kimmy checks her watch. "I'm going to run. Tristan's in the kitchen."

"Great. Thanks."

I move to the kitchen. Tristan, still dating Kimmy, is at the table.

He looks up when I enter. "Ready?"

"As ever."

"Pumped?"

"You bet."

One of the only legitimately exciting things that has happened since the day I got the big fat NO is I studied for the driving test and passed the written part. Turns out, Ian had been right, and I got accommodations for the dyslexia. I was dying to tell him after. But of course, I couldn't. He thinks I'm living it up in Nashville as a country star. Me passing the written driving test in New Jersey isn't logistically feasible.

I'm taking the driving portion of the test today. Tristan's taking me there. Turns out he's part of a band, and he's had me sing with them a few times. I like the camaraderie of the guys and I like Tristan. I've even started composing a few songs.

He drops me off in front of the DMV, pushes a lock of hair off his face, and holds up a hand. "Slay it, Bec."

I slap his hand back. "You know it."

Two hours later, I emerge with a newly minted driver's

license. My smile is so broad in the photo, I look like I'd just won lifetime passes to Disney World. I feel legitimately happy for the first time since, well, the obvious.

Kimmy, because she's the best aunt ever, lends me her car and I *drive* to my class at Music All Around. I feel the latent teenage coolness of swinging my keys as I walk toward the building. *I can drive.* No more bus schedules. No more Ubers. Freedom to go wherever I want, whenever I want. I'm desperate to tell Ian. In my head, I start to concoct some story that would put me at home long enough to get a license. What's one more lie?

I open the door and forget about the story and the lie. Olivia, who's almost never there, is standing with an older woman I've never seen before.

"Bec!" Olivia sings out. "You're here early."

"Yeah." My voice comes out tentative. Why is she here? And who is this woman?

I make my way toward them. Olivia looks very Olivia-ish in bell-bottomed jeans with flowers stitched up the side and a poncho. Her hair is piled on her head in a messy bun. The woman, in contrast, has on a sweatshirt with fall leaves embroidered on the front and thick, white orthopedic shoes.

"This is my Gram Gram, Margaret Caddell." Olivia swings a hand toward the woman.

The name rattles in my head. Margaret Caddell. Margaret Caddell. Oh. Margaret Caddell. *The owner.*

The owner who I've never met. The mentioned-by-name-only woman. Why is she here?

Margaret holds out a small hand; a gold charm bracelet hangs off her wrist. "Nice to meet you, Rebecca."

I take her hand in mine. "You too, Margaret."

The charm bracelet jingles as we shake. She lets go of my hand. "Call me Margie and sit. Please." She gestures to the folding chairs set out for parent observers. We all take seats.

Margie folds her hands. "I was hoping to speak to you."

My heart stops. Am I getting fired? Shit. No. I don't want to be fired. I like coming here. As sad as it might seem, teaching these classes is the main highlight of my week at this point. I can't lose this job. I really can't. I open my mouth to protest what feels like the inevitable but all that comes out is "okay."

"I'm selling the business," Margie says emphatically. "It's too much for me, and Olivia," she puts a hand on her shoulder, "is moving."

Olivia shrugs. "I'm moving to Tallahassee." I don't react right away, and she adds, "it's in Florida." She says Florida in a way that makes it seem like a foreign word: FLOR-I-DA.

Margie gives a small eyeroll. It's a very un-Gram Gram-like thing to do; it makes me smile.

"So," Margie continues. "I'm looking for a buyer. I thought I'd start with you."

"Me?" Ridiculously, I point to myself.

"Yes, you." She gives a warm smile. "From what I hear from our parents, you're great with their kids and you know your music." She looks out the window and back at me. "You may not realize this, but since you started teaching here, class size has expanded for the first time in a decade."

"I—" I open my mouth and shut it, not sure what to say. Buy the business? With what? The couple thousand bucks I've got in savings? I'd planned to use that for a car. "I'm not sure I'd be able to do that." I pause. "I mean, what does a business like this cost?"

Margie smiles again. "Buy might have been the wrong word."

"She wants to give it to you," Olivia says matter-of-factly.

Another little eyeroll from Margie. Love this woman.

"Not give exactly," she says. "You would take it over. The lease, the insurance, all costs, the classes. Everything."

I tip my head, processing. Unless Margie is my life's version of a fairy godmother, there has to be a catch. "What would you get?" I ask finally.

"I'd walk away, officially retire, and know the business I started is in good hands." She must take in my doubtful expression. "I could pay money to have it appraised and sell it to the highest bidder. But I don't want to do that. I want Music All Around to go on with an owner who loves music and children as much as I did when I started it. And Rebecca"—she reaches out and puts her hand over mine—"I think that person is you."

CHAPTER 42

I

an

At the Mrs. Fishes plant in Cape May, Brenda watches the packaging line from her vantage point behind the glass.

Kimmy holds out her arms. "This is where the sausage is made."

Brenda laughs.

Over the past weeks, Brenda has been talking to Kimmy almost daily. Turns out, starting a frozen food business is complicated and expensive and not something Brendan and Julian could realistically tackle. But partnering with an existing frozen food business? That's another story. I'd recalled Kimmy's desire to expand and put her in contact with Brenda. And here we are. Watching fillets of fish on a conveyer belt at a processing plant outside Cape May. Julian's back in the Vine-yard, taking care of Casper and the catering business.

Brenda watches, transfixed. "It's such a different side to the food industry."

"It's profitable," Kimmy says, her voice all business as it

always is when it comes to money. "And it's needed. People don't have time to cook like they used to."

Brenda and Kimmy are at the beginning stages of creating a Mrs. Fishes Trans Meal Line. The name's a secret play on Brenda's background—one she loved. The brand also highlights the fact that Brenda's dishes won't feature fish.

Kimmy waves a hand. "Come on. You've probably seen enough frozen fish for one day."

She walks us out and Brenda profusely thanks her. We stand in the parking lot after, the fall sun beating down on us in the crisp air. "I'll see you tomorrow?"

Brenda gives a wide smile. "For the pre-Thanksgiving Thanksgiving? Wouldn't miss it for anything."

This is an understatement. Brenda is over-the-top excited about the pre-Thanksgiving Thanksgiving. Of course she is. It's new people and socializing, her lifeblood. I'd rather go home. All my memories of Kimmy's place and of Cape May are intertwined with Rebecca. I know she won't be there; she's in Nashville. It's probably for the best. I'm not sure she wants to continue our friendship. She's all but ghosted me since making the show.

We say our goodbyes to Kimmy and drive to Shelly's by the Sea. Notwithstanding the ceiling caving in and the unsettling memory of a midnight Lou at the foot of my bed in his headlamp, I booked rooms there. I had to. Brenda is a classic bed-and-breakfast girl. Last night, she stayed up late playing cards on the porch with strangers. The night before she went on the same haunted tour I'd refused to go on all those months ago. She laps up the extra socialization; I beg off and watch television in my room. It's a win-win.

Sue and Lou are on rockers out front when we arrive. Sue gives us a big-armed wave. "Ian, Brenda. Hello!"

"Hey." My tone is uninviting. I can't muster Sue-Lou small talk right now.

But of course, Brenda's game. "Sue, Lou," she says, "good to see you. How's your day?"

Lou gives a detailed account of their morning. Sue gets up, moves to a long table, and spoons warm cider from a Crock-Pot into thick mugs. She holds them out. Brenda grabs one with a smile. I take one reluctantly and internally calculate how long I have to stand with it before I can beg off to my room.

"We're making oversized terrarium centerpieces at the civic center this afternoon," Sue volunteers. "Care to join?"

Hard no. I sip the cider.

"We'd love to," Brenda says.

I spit out the drink.

"Sorry." I grab a napkin from a nearby table and wipe my mouth and coat. "Went down the wrong pipe."

A discussion about crafts ensues. Not just terrariums. Suncatchers. Scrap-fabric magnets. Coffee cozies.

I'm done. I hold up a hand. "I'm out on this one. I think I'll go for a walk."

"Beautiful day for it," Lou says. He looks at the sky, and for a moment, it looks like he might ask to join.

Please no.

I'm already off-balance being here without Rebecca; I do not want to spend the afternoon with Lou.

"We'll be at the civic center if you change your mind," he says.

Phew.

"Terrariums available until four," Sue chimes in. "But the good stuff gets taken early."

"Good to know." Brenda grabs my mug and I step off the porch.

I start down the sidewalk. Sue, Lou, and Brenda are still in earshot, talking like best friends. I don't want to join them. I viscerally do not. But in a weird paradox, I'm lonely for *not* joining them. It's the enigma of the socially reticent. You *want* to be alone, but the isolation makes you sad anyway.

I walk to the Washington Mall, decorated for fall with big pots of mums, scarecrows, and arrangements of pumpkins. I picture Rebecca vividly in my mind. I do a reasonably good job of putting her out of my mind at the Vineyard. But here? She's everywhere. At Della's. In the pair of ridiculous turkey flip-flops on display at a storefront. She's in the card store where we went to get a birthday gift for Mark, on the bench where she belted out a stanza of her audition song. I see her sipping a beer at the Ugly Mug. I hear her laugh, cracking up at a T-shirt in Just for Laughs that says: "Hedgehogs. Why Don't They Just Share the Hedge?" I get a whiff of a coffee she liked from Coffee Thyme.

Then, I swear, I see her for real.

I stare at the Rebecca doppelganger, striding down the street, a plastic Della's shopping bag swinging in her hand. It can't be her. Can it?

I cup my hands around my mouth. "Rebecca."

The woman does not turn around. I stride-jog in her direction.

"Rebecca."

The woman turns and my heart leaps. It *is* her. I catapult in her direction and wrap my arms tight around her shoulders. I'm so unbelievably happy she's here, I can't think. Then I release her from the hug and—

Oh.

She is *not* happy to see me. She actually looks almost horrified. I drop my hands, my mouth agape like a stuffed fish.

"Ian," she says finally, "what are you doing here?"

"I—" I start. I can't formulate a coherent sentence. I'm still processing her obvious displeasure at seeing me.

"Are you here with Audrey?" She scans the immediate area.

"I—no." I shake my head. "I'm here with Brenda. She's been

meeting with Kimmy about—" I stop the explanation. "Wait, what are you doing here?"

She hesitates. "I'm here for something at Kimmy's."

She doesn't elaborate.

"Are you mad at me?" I blurt out the question, regret it as soon as I do. What kind of question is that?

She shakes her head. "No. Of course not. I just—"

She closes her mouth, doesn't finish the sentence. We stand, staring at each other in silence. It's almost as awkward as when we first met on the bus.

"Why would you think that?" she asks finally.

"You didn't return my calls or texts." The words sound pathetic and clingy as soon as they leave my mouth. I wave a hand. "Never mind. I know how busy you are."

"Yeah." Her face clouds.

A flash of worry hits me. "Is it okay?" I ask. "It's not too insane?"

"Oh. No. It's fine." She shakes her head. "Why are you here again?"

"Brenda and Kimmy might team up to create a frozen food line."

"Wow." She scrunches up her nose. "Kimmy didn't mention that."

"She probably didn't get a chance to tell you. Should we"—I incline my head to the coffee shop—"get a cup? I want to hear about everything."

"Oh." Her eyes widen. She takes a step back.

The hint I've been getting for weeks—SHE'S NOT INTO YOU, BRO—blares in my head.

"I would," she stammers, "but I have to get this home." She holds up the Della's bag. The plastic is thin. A bottle of cheap shampoo and a pack of M&Ms are visible inside.

Rebecca glances at the bag, seems to realize that there is nothing perishable inside. "Um. Anyway—"

"Go." I force a smile.

She takes a few steps and turns. "Good to see you again, Ian."

"You too."

She walks away, and God, I'd imagined this reunion a hundred different ways. We'd talk nonstop. I'd hear about *Country Clash*. I'd tell her about the Audrey breakup. Never once did I think she'd walk away, a bag of lame excuses dormant in her hand. I'd really believed we could pick up where we left off. Maybe even—

I don't go there. Because the reality is clear.

Rebecca's done with me.

CHAPTER 43

R*ebecca*
I walk, fast, away from Ian.
God.
I'm a jerk. A cowardly, lying jerk. The look on his face. Ugh. It's like I kicked a puppy.

No excuses, but I *was* surprised. In my mind, Ian was in Nebraska, snuggled up with Audrey and those cats with the ridiculous names. I didn't think he'd be here, and I choked. I could have, should have, told him the truth.

It's not like my life is a complete disaster. I've got my driver's license. And an offer to take over Music All Around, one I'm still wrapping my head around. If I had known I was going to see him, I'd have been more prepared. I *might* have mustered the courage to swallow my pride and just tell him already. Instead, I'd hurt him. Again.

Anger at the blindside whips through me and I pull out my phone. I punch Kimmy's name with my index finger.

"It's Kimmy."

"Why didn't you tell me Ian was here?"

"Rebecca?"

"Why didn't you tell me Ian was here?" I repeat.

"Ian? Does it matter?"

Her tone is quizzical and I realize the obvious. She doesn't know about my feelings for Ian. I've been so consumed by them, I'd forgotten it's not common knowledge. As far as Kimmy knows, Ian's that uptight temp from corporate neither of us cared for all that much.

"I just saw him. I was surprised," I say, recovering.

"Well," she says breezily, "I'm working with his sister on a potential frozen food line. She came for a tour. I didn't know he was coming with her." She pauses. "Is there a reason you wanted to know?"

There's a teasing lilt in her tone, as if she's guessed my feelings. But I'm in way too deep to consider the situation funny. I love a man who's in love with someone else. I've lied to him up to and including five minutes ago when I said that I couldn't get coffee.

"I invited them both to the pre-Thanksgiving Thanksgiving."

What? No.

I cannot come clean with my parents and brothers AND Ian and Brenda all on the same night. I visualize how it would go. I'll tell them the truth: I've been lying for months. I made up the people and the bands and the experiences. No, I don't wear red cowboy boots. No, the band doesn't sing the song "One Fleeting Summer"; that's just a song I composed. And no, we're not called Ghost Town. We're not called anything because the band I'm allegedly in *does not exist.*

Ian will look perplexed, my Dad and Mark disappointed. The glimpse I've had of my mother's approval these past months—poof! Gone. Lily will be hurt I didn't tell her, and John, like a self-proclaimed white knight with all the answers, will trot out his gift of a paralegal job. Brenda will most likely believe I'm not good enough for Ian, friends or otherwise. And rightly so.

I can't do it. At least if they all found out when the show aired, I wouldn't be there to witness their reactions. I could come clean one-on-one over a phone line, or better yet, a text.

"Rebecca? You still there?"

"Yeah. Sorry."

"I'll see you tomorrow?"

"Of course," I lie. There is no way I'm going.

I click off and start the walk back to the duplex, my mind searching for a valid excuse not to attend the pre-Thanksgiving Thanksgiving. I can't claim a family emergency because, duh, my family will be there. And Kimmy, my boss, knows I wouldn't have a work emergency. I could say I had to get back to the band, but Kimmy's head would explode if I did that. She'd probably spill the beans and stage an intervention—the whole lot of them showing up at my doorstep with platitudes and sympathy, which, I'm pretty sure, might be worse than me just taking my lumps in the first place.

The only viable excuse is illness. But how ridiculously fake does that sound?

I reach the duplex. Renee, the new renter on what I'll always call Ian's side, waves from her front window. I wave back. I'd gotten used to Renee, a friendly enough older woman *very* into her two parakeets. But now that I've seen Ian, felt his arms wrapped around me, I viscerally wish he were here. That he'd swing open the door with some dish in his hand and say, "Bec, try this." Or "What's on tap this time?" in relation to our next fun lesson. I want to see his smile, hear his laugh, ask him his thoughts about the Music All Around opportunity.

I push the door open, collapse onto my couch, and pull out my phone. I stare at my contacts, hover my finger over Ian's name. I could just call him. I close my eyes and press. It rings; I hang up. I'm not ready.

I move to the bedroom and find my composition notebook. Composing has become an outlet for me, one of the few things I know can remove Ian and the upcoming pre-Thanksgiving Thanksgiving from my mind. I work on melodies, harmonies, band parts for my favorite song, my eventual intention to play it with Tristan and the guys. I work until the notes blend together, until the words stop flowing, and the creative well is momentarily tapped dry.

I lean back on the bed, close my eyes, and reflect.

I set an intention, and when I open my eyes, I've got a plan.

CHAPTER 44

Ian

I   "You have to go." Brenda sits forward in her rocker on the porch of Shelly's. It's the morning of Kimmy's party.

I shake my head. "You didn't see her face. I don't know what I did, but it's clear she was not happy to see me."

"You need to get to the bottom of it."

"I tried. She said nothing was wrong."

Brenda blows on her coffee. "Most women will say nothing is wrong, Ian. You have to be persistent."

A couple walks by on the sidewalk, coats wrapped around them, their breath smoky in the cold. They give a friendly wave. Brenda waves back.

"She doesn't know you broke up with Audrey, right?"

"No. I'd planned to tell her. There was never a good time."

This is true. She was clearly rushed the few times we spoke. And giving the news now would seem a desperate attempt at—I don't even know what. Winning her back seems about as likely as me becoming a socialite.

"Don't you think you ought to tell her? Who's to say she

doesn't have the same feelings for you? You remember how it went with Julian, right?"

"Of course."

It's their favorite couple story. They worked together in the kitchen at an upscale restaurant on the Vineyard. Brenda was certain Julian was in a relationship with the sous chef, Brianna. They came in together, left together, and laughed endlessly at jokes no one else got. It seemed clear they were dating until she got an invitation to Brianna's wedding. Turns out she and Julian were platonic roommates, sharing the cost of exorbitant Martha's Vineyard rent. She and Julian sat together at the wedding and discussed food the whole time. The rest, as they like to say, was history.

"If Brianna had never gotten married that summer, I'd always have assumed he was taken. Maybe that's what Rebecca's thinking."

I shrug like I'm considering it, but I'm not. The horrified look on her face followed by the fabricated excuse was all I needed to see.

Brenda drains her coffee and stands. "Okay. I'm going to get ready."

"Now?" I look at my watch. It's not even 8:00 a.m.

"I'm going early. I'm making some dishes for the party."

Of course she is.

She kisses the top of my head. "See you there?"

It's both a question and a warning. I don't respond.

I return to my room at Shelly's, lie on the bed, and look at a stain-free ceiling. The more I think about it, the more it seems Brenda's right. I have to confront Rebecca. I need to know what I did wrong.

I arrive at the party and scan the room for Rebecca. She appears not to be here. But she can be flighty with start times, treating them as suggestions rather than mandates. I imagine she'll walk in any minute in one of those colorful getups I'd found so disconcerting when we first met. I'll see her and what? For all I know *she* has a boyfriend. Which would explain a lot about why she acted so weird. Maybe he'll come here too, some muscly bass player who doesn't need lessons to be fun.

Brenda, the epitome of grace among strangers, grabs my arm and pulls me into her group. She introduces me to Tristan, Kimmy's boyfriend.

"You," Tristan says, jutting out his hand, "were at the foam party."

"Yes." I grip his hand and shake. "I'm Ian."

"Rebecca's friend."

"Yes. Is she here?" I look around the space.

"Supposed to be."

She'll be here. Of course. It's *her* family. And she said she was coming.

My heart beats in a rapid spurt. Conversation goes on around me but all I do is scan the room for Rebecca. I want to see her, and I don't want to see her in equal parts. It's unsettling and eventually, I sneak out and head to the beach. I sit in the identical spot I'd sat with Rebecca, the place where I'd made her that balloon seahorse, where we'd come up with our deal—guitar lessons for fun lessons. I had no idea that silly agreement would end up altering the course of my life. Without it, I'd probably be engaged to Audrey right now.

"Hey."

I turn; it's Brenda. She plops onto the sand beside me, puts her hand on my shoulder. I appreciate that she doesn't say anything. Waves crash on the sand.

"She there?" I ask finally.

"No." Brenda pulls her coat tighter. "Not yet."

"She probably knew I was coming." I rake my hair with my hand. "I have no idea what I did. We were friends, real friends. I told her things I've never told anyone else. Now it's like I repel her or something."

"Do you think the fame has gotten to her? Making the show and all?"

I visualize the sadness that crossed her face during our brief encounter outside the Washington Mall. "I don't think so. If anything, she seemed to be exhausted by it." I exhale. "But what do I know, really? She's barely talked to me."

"I'm sorry."

"Thanks." I trace a circle in the sand with my finger. "I'm going to die alone."

"What?" Brenda pushes at my shoulder. "No."

"I'm serious. I'm socially awkward. I hate social events. And I clearly have some deficit when it comes to interpersonal relations. I mean, I actually thought Rebecca was into me."

"So did I."

"Well, that's good. At least I'm not totally crazy." I stand and brush sand off my jeans. "We should get back."

I hold my hands out, and pull Brenda to her feet. "I don't even know what I'm going to say if she's there."

"Maybe hello?" She teases. "Extra points if you use her name: Hello, Rebecca."

I shake my head. "Shut up."

"Just saying. Things don't have to be as hard as you make them."

I don't comment. I know she's right.

We reach the front step. Our phones ding with a text at the same time.

"Probably Kimmy looking for us," I say and pull out my phone.

I glance at the text. It isn't from Kimmy.

It's from Rebecca.

I'm sorry. Meet me at Stingray Bar at 8:00 p.m. tonight. I can explain.

I look over. Brenda's staring at the same text, also from Rebecca.

I push open the door, the text on my mind. When we rejoin the party, it becomes clear that everyone has received the same message we did.

"She's not answering," Mark says. He holds up his phone. I assume he's talking about Rebecca.

"Well, we have to go," her dad says. "No one has plans at eight."

"I might," John bursts out. "It's kind of bullshit, you know."

Lily puts her hand on his arm. "She says she's sorry right in the text, John."

A ridiculous conversation ensues as to whether Rebecca's request is or is not bullshit. I tune it out because, regardless of how her family comes down on the issue, one thing's for sure.

I'll be at Stingray Bar at eight.

CHAPTER 45

R*ebecca*

"You ready?" Sal, manager of Stingray Bar, sips a whiskey from a thick tumbler. He's wearing all black and has thick stubble on his face and jaw. He skims his hand over it, both of us at the obscured manager's table tucked in a back corner of the bar.

I sip my room temperature water with lemon, tilt my head toward Sal. "Is this a bad idea?"

It's a ridiculous question. I barely know Sal. I met him once, through Tristan, after the band played here a few weeks back. My first gig with them.

"I'm not sure how you singing could ever be a bad idea." He takes a drag of his cigarette, the embers bright in the dark room. "You got the pipes. May as well use 'em."

It's the perfect thing to say and I smile. Truth is, I don't know if anyone from my family is even here. I doubt Ian is. But the show must go on, right? "I'm ready."

Sal sets his lit cigarette in a groove on the ashtray in front of him. He drains the remainder of his drink and stands. "Okay then."

I follow as he navigates his way in the near dark, around tables crammed with people. It smells like alcohol and bar food and an odd mix of sweat and perfume and cologne. I hug my guitar, it's hard surface tight against my chest.

I don't see any of my family members. I do think I see Ian. Over and over. But it's never him.

Sal reaches a small stage and steps onto it. He's illuminated by the single spotlight. I know, from having sung on that stage weeks ago, he can't see anyone past the first table or two.

He steps to a microphone. "Hey all. Sal Rissi here."

There's a smattering of cheers.

"We've got some live music tonight."

More cheers.

"And let me tell you, this one can sing." He throws out a hand toward me. "Rebecca Chapman."

I step out of the darkness, my hand gripped around the neck of the guitar. I step onto the stage and see them then. My family. Clustered near the stage, faces highlighted in the bright glare of the spotlight.

Sal leans over. "They were looking for you, so I seated them in the front." He taps me on the shoulder.

Great. If they came, I wanted *not* to see them. But there they are, ducks in a row, all but Kimmy clapping with the kind of reservation you'd expect from the royal family. But there's no Ian. This throws me off. More than it should.

The applause dies down. It's time for me to step to the mic. I know this. It's not rocket science. But I don't move. I stand there instead, frozen with insecurity. My mouth goes dry. Sweat pools in my arm pits. I inhale, my breath shallow.

Doesn't matter that I'm nervous. I have to do this. I step to the mic and start "Jailhouse Rock," the audition song. I belt out the words, and after, there's applause. Real applause. It's the lifeblood of entertainers, and it buoys me. I am a singer. The world may not know me, I may not ever sing on a grand stage or be on television, but tonight, in this moment, I'm doing what I love.

"I've got a new song to sing tonight. Composed by yours truly." I hit my chest with an open palm; there's a smattering of cheers. "I've struggled the past few months." I look to my family, then past them, to the dark. "Has anyone out there ever told a lie?"

There's some applause, not a lot, because as a general rule, people don't want to admit to being liars.

"If you have, you know how it goes. How the first lie leads to another and another and another." I grip the guitar. "My original song, "Tangled Mess," is for all you liars out there. I'm coming clean tonight."

I glance at my family, then start to sing the truth. I lose myself in the words, in the refrain, in the carefully orchestrated verses. Words flow out of me. I sing about lost dreams and saving face and guilt and hiding and remorse. I sing about truth. I'm fully in the moment and the song, and when it's over, there's a crush of applause. I stand, sweaty and breathless. Nothing to hide.

I glance at my family, all on their feet, a standing ovation.

It's not *Country Clash.*

But it's enough.

CHAPTER 46

I an "Tangled Mess." A heartbreakingly beautiful song. Rebecca's delivery was stunning. She's breathing heavy on the stage, beads of sweat across her brow. The guitar hangs around her neck. She glances down at her family, all of them standing in ovation. Her face erupts into a smile.

Brenda touches my hand. "Beautiful," she mouths.

Rebecca takes a sip of water, sits on a stool, and sings a second song, then a third. She looks like a pro up there. I'm swollen with pride on her behalf. She finishes her set by singing "Tangled Mess" a second time, a quieter version, just as beautiful as the first. She steps off the stage and is immediately swarmed by her family. I hold back, not sure of my place in this moment of familial approval, one I know she's craved her whole life.

"You should go." Brenda nods in Rebecca's direction.

"I don't want to interrupt."

"She invited you."

I say nothing.

"She wants you here."

I shrug, still unsure.

"Damn it, Ian. Stop playing it safe." She orients me in Rebecca's direction, gives my back a not-too-subtle nudge. "Go."

I take a step forward. Rebecca looks up; her eyes lock with mine. She smiles. My heart lifts.

I push through the crowd. She pulls the guitar off her neck and hands it to her dad. When I reach her, she wraps her arms around me. "You came." Her voice is soft.

"Of course I did."

"I'm sorry."

"Don't. I get it."

"But—"

"It's all right." I step back and look at her. "But just know, you don't have an excuse to avoid me now."

She takes both my hands in hers and squeezes them. "Trust me, I won't. I've missed you, Ian."

I put my arms around her and squeeze. "I missed you too." I let go. "You were amazing up there."

She shrugs.

I push at her shoulder. "Come on. You know it."

Her face reddens. "Okay. I did pretty good."

The man who introduced Rebecca comes up behind her and claps her on the shoulder. "Unbelievable. We don't get a lot of performances like that at the Stingray, you know."

Rebecca smiles in a way that could light up a room.

"I got a big table in the back freed up. Drinks for you and your family are on the house."

"Wow." Rebecca touches his shoulder. "Thank you, Sal."

He smiles. "I got to keep you coming back." He shakes his head. "That was unbelievable."

My phone pings. I pull it out and glance at the screen. A two-sentence text from Brenda: *I took the car. Go home with Rebecca.*

I shake my head. I wish it was as easy as that.

Rebecca gestures to her family with a big-armed wave, and collectively, we make our way toward the table. Patrons stop Rebecca every few steps. They love her song. They love her voice. They love her and her candor and her willingness to be vulnerable.

I'm not surprised. I know how it feels to love Rebecca Chapman.

At the table, with her family, it's obvious no one cares about the lie. It's brought up only in the context of how *Country Clash* missed out. There's vigorous agreement on this, and the group, who probably wouldn't have watched the show to begin with, nonetheless agrees to boycott it.

"What's next?" her mom asks. The tone is different from the way it had been at that lunch at The Mad Batter all those months ago. Not "what's next" because you need guidance as to a *real* career. It's a "what's next" because, wow, you've got a talent to share with the world.

"I have something in the works." She gives a sly smile. "It's a business deal. But I'm not ready to share."

Mark bangs the table. "Come on, Sky Gold. Don't keep us hanging."

I don't know what Sky Gold means, but Rebecca throws her head back and laughs.

"If you need help, ask," her dad adds. He reaches across and puts a hand over hers. "Please. I'm sorry we didn't do more for you before."

Rebecca looks to me. "Probably a good thing. Otherwise, I may not have convinced Ian to help me out."

John looks to me. "How did she convince you to give her music lessons?"

"She was bad," I say. "I couldn't listen to it."

Rebecca taps my shoulder, her cheeks pink. "Shut up." She looks to her family. "I was, though. So bad."

"Pitiful."

We jointly share our deal on the beach all those months ago: fun lessons for music lessons.

"And did you get the girl?" Mark looks at me.

The girl. Incredibly, for a moment, I don't know who he's talking about. Then I realize he's talking about Audrey. "We broke up."

"Oh sorry, man," Mark says.

"It's all right." I don't go into any level of detail. "It wasn't because I wasn't fun," I add and there's a smattering of laughter. "I had a good teacher." I look to Rebecca.

She's staring at me intently. "You broke up with Audrey?"

"Yeah, I—"

"Why didn't you tell me?"

"You were busy."

Her face falls. I open my mouth to say something else, but a man taps her shoulder. She turns; he gushes about the song. She's drawn into a conversation about it. I'm glad for the interruption. A crowded bar, surrounded by her family, isn't the right place for the conversation we need to have.

She was honest.

I need to be too.

CHAPTER 47

R*ebecca*
I stop at the claw machine, stationed by the doorway of Stingray Bar, and nod to Ian. "One for the road?"

He smiles. "Do I have to get inside that thing?"

"Hmmm." I tilt my head and put my hand on my chin. "I don't think you could fit in this one."

"All right then."

It's just him and me now, my family having just left the bar. My emotions are...all over the place. I'm relieved that I no longer have to carry around that burdensome lie. I'm proud of my performance tonight, proud that, for the first time, I sang an original song. I'm shocked too.

Ian is no longer with Audrey.

I've repeated the fact to myself at least a dozen times since he said it.

Ian is no longer with Audrey.

Of course, I don't know the details of the breakup. Maybe *she* wanted it. Maybe he's heartbroken. Maybe he wants another round of fun lessons to win her back. Any of these things are possible. But a gut feeling tells me that's not it.

I pull four quarters from my purse and drop them in the machine. Ian takes the control and navigates the claw over what he correctly guessed I would want—a stuffed pink dolphin. The claw drops and grips the dolphin. He pulls it up, the dolphin in its grasp before it falls lifelessly back down.

"I'm trying again." He fishes in his pocket for change. He inspects the handful, then looks to me. "Got a quarter?"

I hand him one. "Addict."

Ian grabs the control again, hits the button to drop the claw. It lowers and grips the dolphin. "I've got it." The stuffed pink toy is in the grip of the claw, suspended by its tail. Ian hits the lever. The mechanical arm moves the dolphin toward the edge.

"Oh yeah," I say. "Almost there."

The dolphin drops. Ian throws his head back. "No." He looks to me. "One more."

"Absolutely not." I grab his hand. "Let's get out of here."

We take a step toward the door. Ian stops.

"No," I say with mock firmness. "I'll buy myself a pink dolphin if it's that important to you."

"It's not that. Though I very much do want you to own a pink dolphin." He looks at the door. "I don't have a car. Brenda took it." He reaches in his pocket and pulls out his phone. "I'll call an Uber."

I jut my hand out and put it over his. "No need. Follow me."

I push open the door and lead him through the parking lot.

"Are you leading me to some remote location?" he asks. "'Cause I'm not cool with that."

I look back and smile. "You'll see."

I stop in front of a cobalt blue Ford Escape.

Ian looks at the car, then at me. "No," he hisses.

"Yup."

"When?"

"Last week."

"Last week. Wow." He's stares at the car. From the expression on his face, you'd think it was a Maserati or Ferrari instead of a used Ford with *lots* of mileage. He taps on the hood.

I dangle the keys before him, the keychain he got me at Califon Beach on the end.

"You kept it," he says, surprise in his tone.

"Of course I did." I grip it in my hand. "Come on. I'll take you ∙ for a ride."

I navigate the car from the outskirts of Wildwood toward Cape May. "I got an accommodation for the dyslexia, you know. For the written part."

"That's so awesome."

"Thanks for the tip."

"Of course."

I drive toward our beach, the one near Kimmy's house. On the way, he tells me about Brenda's frozen food line, about living in Martha's Vineyard, about Casper.

"Tell me the cat isn't white."

"She is."

I smirk. "Only you."

I tell him about the offer to take over Music All Around.

"You have to do it," he says.

"I know." I've already decided it's a yes.

I pull into a space directly in front of the beach. We both get out and walk along the paved promenade, our breath smoky puffs in the air. The moon is full, bright stars scattered across the sky.

"And Audrey?" My heart beats, hard, in my chest. "What happened?"

Ian takes a few steps before speaking. "Audrey's dad gave me her grandmother's ring." He pauses. "For an engagement."

"Oh."

"Audrey found it in my bag. She thought—" He stops. "Well,

it's obvious what she thought. The moment was right. She'd all but told me she'd say yes and—"

I wait. My breath catches.

"And I couldn't do it. I couldn't ask her." He stops, turns toward me, takes my hand in his. "It wouldn't be fair to ask her," he says, "because I'm in love with someone else."

My heart leaps in my chest and for once I don't question anything.

"I'm in love with someone too," I say. "My guy is tall. He's *a bit* standoffish but in the most lovable and endearing way. He's kind, patient, and quite the guitar player."

Ian squeezes my hands. "My love interest is stunning, talented, and quite, shall we say, unrestrained. She is marvelous." He looks into my eyes. "I can't tell you how much I've missed her."

"She missed you too."

I angle my head up and his lips meet mine.

I'm home.

EPILOGUE

Six months later
Rebecca

Ian zips up my dress, the green one he loves, the one he calls "the mermaid." He kisses my cheek. "Stunning."

I move back and straighten his lapel. "Wait until you see my date," I say. "He's a hottie."

He smiles, the adorable, lopsided one that has not grown old. "I can only image how great he must be to snag a girl like you."

I shake my head.

It's been six months since that epic November night and we're going to a wedding. Not ours, not yet. But it's coming. We've looked at rings. And we live together, still in that same duplex, sharing the same side this time.

The wedding is Kimmy and Tristan's. Huge mic drop because Tristan is WAY younger than Kimmy. It's so very her. But I know they love each other.

I know this because I see Tristan all the time. I'm still in the band with "gigs"—I love calling them that—a few weekends a month. And Tristan works for me part time. Yup. I am the OWNER of Music All Around. I made a bunch of moves out of the gate and am making real money now. One was to hire Tristan to teach a teen class. Brilliant. The class got so popular, I had to add another. And a waitlist. I opened a second location in Cape May Court House, more of a year-round community, and use the existing venue for weekly summer camps. I have a staff of three that doesn't include Olivia. I try to be a good boss. I'm planning to have a foam party to celebrate our first six months in operation.

Ian is in charge of the Trans Frozen Food Line for the Brenda/Kimmy deal. The brand just came out and it's wildly popular. I might be their best customer. I haven't given up my love of frozen meals.

In a weird twist of fate, my parents are encouraging the whole music endeavor now, each shooting off texts or emails with audition information a few times a month. I laugh every time I get one. I would have given a limb for this kind of validation six months ago. I don't need it anymore. I love my life. I love being with Ian, running my business, living in Cape May. We walk the promenade every morning, play Skee-Ball at the arcade, and have our own mugs at the Ugly Mug bar—something reserved for the lucky few or whoever paid the most—Ian won't tell me how he got them. Every few weeks we have cocktails with Sue and Lou on the porch of Shelly's by the Sea. They finally convinced Ian to go on the haunted tour *and* play cards. He grumbled that he didn't like either, but he did. I know.

Whatever it was all those years that drove me to seek fame and validation, that made me believe my only pathway to success was making it on *Country Clash*, it isn't a part of me anymore. I'm happy.

Ian takes my elbow and escorts me toward my very fancy cobalt blue Ford Escape, of which I am still incredibly proud.

I hold open the door for him because I'm driving—duh. On the way to the wedding venue, we pass a sign for a mystery bus tour. I nod toward it. "I think you're due for another fun lesson, Mr. Ledger."

"Really? Lost some skills, have I?"

"I think so. You did refuse to go to Sue and Lou's American History party."

"So did you, as I recall."

"Nope." I shake my head. "Love history."

He snorts because he knows that's not true.

"What about a nude beach again?" I ask.

He angles his head; I see his smiling face in my peripheral vision. "Whatever it is, clothed or unclothed, past or present, if it's with you, I'll do it." He pauses. "I love you, Rebecca."

I pull into the parking lot of the church, park the car, and look at Ian, a man I detested, now the center of my world.

"I love you too, Ian."

THE END

ACKNOWLEDGMENTS

My fourth full-length novel! I can't believe it, and of course, I would not have been able to get it out into the world without help. A heartfelt thanks to the following people:

My cover artist: Jena R. Collins. I am routinely blown away by your designs (both for my books and others you have done). Your talent is remarkable and I feel grateful to have you design my covers.

My editing team: Shelly Davis of *The Detail Devil*. Thank you for your attention to detail and thorough work in editing *Fun Lessons*. As a big picture person who is sometimes blinded by creativity, your contribution is something I very much need. Thank you.

My author team: Thanks to Wendy Rich Stetson, Susan Reinhardt, Judy Mollen Walters, Jan Heidrich-Rice, Carmen DaVinleam, and Maria Imbalzano for taking the time to read my book in advance and provide meaningful reviews. I so appreciate your time as I know author days are filled with *lots* of reading. A special thanks to Wendy for my front cover blurb. I love it.

My advance reader team: Thanks to the following people for joining my advance reader team to provide some pre-publication publicity to the book: Deb Hanlon, Jody Giedraitis, Katie Lippman, Terri Grant, Vickie Waters, Francene Katzen, Krissy Cx, and Gina Pelz.

My children: Cassidy, Katie, and Kevin for patiently listening to my story ideas and giving input. A special thanks to Katie for reading a gazillion iterations of this book and providing valuable insight.

My husband: Jake, I am so lucky to have you for countless reasons, but in this context, thank you for your support of my writing dream. Love you.

A NOTE FROM THE AUTHOR

There are millions of books out there and I don't take it lightly that you took the time to read mine. If you enjoyed *Fun Lessons*, you can find links to my other books on my website:

www.leannetreese.com.

I would also be deeply grateful if you would leave a review on your retailer of choice. Reviews help other readers find my book.

Thank you again for taking the time to read *Fun Lessons*. I had a blast writing this book and was happy to send Ian and Rebecca out into the world to tell their story.